The PASADENA PLAYHOUSE

A celebration of one of the oldest theatrical producing organizations in America.

WRITTEN & EDITED BY
JUDY O'SULLIVAN

ISBN: 0-9633603-0-2

Published by:
The Pasadena Playhouse
39 South El Molino Avenue
Pasadena, CA 91101

Printed by:
Welsh Graphics
Pasadena, CA

Designed by:
Lizardi Communications, Inc
South Pasadena, CA

T heatre "opens the temple
doors and enables you to walk with those
who have come nearest among
men to what men may sometimes be."

MAXWELL ANDERSON

Acknowledgements

Judy O'Sullivan

I appreciate David Houk's genial hospitality and valuable time. I am grateful for Lars Hansen's enthusiasm, trust and chivalrous faith. And without Peggy Ebright's files, personal papers and charm, this book would not have been possible.

I would like to thank Lawrence O'Sullivan for being there, in my life, and at The Pasadena Playhouse in memorable productions.

Gail (and Dorothy too!) Shoup gave enthusiastic and diligent help and support. His beautifully researched and definitive 1968 doctoral dissertation, The Pasadena Community Playhouse: Its origins and history from 1917-1942, is a treasure. As is his collection of photographs and memorabilia in protective custody at The Huntington Library. Visual documentation is worth a thousand words.

Diane Alexander generously allowed me access to her slides and the use of several anecdotes from her book Playhouse.

Ken Rose gave whole-heartedly of his time and eleven-year's worth of production stills. He has an elephant's memory, a passion for detail, the soul of a romantic, and is as solicitous as any devout Southern gentleman can be.

Many others sifted through old production stills and were moved to graciously share their personal stories: David Banks, David Crandell, Terrence Beasor, Raymond Burr, Gene Hackman, Jon Jory, Randy Kone, Mako, Stuart Margolin, Rue McClanahan, Charlotte Stewart, and Kevin Tighe.

Thanks, also, to the other helpful people who were not put off by either my intrusive presence or incessant phone calls.

Special thanks to copy editors extraordinaire Alison Canchola, who paid attention those years in grade school when the nuns taught grammar, and Hermione Wise.

Finally, I'd like to express my admiration and respect for the very fine designers of the book, Lisa, James, and Ben Lizardi—an extremely talented and lovely family.

Contents

In Appreciation
JASON ALEXANDER

Introduction

The publication of this handsome commemorative book kicks off the celebration of the Seventy-fifth Anniversary of The Pasadena Playhouse. Whether you glance quickly through the wonderful photographs, the production listings, or read the informative text in depth at your leisure, it is a most pleasurable trip back to our future. The quixotic history is here: Gilmor Brown's modest beginnings at the old burlesque house on North Fair Oaks Avenue, the triumphant early years on South El Molino, the decline and fall, the dark days, and the rising of the Phoenix. The restoration is detailed, and the Mainstage productions from 1917 to the present are carefully documented.

Here at The Pasadena Playhouse, we are custodians of an illustrious past. We have a responsibility to the future, but our main concern is today. We work daily on being financially viable, and artistically successful for those who will follow. I am very proud to represent the hundreds of people who make up The Pasadena Playhouse family during its Diamond Jubilee celebration.

Sincerely,

David G. Houk

In Appreciation
AMERICAN ACADEMY OF DRAMATIC ARTS

Prologue

The Pasadena Playhouse seems something like a cathedral. It inspires the same breathtaking awe and with a kind of mystical synergy becomes more than the sum of its parts. The buildings can't be separated from the age-old ritual of acting out stories in a way that leaves an indelible mark on the soul. This magic transcends reality, and you know only that being there is a lofty experience. Well, every theatre captivates. But it is especially true on South El Molino where stately palms, half-dressed in fronds, remain resolute sentries seemingly guarding the street entry and no doubt the alluring secrets of days both glamorous and dark. Maybe it's the seductive Spanish architecture. The pastel stucco absorbs the gauzy twilight, and in the protected courtyard, a baroque fountain sprays a fine mist of memories. Ahead, the arcades deepened by violet shadows seem to lead inward to hushed and sacrosanct places. Crossing the flagstone it is easy to imagine a bygone era. Hear the strolling musicians. See the elegant patrons mingling with dazzling celebrities whose laughter floats on the silken air like stardust.

And although the cast of characters changes from time to time, The Pasadena Playhouse remains the same. Once encountered, it proves unforgettable.

In Appreciation
WALLIS ANNENBERG

The Great God Brown

Many legendary figures thread through the history of The Pasadena Playhouse. Their colorful lives weave an enchanting tapestry. But it's Gilmor Brown who emerges from the vivid background as an omnipotent, almost mythological character.

Brown breathed his life's breath into the several stages and the acclaimed School of Theatre Arts and brought international attention to 39 South El Molino for three decades. Nicknamed "The Great God Brown" early on, from the title of Eugene O'Neill's play, his ghost is said to hover backstage now, and to stand watch over his corner office on the third floor of the theatre he believed his own. In a way it was.

O Pioneers!

The story begins in a little house on the prairie.

Emma Louise and Orville A. Brown already had one son when George Gilmor was born in 1886. They were no doubt pleased to have another boy who could eventually help out on the homestead, where raising sheep and wheat provided a meager living.

The Voice of the Prairie

Growing up twelve miles beyond the German settlement in New Salem, North Dakota, Brown had a front-yard seat to real-life theatre. With an artist's eye, he witnessed the spectacle of nature played against the neutral backdrop of an endless sky.

Lightning danced and thunder roared. Winter blizzards howled past, leaving behind a pristine white silence.

Spring dyed the pasture green, and then blue and yellow wildflowers polkadotted the land. After the hot sun baked the ground, swift summer storms of swirling dust and fire balls devastated animals and crops. People died as well. Brown watched the violent end of a young friend dragged to death by runaway horses.

His sponge-like imagination absorbed the graphic sights, the discordant sounds, the drama. Scarred by hardship, yet toughened in the way a young willow is, Brown grew to be of slender build, a dreamer. He has characterized himself as a lonely and moody child until the family relocated in Denver six years later.

True West

At the turn of the century, Denver was still the "wild west." The bawdy saloons and grand hotels downtown beckoned young Brown. Flickering gas lamps cast spidery shadows and women's laughter made men smile. Decorated in golds and

Brown's mother had great expectations for her second son, Gilmor.

The young Brown characterized himself as a lonely and moody child.

In Appreciation
MR. & MRS. DAVID HOUK

Brown sneaked inside the vaudeville at Elitch Gardens and found religion.

At seventeen, Brown enrolled at the Johnson School of Music, Oratory and Dramatic Art.

yards of plush red brocade—Brown later had a penchant for garish design—there was a dramatic suspension of reality in these barrooms and busy lobbies. The curious youngster took in everything: the sleek ranchers and weathered cowboys and fancy made-up women whose skirts rustled as they walked. These early images inoculated him against the ordinary.

Brown sneaked inside the vaudeville at Elitch Gardens and found religion. The comedy, the pantomime, the song and dance, the acrobats and performing animals spoke to his soul. Already different from his peers, he distanced himself further, reading plays in seclusion. Imaginary lives became more real than reality. He expressed his pent-up feelings in several melodramas and tragedies.

Vanities

With his mother's prodding, Brown convinced the neighborhood children to become the Tuxedo Stock Company and staged shows in the family basement, acting and directing himself. These were good enough to attract the attention of the pastor at St. Mark's, who asked the fledgling group to perform for his Episcopal parishioners. Dr. Houghton liked the sensitive Brown and accompanied the good-looking lad to a church camp in the nearby mountains.

Another Part of the Forest

There, deep in the forest, a mesa-top rose sharply to stage height against the dark shapes of silhouetted trees. That was enough for Brown. With males acting the female roles, blankets for togas and flashlights as "spots," lighted above by the moon and on either side by blazing bonfires, Greek tragedy struggled to life.

Stage Struck

Through his self-conscious adolescence Brown seemed vaguely out of sync. His passion for theatre consumed him. Touched by a professional touring troupe production of *Becky Sharp*, he confided to his mother that he would become an actor. The shy teenager kept meticulous scrapbooks of performers' press clippings the way others his age collected sports heroes.

Beyond the Horizon

At seventeen, after much agonizing but with his mother's blessing, Brown set off for Minneapolis and enrolled at the Johnson School Of Music, Oratory and Dramatic Art. He seemed to have found his niche. His interest in drama led him to Chicago and the Chicago Auditorium where he concentrated on Shakespeare. While in this cosmopolitan city he was exposed to a mind-boggling potpourri of the performing arts, ranging from the circus to New York's touring Metropolitan Opera Company. Within a few short months, he saw Sarah Bernhardt, Yiddish theatre, and a Russian interpretation of Ibsen. A celebrated European actress spoke to Brown's class about limiting drama to a very small platform. Brown later said he remembered her words when he started the Playbox theatre. He tried his hand at directing before leaving school behind, impatient to get on with his life. Perhaps success would compensate for his self-imposed sense of isolation.

Days Without End

Brown hit the road, touring the U.S. with a troupe of English actors—including Sidney Greenstreet, who went on to make several Humphrey Bogart films. The repertory company brought Shakespeare to college campuses. Intuitively, Brown discerned the differences between himself and the *chic* and urbane students whom he encountered.

Instead of brooding, Brown traveled to Canada and learned stage technique. To raise the dramatic stakes, spot the main character during emotional scenes, go to black on the rest of the stage. To startle the audience, try a full-volume declamatory style and raging diatribes. On this gig, Brown's job included talking second-hand store owners into "loaning" set furniture for an evening's performance; he knew these pieces couldn't be returned as promised, since the company needed to catch a train soon after the final curtain.

Company

Whenever Brown ran completely out of money he returned to the solace of his parents' home. But he felt restless there; and he always headed out again in search of an elusive belief, nurtured by his mother, that his differences made him special. Driven throughout his twenties by a vague idea of fame and fortune, he joined with various companies, some first rate, some not. His blonde good looks, a developing acting style, and persistence—tempered with a still-boyish charm—eventually brought him some recognition throughout the United States.

Rising now from smaller parts to the romantic leads, like hundreds of actors before and since, Brown decided to take a stab at the Big Time. He made the rounds in New York. Doors were slammed in his face.

The rejection was humiliating, the city frightening, but Brown refused to be discouraged. His practical solution was to form his own company. He returned to Denver, determined. With his mother's backing, he convinced his immediate family and some semi-professionals to become The Comedy Players. Optimism, ingenuity, folding scenery, and a few costumes accompanied them across the country. Somewhere along the way, Brown's brother Frank secretly married Virginia Lykins, the leading lady. At the first performance March 26, 1909, in Savannah, Tennessee, Brown gave himself top billing. A subsequent review in

Brown became a leading-man.

Actress Virginia Lykins secretly married Brown's brother Frank.

In Appreciation
LINDA BAKER & J.B. SUMMERS

the Evanston, Wyoming, *Leader* noted, "The simplicity, earnestness, and remarkable good taste which mark the productions of this company reflect great credit on Mr. Brown, the star, and stage director." Despite such positive reviews, the company broke up for lack of money.

Down the Road

Brown refused to give up. Hitting the road again and again with this company or that, he proved himself a tireless worker as actor-manager. Like Professor Henry Hill, his arrival in a Midwestern town was much celebrated. He staged several highly successful and completely original outdoor pageants.

In 1912 he put together a whimsical *A Midsummer Night's Dream* on a riverbank in Kansas with a cast of one hundred townspeople. Over two thousand others paid to see the show. The following year, as a member of the Crown Stock Company he played Pasadena, noting that it was a fine city.

As Brown's prestige grew, so did his circle of influential friends. During a two-play festival in Rochester, Minnesota, in 1916, the wealthy Mayos offered to build a cement stadium for his use if he would stay. Life on the road was difficult. In previous letters home, Brown had complained of the "ghastly awful places" he had to endure. But he dreamed of settling elsewhere.

Over two thousand paid to see the show.

California Suite

The time came for a career move. Brown boldly rounded up his old company and headed west, possibly intrigued by the developing film industry. Pasadena was not chosen at random. He had decided during his previous stay to come back. Brown was looking for an upscale place to call home.

Admit One

Pasadena abounded with culture and the well-bred kind of people who would support the arts. The abundance of churches seemed a good omen, as did the formidable high school buildings. The massive stone Pasadena Public Library was a monument to gentility. And on the wide tree-lined residential streets, especially Millionaire's Row, there were baronial mansions. A place like this, where the grandiose luxury hotels with acres of flowering gardens enticed thousands each winter, could subsidize community theatre. Community theatre was definitely coming in vogue, as surely as the era which had generated traveling troupes was fading.

Enter Laughing

Brown was thirty years old and knew what he wanted from the Crown City when he stepped off the train with "The Gilmor Brown Players." In the hills above Hollywood, actors on horseback shot it out with six shooters before a moving

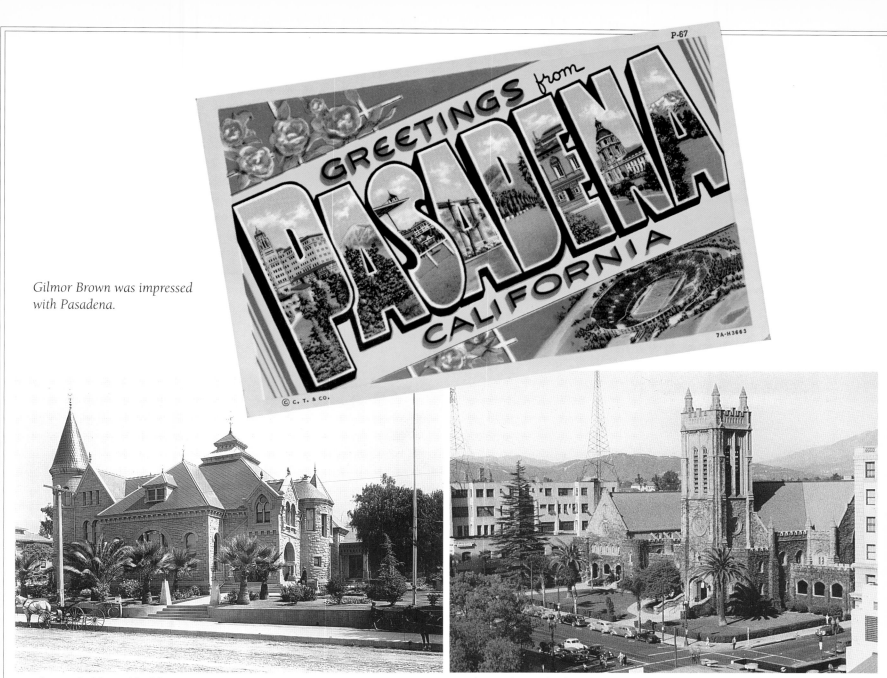

Gilmor Brown was impressed with Pasadena.

The castle-like public library.

The Gothic-style churches.

And the formidable school buildings.

In Appreciation
MEREDITH BAXTER

P-10—Air View of Pasadena, California, Sierra Madre Mountains in the Distance

1A-H477

13366 EAST COLORADO ST., PASADENA, CAL.

Panoramic postcards from Pasadena seduced wealthy Easterners.

In Appreciation
JODI BENSON

Brown traveled with his troupe across the country.

VOICES OFF
Professor Gail Shoup, formerly of The Pasadena Playhouse, which was the subject of his doctoral dissertation, is now a well-traveled and well-versed authority on Asian Theatre at Cal State Long Beach.

Shoup believes it is because Brown was very good at what he did, you might even say, "a benign opportunist," that he was able to accomplish so much in Pasadena.

camera. Overseas, French and German soldiers fought for real. These events hadn't touched Pasadena yet. Nor had Brown's presence. The troupe glanced tentatively around the quaint Pasadena station. It was a hot fall day; the pungent smell of star jasmine lingered on the sultry afternoon air. To the north, the San Gabriel mountains loomed large, a purple sawblade of color slicing the vivid blue horizon. It must have seemed like paradise.

Blind Ambition

Brown possessed the charisma to charm local citizens, and the know-how to make theatre happen. He had been baptized into the business by total immersion.

Intelligent and quick, he had a working knowledge of the major plays and diverse acting styles. He had performed, directed, and stage managed. And he had developed a knack for pleasing civic organizations. He was sure he could support himself. Brown later said, "I learned so much from it (road productions) particularly about the people to interest in a theatre…and…I think it was on that, that I founded The Pasadena Playhouse."

Talley's Folly

Booked for a thirty-five week season at the old Savoy theatre—formerly a dilapidated burlesque house named Tally's—on North Fair Oaks Avenue, Brown set about to carve a place for himself and to turn Pasadena into a theatre town. So what if it was three thousand miles from Broadway, the climate was better.

The season ended in May, but Brown stayed on until his death. Brown may not have been "born great," or had "greatness thrust upon" him, but he recognized an opportunity when he saw it. "Achieving greatness" quickly followed.

Summer home of chewing gum magnate William Wrigley Jr. built in 1914, presided over "Millionaire's Row."

The Rite of Passage in Pasadena

The mansions on Orange Grove Avenue echoed the palatial European architecture reproduced on the Atlantic's Gold Coast. The wealthy residents here took their cultural cues from the East as well. When Grand Avenue was cut through, more of these homes were built.

The new street was known as "The Fifth Avenue District." Then along came a group of bohemians, artists and musicians. They erected rustic bungalows out of natural materials behind Grand on the east bank of the Arroyo Seco.

Making History

These settlers, collectively labeled "The Arroyo Culture," espoused an accessible approach to art. The Crown City quickly became "The Athens of the West." George Bernard Shaw wrote to Upton Sinclair about "all sorts of interesting people being at Pasadena." Alice Coleman Batchelder, whose chamber concerts were later held at The Pasadena Playhouse, was a member of this group. She declared, "Let us cease to lament our distance…from the East and stand shoulder to shoulder in making of Pasadena a worthy center of art." It was a perfect entrance line for Gilmor Brown.

Much Ado About Nothing

Several thespian groups already thrived downtown. Young men interested in sociability and music and dramatic art had formed The Cauldron Club. The Pasadena Dramatic Club dabbled in theatre. The previously quoted Mrs. Batchelder was a patroness of The Children's Theatre Society. Even the Valley Hunt Club got into the act with "entertainments." The Thalia and Cue Clubs and The Maskers met regularly. Brown did not need much of a suitor's line to woo this audience. Ah, yes, Pasadena fit him like a silk glove.

Taking Stock

Mrs. George E. Hale, wife of the astronomer who established an observatory on Mt. Wilson in 1903, has been quoted as saying that her friends were most enthusiastic about Brown, and willing to aid him.

Brown's troupe, now calling itself The Savoy Stock Company, opened to a crowd of well-dressed women and their reluctant but curious husbands at the dowdy burlesque house on North Fair Oaks. It was September 17, 1917. The former bill of ribald comedians like Fatty Arbuckle and Nan Halperin and scantily-clad dancing girls was gone, except as the subject of titillating gossip.

Aristocrats

The novel company was quasi-democratic. Semi-professionals and professionals mingled with the socially prominent. Lillian Buck, who had previously worked for Brown in a Shakespeare festival in Rochester, Minnesota, became the company's leading lady by contributing five

Ernest Batchelder led the Arts and Crafts Movement to the east bank of the Arroyo.

Standing Room Only at the Community Playhouse.

In Appreciation
THE BROTMAN FOUNDATION

19

MISS MARJORIE SINCLAIR
Whose Song Numbers and Comedy Scenes Prove Big Hits
Rollicking Production.

A reluctant debutante.

hundred dollars to the pot. Brown and John Allard, a sometime film actor, played the romantic leads. The local Maskers provided the two elite recruits. The first, Wendall Wilson, worked professionally the rest of his life. Brown's biggest catch was the formidable president of the club, Miss Marjorie Sinclair herself. Marjorie Sinclair's popularity and her connections at several newspapers bought out the aristocracy and the press.

Little Shop of Horrors

Brown's parents and brother busied themselves running the theatre's box office and cigar store and collecting tickets while Brown whitewashed the stigma of the previous "girlie shows" with classics. Proper Pasadenans continued to brave the somewhat scandalous North Fair Oaks area in pursuit of art, perhaps a little excitement, and the fun of seeing their friends on stage. With a faithful audience building, and truly lavish productions, the ex-burlesque house was quickly christened "The moth-eaten temple of drama."

Tricks of the Trade

As America prepared for war, Brown staged *Crucifixion* championing peace. It may have been a marketing strategy rather than a political statement.

The huge cast allowed him to offer parts to the more reluctant townspeople who hadn't already come forward. Brown guessed that even the most conservative

banker had a little ham in him. He proved to be right.

When a traveling troupe at The Raymond Theatre further down on Fair Oaks drew paying customers away, Brown countered with other ploys. He staged a pageant for the Red Cross and presented original plays by Pasadenans. There were amateur nights, and pie-eating contests. Brown even had the actors do their makeup on stage in view of the audience before the show, and host monthly receptions. A theatre critic for the Pasadena *Star News* wrote, (they) "appeared to be a very pleasing and interesting feature" in "Pasadena dramatics."

Design for Living

The run closed in early May and Brown was heralded as a success. But money-wise the season was a flop. A generous donation of five hundred dollars from a prominent attorney kept the creditors from the door. Undaunted, Brown stayed put. He had made influential friends and foresaw a real future here. *The Dramatic Mirror* gave him *carte blanche*, saying that a community theatre would "take an interesting place in Pasadena's dramatic affairs."

Brown called a town meeting in the summer of 1917 to establish a Community Playhouse and an *esprit de corps*. He vowed theatre belonged "to the whole community and is designed to express the big art of friendship." He stressed the non-profit aspects of his "civic enterprise," adding that his endeavors were "for all recreational and artistic interests of the community."

Tomorrow the World

On November 20, 1917, Brown's newly christened Community Players opened four one-acts at the staid Shakespeare Club on South Los Robles. Martha Graham, a dance student, made her stage debut and spoke the Community Players' initial words. Many of Brown's well-known actor friends appeared without pay, contributing to the overall fervor and financial success. Encouraged, Brown looked for a space of his own, and soon moved back to the old Savoy.

Second Chance

Brown recognized this dilapidated burlesque house as having once been quite grand. He moved his company into the pseudo-Spanish-style structure, renamed it the Community Playhouse, and put out a call for hard-working volunteers. The soon-to-be transformed building wasn't perfect, but it suited his purpose quite well. High above an entrance arch were two decorative red-tiled false roofs. Inside, capping dark and peeling walls, an ornate skylight outlined with plaster rosettes held electric light bulbs. These matched the designs in the straightforward proscenium, and a proscenium was all he really needed.

Brown's Community Players debuted at the erstwhile Shakespeare Club.

Brown transformed a dilapidated burlesque house into a renowned theatre.

In Appreciation
PAUL BURKE

Although the *Pasadena Independent* described the run-down ex-burlesque house as "the little brick theatre…with its creaky (wooden) seats and its torn and faded carpets," Brown was never one to complain. He got down to the business of creating theatre. (In the '70s, having come full-circle, X-rated adult movies were the bill of fare here. Eventually, in the name of progress, the Community Playhouse was torn down to make way for Parson's parking lot.)

A Renovating and Redecorating Committee spent $273.81 upgrading the interiors following the first season.

Beyond the Fringe

Not much could be done about the shallow 30-foot stage at the Community Playhouse. It was a director's nightmare. At one time Brown said his stage pictures had the quality of a Greek frieze. Scenery was pushed against the rear wall to provide maximum depth. Crossing from stage left to right, an actor needed to exit into the back alley and then re-enter on the opposite side. When it rained, a volunteer waited outside with an umbrella. Storms also brought the annoying sound of water dripping into buckets lining the attic.

Backstage the conditions were equally primitive. There was one unisex bathroom, and the dressing rooms located in the dank basement were

Large casts meant there were more roles to go around.

In Appreciation
JOLENE BURTON

reached by treacherously narrow stairs. The lighting equipment was minimal. A loft held an act curtain and there was barely room for scenery to fly. Other scenery was stacked. A traveler or draw curtain could be used.

There were neither false boxes nor proscenium doors, and the stage had no apron.

The Play's The Thing

So it wasn't an ideal theatre, and there was never enough money, nor enough of anything for that matter, but there were twenty-eight memorable productions the first season. Brown chose traditional Shakespeare, Sheridan, Moliere, Chekhov, and Yeats. Then he opted for two new plays by Oscar Wilde, an adaptation from Dickens, and rounded out the bill with the popular *Mrs. Wiggs of the Cabbage Patch, Alice in Wonderland* and *Rip van Winkle*.

Benefactors

Now Brown reorganized his volunteers, who incorporated in the fall of 1918. They called themselves The Community Playhouse Association of Pasadena. A board of directors composed of nine leading citizens was drawn from the fifty members. Mrs. Aline Barnsdall donated two thousand dollars. That was enough money for another season.

Pasadena Follies

Next, stressing the joy of creative involvement, Brown invited Pasadena artists to design sets, and society matrons to dress the stage and the actors. His wish seemed to have been their command. *Voila!* Exquisite antiques, heirloom furniture, and brocade drapes from local living rooms soon appeared on the narrow stage. Period costumes were created from donated velvet by a busy "sewing circle." Dozens of uniforms handmade in the finest wool and beautifully stitched silk togas and satin capes became a part of the permanent wardrobe collection. Brown eventually had to rent a warehouse for shop and storage space on the alley half a block north, which remained in use long after the move to South El Molino.

As a way of insuring local support, Brown had sworn he would continue to cast ordinary citizens in both major and minor roles. He kept his word, juxtaposing various professionals and amateurs. Some business men were so smitten with the theatre that they abandoned successful careers. Samuel Hinds, trained as a lawyer, ended up in films.

Mama's Bank Account

Some husbands feared their equally smitten wives might abandon their families or at least plunge them into debt. Several otherwise sensible ladies spent hundreds of dollars outfitting themselves for roles.

The Pasadena Playhouse gamely entered the 1921 Rose Parade.

Lawyer turned actor, Sam Hinds.

In Appreciation
CENFED BANK

STAGE WHISPER: GAIL SHOUP
"Although the Community Playhouse, when using the old Savoy theatre, was a totally inadequate plant, the product turned out by its players was superior to the work done by many groups using far better facilities."

GILMOR BROWN *wowed 'em in* The Merry Wives of Windsor.

A Few Good Men

Brown knew how to please and tease audiences with some Shakespeare and Shaw. The guaranteed "tear-jerkers," *Rebecca of Sunny Brook Farm*, *Little Women*, and the Dickens Christmas story *Cricket on the Hearth* were repeated each season. A Gilbert and Sullivan operetta would be followed by serious drama. Brown cleverly utilized new plays whose rights could be had for little or no money. Often lacking the budget to pay huge dramatic royalties, Brown is said to have used black market copies of New York's hits available from a Chicago outfit which provided a stenographic transcription. A false title was concocted and the author's name changed.

The Knack

Brown's reputation grew. New York playwright Montague Glass waited in line at the box office for half an hour once before getting a last-minute cancellation. He was so impressed with the "honest acting" he saw that he wrote about it in the October 1920 *Theatre Magazine*. Their April issue the year before had carried a description of Brown's "experiments in lighting, setting and producing." Some experiments were born out of necessity. Brown hadn't learned innovative thinking on the prairie of his youth for naught. He shone colored lights on a backdrop of white drapes in *The Tempest* because there was

but sixty-eight cents in the scenery budget. The production was lauded by the drama editor of the *Los Angeles Times*.

Brown staged a stark five-level expressionistic version of *King Lear* on a cubistic and brightly colored set. Pulsating drum beats and brass underscored the dialogue. This seemed rather audacious for Pasadena. Audiences and critics alike either loved or hated the work, but Brown was credited for his boldness.

A 1922 production, *The Yellow Jacket*, astonished audiences with authentic costumes and extravagant properties furnished by the importer, F. Suie One.

Brown also staged the first of many outdoor productions, *The Merry Wives of Windsor*, in conjunction with the city, on a hilltop in Brookside Park. He played Falstaff himself.

A Dream Play

Eugene O'Neill granted Brown permission to give the first Pacific coast production of *Beyond the Horizon*. Established playwrights were rarely this generous to non-professional little theatres.

The premiere of Strindberg's *Lucky Pehr* followed, receiving national notice in *Billboard*, *Variety* and *The Christian Science Monitor*. Maurice Browne, who founded Chicago's Little Theatre, claimed Brown had put Pasadena on the dramatic map of the country with "the succession of worthy plays you have produced …something all too rare…."

In later years, a play selection committee made suggestions, but Brown virtually did his own thing, producing an incredible two shows a month.

The Subject Was Roses

As proof of civic spirit, The Pasadena Playhouse entered the 1921 Rose Parade. The small float designed by F. Tolles Chamberlain consisted of three sculptural figures representing Pasadena, Drama, and Music. Thirty-two actors and theatre personnel, wearing Grecian costumes and carrying banners and garlands of flowers, marched behind. It cost The Pasadena Playhouse $350, despite $500 worth of donations.

How To Succeed In Business Without Really Trying

Brown, a celebrated figure in four short years, was now financially stable enough to hire a music director, a children's theatre director, and a business manager who served also as a promoter. Hans Strechhan in the latter position was soon called the "country's foremost little theatre publicity director—a master of the art" by *Little Theatre Monthly*. He was able to place stories nationally in *Drama*, *Theatre Arts*, and Hearst's *American Weekly*.

Strechhan deserves credit for much of the Community Playhouse's early notoriety. This industrious, somewhat burly man gave his energies entirely to publicity and worked tirelessly until he resigned just prior to the move to South El Molino, possibly because of a personality conflict with board members. In three years, 1919-1922, Strechhan increased membership by over three thousand percent, attendance by four hundred percent and receipts by three hundred percent.

Dedicated to the End

Charles Prickett, who had been a volunteer from the beginning, acting and sweeping out backstage, made a cunning assistant business manager. He assumed most of the financial responsibilities from the start, eventually moving up to general manager. With Prickett skillfully handling the finances, Brown was free to completely devote himself to art.

The Odd Couple

Theatre takes a money man and an artist. Brown dreamed big and Prickett usually found a way to pay. Prickett's practicality often put him at odds with those of artistic temperament. Prickett has been quoted as saying, "It's not always easy to curb the demands of the enthusiast." Brown and Prickett had an uneasy relationship characterized at times by bitter fighting, but in his thirty-three years Prickett rode out a death-defying roller coaster of crises and kept The Pasadena Playhouse open for all but two weeks during the late '40s. Years of ledger sheets testify to Prickett's contribution.

Gilmor Brown *and* **Charles Prickett**.

VOICES OFF
Ken Rose *put in almost eleven years at The Pasadena Playhouse, mostly during the '50s as a student and instructor. Now owner of the Off Ramp theatre in Hollywood, he swears, "Gilmor would have tea with those little old Pasadena ladies, and charm them to death. You can't imagine how good he was. They would be begging to donate whatever he asked for. It was amazing. They never let him down. You had to see it to believe it."*

In Appreciation
COUNTRYWIDE CREDIT INDUSTRIES

In Appreciation
DAVID MILLER CRANDELL

Pasadena Community Playhouse

"A CIVIC ENTERPRISE"

THE PASADENA COMMUNITY PLAYHOUSE ASSOCIATION is a non-profit organization, legally incorporated to foster educational recreation for adults and children. Its purpose is not to make actors but to afford individuals opportunity for self-expression in the Allied Arts of the theatre. The Players—all volunteers—are amateurs in the best sense of the word, as they play for the love of it rather than as a business. Democracy being the Association's ideal, it welcomes as members—Active or Sustaining—ALL who desire to participate in or encourage the communal endeavors for which it stands.

THE GOVERNING BOARD.

Fifth Season   Fourth Regular Production

"KING LEAR"

By William Shakespeare

Eleven Performances   -   January 26 - Feb

COMING

"TOO MANY COO[K]

By Frank Craven

Third Special Production   Week

"GOOD GRACIOUS, ANNA[

By Clare Kummer

A modern King Lear horrified Pasadena but delighted most critics.

"The liveliest thing I have found in Western America is the Pasadena Community Playhouse."—John Drinkwater

---

"Lear" and the Moderns at Pasadena.

S. P. Times

The staging of Shakespeare's "King Lear" is a feat that must always be admired for its heroism, no matter what the results. If this is true of a company who have at their disposal every resource of stage machinery, and who, moreover, proceed in the traditional manner, cutting the play ruthlessly and setting it realistically—what then shall we say of a company who undertake to give the play entire, with symbolic sets and costumes, on a small stage, and with practically no mechanical aid whatever?

This is what the Pasadena Community Players have tried to do in their present production of "Lear," and the results are very interesting, even though one chooses to quarrel violently with some of their methods. Their break from tradition is most decisive, and the whole effect is something which you are likely either to love or dislike intensely—a sure sign of vitality.

The chief difficulty is one of dimensions. "Lear" is a tremendous drama, both spiritually and physically; it seems to demand big and simple backgrounds on the one hand, and much cutting on the other. Above all, it does not want the grotesque emphasis, or any irritant extraneous to its nerve-racking theme.

GIVE OLD PLAY SETTING OF NEW ART

Star News. Jan. 27 1922

Community Players Give "King Lear"; Drama Sets New Mark

• VERSATILITY IS STRONGLY SHOWN

Gilmor Brown as Lear Is Cast in Role for Which He Has Great Love

Daring along the trail of the high arts is dynamite that blasts the way to progress. It makes incredible things possible and the impossible practical. To harness a story of the times before Christ to stage settings evolved in the hectic times of the Twentieth century and popularly known as "impressionistic" or "cubist" or "futuristic" or anything else of that fin de siecle trible and have the twain haul out on the stage an old classic like "King Lear" and "put it over" is an achievement in modern stagecraft.

There is another important—tremendously important — mark to be credited to the triumph of the Pasadena Community Players in their presentation of this old Shakepearean tragedy last night — the versatility they have demonstrated in the weird offering of stage settings. Of one gigantic and impressive combination of stairways, pedestals and hangings, set forth in a geometrical crazy-quilt of color, the Players have developed a throne room, a castle interior, a castle exterior, a stormy heath, a shack, both interior and exterior, a battle ground or two and, yet again, two other and distinctly different castle interiors.

One would say, "It can't be done." The answer is, "It has been done in 'King Lear' by the Pasadena Community Players." A visit to the Playhouse any evening this week will be convincing evidence it has been done cleverly well.

With willing and enthusiastic praise to Gilmor Brown and Eloise Sterling for the remarkable success they have shown in staging this thrilling drama of the immortal bard, the hats of art lovers will be doffed all this week and next to the production and costume innovations developed by Frederick Eastman and the scenic effects that are credited to F. C. Huxley and H. E. Billheimer and to H. Arden Edwards for the painting.

Not only is the daring, above mentioned, evidenced by the scenic effects, but is demonstrated by a departure in the entire presentation of "King Lear," doing away entirely with numbered acts and scenes, just as Shakespeare is said to have done. As far as study of Shakespeare's manner of offering his tragedies can proceed, the Players have followed it.

In Appreciation
ANTOINETTE & BILL CRAWFORD

The national press covered the laying of the cornerstone at the new Pasadena Playhouse.

Extravagant costumes enhanced
The Yellow Jacket.

Unseen Friends

Lenore Shanewise, Maurice Wells, and Ralph Freud started out assisting Brown and became integral parts of his success. Shanewise directed over two hundred productions; Wells, over sixty. Freud made his first appearance in *The Yellow Jacket* and ultimately did more full-length roles than anyone but Brown. Freud directed and co-directed as well.

Brown knew the value of a good technical director. Frederic Carl Huxley, for whom one of the small theatres was named, was ultimately hired and stayed with The Pasadena Playhouse until his death in 1949.

This Property Condemned

Eventually, the house outdrew its space, which the fire department had already condemned. Brown envisioned a new permanent theatre. He talked of a multi-stage complex, "the largest working plant in the universe." He presented a grandiose plan, budgeted at $300,000, to The Community Playhouse Association of Pasadena.

Angels Amongst Us

A fund drive commenced to raise money for the building. In 1922, three board members made a payment of $1,500 toward the property on South El Molino with 110-foot frontage. It was 195 feet deep. The balance of the $23,000 purchase price was contributed in early 1923 by sixty-six donors. Encouraged, the Community Playhouse incorporated a holding company called The Pasadena Community Guild with the authority to raise money for the new building. Over $20,000 was raised by the sale of stock. A door-to-door campaign, chaired by Mrs. Hale, began with local newspapers charting the progress. The academic community pitched in and made over a hundred contributions. Mrs. Robert Millikan gathered $125,000. Yet amazingly, most of the money came from smaller subscriptions of fifty cents or a dollar.

As You Like It

The Littleton Company was hired with Elmer Grey as the project architect. His proposed rendering, (a flip-flop version was later used for Tucson's Temple of

In Appreciation
JOHN CULLUM

Music and Art), appeared in *Billboard*, *Drama Theatre* and *Theatre Arts*. Modification stickers bloomed all over the blueprints. They represented $200,000 in changes. It was raised by first and second mortgages and a loan.

Still, money was needed for seats, curtains, draperies, carpets—there was an endless list. Old friends of the Community Playhouse united to meet this bill of twelve thousand dollars. Indebtedness remained, and money would always be a problem.

A Touch of the Poet

The Drama League of America met in Pasadena in 1924, and PR whiz Stechhan made the most of it. He suggested the laying of the cornerstone for the new theatre, to be called The Pasadena Playhouse, on May 31st as part of the convention's activities. The project, heavily covered by the press, continued to expand. An additional 3,300 square feet was purchased for $4,500. On September 13, 1924, the actual work was begun by the Winter Construction Company, which had built Sid Grauman's Egyptian Theatre.

All's Well That Ends Well

The nostalgic closing night, May 2, 1925, at the Community Playhouse was a sell-out. Rachel Crothers' comedy *Expressing Willie*, the last of 163 productions, left them laughing.

With the move to a new space, Brown believed that at last Pasadena could rival New York and London.

In Appreciation
TONY DANZA

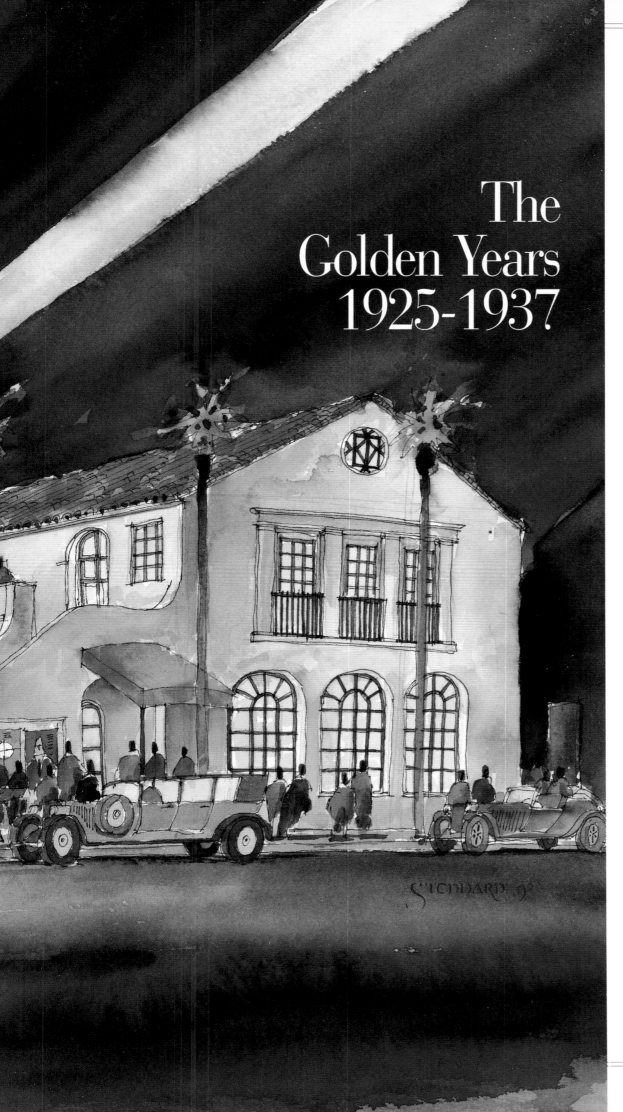

The Golden Years 1925-1937

T here was something exalted about the imposing new theatre from the beginning. Perhaps it was the architectural tribute to California's early religious life. Roofed in vibrant red tile, the two stories of vanilla stucco with cloistered arcades embraced a flagstone-rough and flower-bright courtyard. It could have been one of Father Junipero Serra's stops on the way north. After all, Monterey Road, the old trail that connected the missions, is just a few miles south.

Paths of Glory

With a building as splendid as the address, almost as ritzy as Millionaire's Row, The Pasadena Playhouse blended inconspicuously into the neighborhood. Unlike New York spaces, the rambling structure deceptively hid the modernly efficient plant. Brown went directly into rehearsal and luxuriated in the opulence.

Heaven Can Wait

Silhouetted palm and olive trees fringed the pastel evening sky, and sleek limousines lined the curb on the balmy May night in 1925 when The Pasadena Playhouse opened. Tickets had been pre-sold by mail for five dollars. Hundreds of last-minute patrons had to be turned away at the box office. Stylishly-clad first-nighters, the women gowned in flowing pastel chiffon—the men, black tie—paused in the courtyard. Waterfalls of light fell from large wrought-iron lanterns. Romantic guitar music accom-

Local artist Alson Clark handcrafted the asbestos fire curtain.

The swooping balcony lacked visual support.

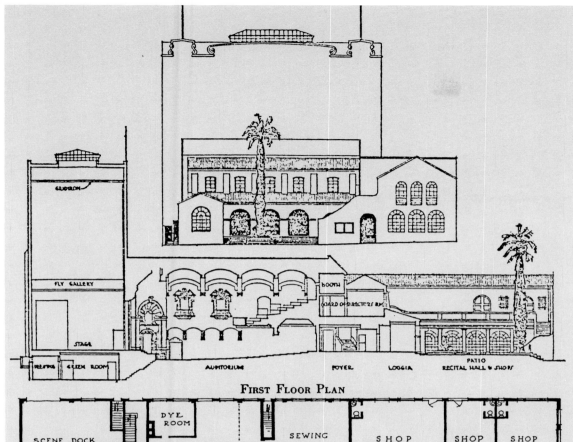

First Floor Plan

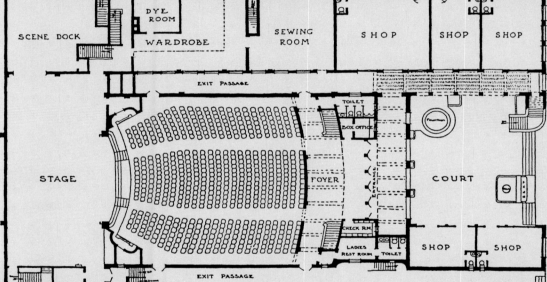

Dimensional Data

Proscenium height .... 20 ft.   Stage depth from curtain... 36 ft.
Proscenium width .... 31 ft. 6 in. Stage height above room floor 47 in.
Stage height to gridiron.... 69 ft.   Back-to-back spacing of seats 33 in.
Stage clear width........ 73 ft. 6 in. Cubage per seat..........1035 cu. ft.

83.5%	BUILDING & FEES	$365,000.	$440./seat
1.1%	STAGE EQUIPMENT	4,000.	5.
2.7%	ALL ELECTRIC WORK	12,000.	14.
3.4%	SWITCHBOARD	15,000.	18.
4.6%	HEATING & VENTILATING	20,000.	24.
2.1%	AUDITORIUM CHAIRS	9,500.	11.
2.6%	DECORATION	11,500.	14.

CUBAGE 860,000. CU. FT.	IN 1925 @ 54.3¢/CU.FT.	TOTAL $467,000.	$530./seat
COMPARATIVE COST E.N.R. JAN. 1 1933	41.6¢/CU.FT.	TOTAL $358,000.	$406./seat

panied excited conversations, tugging at already heightened emotions.

Inside the foyer, the freshly painted walls, still slightly sticky to the touch, shimmered like good taffeta in the golden glow from ornate wall sconces. And, adding a personal touch, there was a handsomely framed portrait of the gracious Gilmor Brown. He seemed to be welcoming his guests.

Patrons gasped as they entered the 820-seat auditorium. Some said it rivaled the garish Opera House in Barcelona. The sight was breathtaking. Architect Elmer Grey had not sacrificed beauty in designing the interior of this working center.

Looking Good

The auditorium had the lush multifaceted look of a sparkling cut-crystal tumbler full of brandy. Geometric floral patterns, drawn to resemble tiles, were hand-painted onto the burlap in the coved ceiling.

Professor Vern Knudsen, an acoustical consultant, had laid two inches of felt underneath, insuring the finest sound. The swooping balcony hovered over the main floor without visual support as graceful as a sizeable bird in flight.

Straight ahead, upon the asbestos fire curtain, a Spanish galleon listed with amber sails unfurled in a vivid aquamarine sea. Handcrafted by local artist Alson Clark (Clark's work includes the

Your Opportunity

YOUR beautiful, long-dreamed of Community Playhouse is open at last. It represents not only the faith of the community in its citizens, but the belief of the community in doing as perfectly as possible whatever it undertakes. Pasadena citizens have put faith, effort and money into this community movement—an enterprise which those who stand closest to it, believe to be in its infancy.

This is your Playhouse, your enterprise, your opportunity. A conservative appraisal of the value of this plant is $400,000. These figures do not represent the actual cost of the Playhouse, because many Pasadena artists and business men have whole-heartedly contributed their services.

Many of you have given and given liberally. There are, however, many more who have not as yet taken advantage of the opportunity to prove their faith in their community and their sense of responsibility toward its undertakings. You can not but be proud of this building, its beauty, its equipment and its promise. Will you not express your faith, your appreciation, your spirit of co-operation by helping to clear your Community Playhouse, now about half paid for, of debt? Any donation, large or small, will help. "SAY IT WITH CHECKS."

MRS. ERNEST WITBECK
CHARLES STANTON
ARY ESTHER MARCELLUS
ELIZABETH FLINT
J. MILTON STEINBERGER
EDYTHE KING
DR. H. F. BOECKMAN
HAROLD CROSS
OBERT LOOFBOURROW
MILDRED SCHEIBLER
ROSE BRIZIUS
ROGER CLAPP
ERRIEN GRUNIGAN
JEROME YOUNG
RBERT ROOKSBY
ARET COLEMAN
AIR MURPHEY
RLE STANLEY
V. HINDS
Y HOLBERT
MACAFEE
ATES POST
AY GLASS
WILLIAMS
MURPHEY
MILTON
NKLER
ATHER
MOND
CAN
ELL
EN

WIGHTMAN
RS. DAVID BLANKENHORN
GEORGE BENDER
MRS. STELLA QUACKENBOS
MARIE HUXLEY
MARGARET R. CLARK
GERTRUDE PETTIGREW
GEORGE C. REIS
MARGARET MILLER
GWYNNE COLLIER
LOIS AUSTIN

L. rangers
Th Enchanted Cottage
Expressing Willie
The Children's Theatre
The Original Plays
The Dark Lady of the Sonnets
Production Group
MILDRED SCHEIBLER, GENEVIEVE GRAYDON, MRS. WILLIAM E. VanDOORN, J. L. JAGGER
MRS. CARL VAN DUGTEREN, MRS. E. B. FUESSLE, MARIE JOHNSON
Costume Group   LORETTA JAPS
The Maid

"THE AMETHYST"

A Comedy in Four Acts

Needles and pins, needles and pins,
When a man marries his trouble begins.

Cast

Harold Brown, an author
Byron Hawksley, an actor
Judge Brewster, a distinguished lawyer
George T. Stockton, a moving picture impresario
Schuyler Hazlett, a young millionaire
Jake Durkin, expert accountant
McPherson, a contractor
Bobbie Crocker, in the smart set
Mildred Brown, Harold's wife
Blanche Duval, a Broadway leading
Amy Crocker, Bobbie's wife
Mrs. Latimer, a society matron
Pamela Gast, in the smart set
Miss Stilson, a stenographer
Miss Klinger, a stenographer
Hilda, a maid
A Script Girl

SAM
FRED
ROBERT

DOUGLAS

ACT I.   A living ro
ACT II. The same
ACT III. The same
ACT IV. A studi

SETTINGS DESIG
by Carl
PRODUCTION
Antha
COSTUME
Carl
SPANISH
Miss
PROPER
ACKNO
i
MUSI

The opening night program included a request to "Say It With Checks."

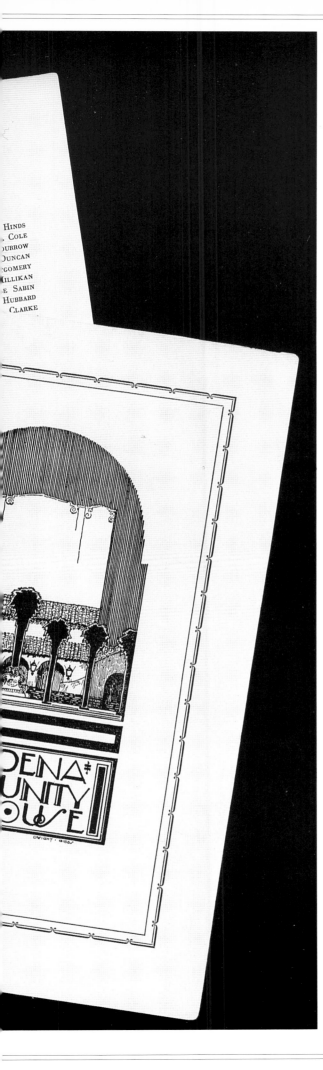

murals in the lobby of what is now Sanwa Bank on Colorado Boulevard), the top two masts extended clear to the proscenium arch.

And what a flamboyant arch it was, scrolled in gold leaf and crowned by an exotic-looking carved Mayan mask. On either side of the Mainstage, black fringed Spanish shawls draped two intricately grilled false boxes topped with lavish cornices. In between, wooden doors fronted an additional 50 square feet of playing area under equally ostentatious "Juliets" or usable balconies.

The Curtain Rises

The program commenced with a salute to the past. Seventy-seven actors costumed as fictional characters from previous productions at the Community Playhouse paraded solemnly down the side aisles, posing onstage to thunderous applause—much as they had at North Fair Oaks. These same actors and their colleagues, 1,200 in all, donated the necessary funds to complete

the tiered courtyard fountain, the baroque central core ringed with molded conch shells.

Silver serpentine stripes slithered across the lavish black velour curtain that rose promptly at eight o'clock to reveal a *chic* Long Island living room. Brown admitted that his premiere production *The Amethyst*, with a cast of seventeen, "wasn't a particularly good play," but felt no one was coming to see the show. Taking a curtain call, he told the audience it was *their* theatre. A visiting New York drama critic reported, "Pasadena has reason to be proud."

Accommodations

The stage provided an extravagant playing area that allowed for large casts and grandiose productions. An entire battle scene could be easily accommodated. A removable forestage covered the orchestra pit. Also, a hinged portion could be raised. (When the auditorium was remodeled in 1965, a much deeper forestage was permanently installed.)

Sam Hinds in The Amethyst.

In Appreciation
BERLE ADAMS

Steps and a short passageway down through the orchestra pit led to the green room below, providing the audience a direct route backstage to congratulate the actors after the performance. This was Brown's idea. He believed that familiarity bred conviviality, not contempt.

Waiting for Godot

The green room was a comfortable lounge. This, the actor's realm, so-called because one of the first backstage waiting areas for performers was painted green, loomed 22 feet by 44 feet and was larger than most living rooms. Above, massive cement ceiling beams painted to resemble wood were decorated with festive hearts, shields, and crests. Huge framed wall mirrors revealed to the colorfully costumed actors just who was the fairest of them all. Red lacquered panel doors lined the walls like tomatoes ripe on the vine. These doors led into 10 three-person dressing rooms, or to corridors that connected a large makeup room, a costume room, and a place for the musicians and ushers. There was even a kitchen for the cast dinners and receptions. A locker room, two sea-green tiled toilet and shower rooms, and two rooms assigned to members of the chorus were spacious and modern.

Behind the Scenes

Backstage was a showcase of the latest technology, unequaled west of

Margaret O'Brian and *John Barrymore*, Jr., in *the famed scene from* Romeo and Juliet *for which these "Juliets" or usable balconies are named.*

The second-floor recital hall was reminiscent of a small church.

The luxurious green room.

Chicago. Designed by Claude D. Seaman, the lighting equipment originally included strip lights in inventive color combinations. Foot and cyclorama lights were concealed. There were more than the usual number of electrical circuits. Four years later Ralph Freud, using a Brunswick phonograph, installed a sound system.

The Chairs

The board room doubled as a library. Comfortable leather chairs clustered around an oak table before an elegant Batchelder tile fireplace decorated with voguish Byzantine peacocks and lovebirds. An outspoken leader in the Arts and Crafts Movement, local craftsman Ernest Batchelder served as president of The Pasadena Playhouse board for years.

An impressive donation of a two-volume autographed set of Eugene O'Neill's works created a need for substantial book cases. Early editions of Shakespeare were added and the library became official. Eventually, the entire area above the foyer was needed to hold the valuable collection which included ten thousand volumes on every theatre-related subject, five thousand play manuscripts, and one thousand rare books and designs for Japanese Kabuki theatre finely executed on ancient rice paper scrolls. It was considered to be second only to the theatre section of the New York Public Library. Later on, students from the School of Theatre Arts would

In Appreciation
FRANK FERRANTE

encounter Beckett, Brecht, Chekhov, and even Pinter for the first time in this small room with the ambience of an exclusive men's club.

A Thousand Clowns

The wardrobe facilities on South El Molino were almost as large as the Mainstage. They provided ample space for costume construction and storage. The wardrobe cabinets and the sewing and dye rooms were located on the first floor of the two-story wing to the north. The structure ran from the scene dock in back to the front sidewalk and was separated from the main building by a covered arcade.

The ever-increasing costume collection was valued at seventy thousand dollars early on. Brown's efficient wardrobe ladies handled more capes, furs, hats, shoes, tuxedos, three-piece suits, silk robes, and Parisian gowns than Bullock's Wilshire. There were enough military uniforms to outfit a small regiment, clown outfits P.T. Barnum might have envied, and more togas than there were Greek plays.

Room Service

Still on the ground floor, closest to the street, were three rental units designated for commercial stores, including a lingerie shop. Across the patio, two others were located in a one-story extension of the main building. (Today La Tienda occupies that space.) A tea room

survived until 1935, serving luncheon and tea and light dinner. The shops closed during the '40s and the space was taken over by the theatre. Later, the first floor of the northern wing became the lobby of the School of Theatre Arts with a receptionist and rows of student mailboxes.

From east to west on the second floor of this wing, there were offices and a conference room; and, closest to the street, there was a long and narrow recital hall, reminiscent of a medieval church. These were reached by an open curving stairway from the patio. The recital hall later became the two student theatres (it now houses the Balcony Theatre), and was used for student productions and to produce experimental works by new authors.

The Price

The *Star News* called the new building a "Monument to Achievement." The organization's land, buildings, fixtures and equipment, as of June 23, 1925, were valued at $382,730.

Still there was a bonded debt of $200,000, and there were interest and principal payments to be made. Charles Prickett constantly battled bankruptcy. A generous gift of $180,000 from Mrs. Fannie E. Morrison paid off most of this in 1930.

View From the Top

Soaring steeple high and sporting sun

In Appreciation
FIRST LOS ANGELES BANK

Charlotte Stewart hopes to read mail from home.

Toga-clad actors await their hour upon the stage.

Ralph Freud served Brown as an actor and director.

VOICES OFF
Fannie E. Morrison's generous donations paid off several debts and made the tower addition possible. Out of deference, all profanity, smoking and drinking were cut from the script when she attended a matinee.

If a swear word did slip from an actor's mouth, she would protest by stamping her umbrella. Also, the fact that she talked continually in a loud voice during the show was overlooked.

Carl Huxley *and* ***James Callahan*** *worked the technical side.*

decks and an outdoor basketball court on the sixth-floor roof, a 40,000-square-foot tower was wrapped around the existing building in 1936. Named the Fannie E. Morrison tower, its benefactor ultimately donated approximately one-third of a million dollars to the theatre. Counting the annex, with its own elevator, Brown now ruled over 70,000 square feet—all under one roof.

Most of the addition was used for production facilities. The new scene shop filled the first and second floors. Properties and furniture moved to the third. Brown selected an office here, as did the other directors. The fourth floor was costume heaven with closets, cupboards, and sewing areas. A permanent

home for the emerging drama school, previously a series of informal classes in available space, was established. Costly up-to-date student classrooms, dance studios, and rehearsal stages occupied the fifth and sixth floors.

The Pasadena Playhouse had become big business. It was one of the largest theatre complexes in the world, and the only facility of its kind west of the Mississippi.

The Film Society

When silent stars tried to speak in the new "talkies," film directors realized that good looks and ability didn't necessarily go together. Sam Goldwyn turned to Brown, who had a reputation for produc-

In Appreciation
THOMPSON & COMPANY

ing classically trained actors that rivaled New York. It has been said that Brown's greatest talent was recognizing talent in others. A geographical and practical link to Hollywood was forged. The theatre and school were dubbed "the talent factory." Brown reveled in this association.

Hollywood agents scouted theatre productions like college coaches at high school games. The studios offered the actors what the theatre couldn't: thirty-five dollars for a day's work. Many actors shot from dawn until dusk at Warner Brothers, Paramount, or Metro, appearing in as many as three films a day, then raced back across pre-freeway surface streets to make an eight o'clock curtain.

During 1921 an early film producer, R. R. Rockett, wrote in *Cinemagram* that Pasadena "will help the movies, in that it will improve the 'raw material' for picture production and make available much new talent for every department of stage and screen."

Believing it to ultimately serve his best interests, Cecil B. deMille helped finance one of the Shakespearean Summer Festivals. DeMille recommended the invaluable experience of appearing on a stage. "I would rather an actor has his training in the theatre than in any other medium."

Stardust

Seemingly overnight, a left turn to the west on Colorado Boulevard from South El Molino Avenue became the well-trav-eled road to stardom for many actors. Blonde Billy Beadle, a South Pasadena kid who attended Pasadena Junior College, took the glittery Colorado Boulevard route (in his case from Brown's small Playbox theatre) to the silver screen; he changed his name to William Holden along the way.

Eventually the opening of the Arroyo Seco freeway made this star trek easier.

Brown's several stages were second home to Dana Andrews, Jean Arthur, Lee J. Cobb, Jean Inness, Victor Jory, Victor Mature, Tyrone Power, Robert Preston, Maudie Prickett, Robert Taylor, and Robert Young. When David Niven arrived in Los Angeles, Goldwyn sent him to The Pasadena Playhouse for experience. At Sunday matinees matrons lined up to ask the suave Victor Jory, a graduate of Pasadena High School, for his autograph. They had seen his film *Gone With the Wind*, but he had won their hearts first on the Mainstage at The Pasadena Playhouse.

The Way of the World

A Hollywood crowd started hanging out at The Pasadena Playhouse. Earlier, Mary Pickford and Douglas Fairbanks, Sr., had attended the 1923 production of *My Lady's Dress*. Both Will Rogers and Charlie Chaplin made memorable visits to the new Playhouse's green room. By the '30s there were almost as many screen stars enjoying nightcaps in the neighborhood bars, say at Albert Sheetz,

Billy Beadle, a South Pasadena kid, changed his name to **William Holden** after appearing at Brown's Playbox.

VOICES OFF
Lawrence O'Sullivan, a student in the late '50s, remembers the sanguine hours spent in The Pasadena Playhouse library. "I discovered Camus there."

BACKSTAGE WITH **ETHEL WATERS**
Drama professor Gail Shoup, formerly an instructor at The Pasadena Playhouse, reports that when Ms. Waters did A Member of the Wedding on the Mainstage she was very ill and needed a tank of oxygen backstage. "After each scene she would collapse into a chair, breathe from the air tube until her next cue and then I'd help her walk back on."

In Appreciation
NORTHWEST ASSET MANAGEMENT CO., INC.

after the show as there were across town at Musso and Frank Grill or The Brown Derby. Nardi's, a hole-in-the-wall, wasn't exactly Sardi's, but it was close and comfortable with a vaguely perverse atmosphere that added to its charm.

Brown received several offers to "go Hollywood." While he enjoyed consorting with those in the film industry, his loyalty was to his own theatre where he had undisputed authority. He had a fascination with celebrities and glamour, however, and was very good at persuading name stars to play "legit" in Pasadena now and then, usually without salary.

The Palace of Truth

In its heyday, The Pasadena Playhouse produced 500 new scripts —claiming 23 American and 477 World premieres. Among these: Noel Coward's *Calvacade,* and F. Scott Fitzgerald's *An American Jazz Comedy: The Vegetable*. Brown befriended a timid, obscure playwright named Tennessee Williams, who tried out several plays on somewhat shocked Pasadena audiences. All thirty-seven Shakespeare plays were staged in their entirety. During the first twenty-five years, The Pasadena Playhouse produced 1,348 plays, an average of over fifty plays a year, with more than six hundred mounted on the Mainstage. (By the '60s this figure exceeded one thousand.)

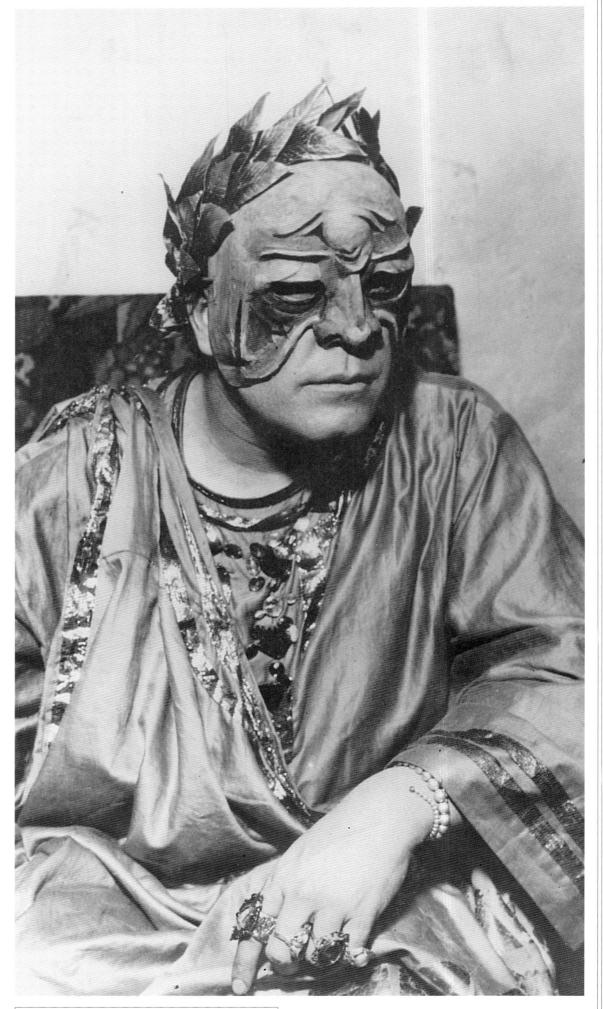

*A masked **Gilmor Brown**.*

In Appreciation
HARRY GROENER

Lazarus Laughed

Perhaps the most notable and ambitious premiere was Eugene O'Neill's *Lazarus Laughed*, a rather tedious epic. The play was only produced twice, in Pasadena and later at Fordham University, causing O'Neill to write that "the cost of mounting such an elaborate play deterred the New York commercial theatre."

Starring Victor Jory and Lenore Shanewise, the saga of the life of Jesus Christ after his resurrection from the dead was timed to open near Easter in 1928. The play, which sought to defy the final reality of death, had 136 cast members, with a chorus and full orchestra. Three hundred masks were used. Only Lazarus was bare faced.

O'Neill once said, "I was visualizing an effect that, intensified by dramatic lighting, would give an audience visually the sense of the Crowd…as a collective whole…" The masks and the costumes and the fact that the play was mostly considered unactable received coast-to-coast press. There were advance bookings from all over the West, and such a demand for tickets that the run was extended.

The production grossed over $35,000 and received world-wide acclaim.

In Appreciation
H. N. FRANCES C. BERGER FOUNDATION

Affairs of State

On March 25, 1937, the legislature resolved to confer upon the Pasadena Playhouse the honor of becoming the State Theatre of California, for having brought "national and international renown to the State of California as a center of dramatic art."

Brown and The Pasadena Playhouse had become legendary.

In Appreciation
PEGGY EBRIGHT

44

The legendary Gilmor Brown as Brutus.

In Appreciation
GREGORY HARRISON

Gwen Horn Willson: THEN

As a drama student in the late '30s, Willson stepped onto the elevator going up and found herself pressed against Vic Mature, Bob Preston, George Reeves, and Don De Fore. "They were on their way to a meeting with Gilmor. I thought I had died and the elevator was transporting me to heaven!"

Gwen Horn Willson: NOW

Willson credits her start in show biz to The Pasadena Playhouse. Currently active in commercials, Willson and the Maytag man rendezvoused in Paris. Most recently, she fooled around with Jack Klugman and Canon Copiers. Stacy Keach, Sr., took her for a second honeymoon on Amtrak, and O.J. Simpson took her for a ride in a Hertz.

IDIOT'S DELIGHT
This bouquet of beauties danced with Robert Preston in Idiot's Delight. Gwen Horn Willson, bottom left, claims, "He could sing and dance every bit as well in the beginning as he did many years later in The Music Man."

In Appreciation
PATRICIA HEATON

Robert Preston *as the Aztec warrior in* Montezuma.

Robert Young *as Marco Polo and in* Street of a Thousand Shadows.

In Appreciation
KATHERINE HELMOND

BACKSTAGE WITH **JON JORY**

Producing Director Jon Jory of the prestigious Actors Theatre of Louisville—home to the acclaimed Humana Festival of New American Plays—didn't feel his childhood distinctive, despite the fact that he was the comely and multi-talented son of Victor Jory and Jean Inness. These Playhouse regulars practically raised him in the green room downstairs. "I'd be content for awhile to sit on those pseudo-leather chairs, but eventually the actor-talk would pall on me and I'd roll my socks into a ball and con someone into a game of 'sock' soccer."

Six-year-old Jory performed in A Christmas Carol, and later in Life With Father. As a young teen Jory naively believed everyone's life was like his. "I had no idea until I was at South Pasadena Junior High that movie stars didn't hang out at everyone's house, come by New Year's Eve, that sort of thing. And I didn't realize my father had a tremendous following. I discovered that about my dad, I think, when Miss Spellicy the English teacher swooned at a parent/teacher conference."

VICTOR JORY AND **JEAN INNESS**

*One of **Jon Jory's** treasured memories is having his mother and father star in Long Day's Journey Into Night at Actors Theatre of Louisville. The small theatre there is called the Victor Jory.*

In Appreciation
EARL HOLLIMAN

48

Lee J. Cobb, *Victory Jory* and **Milburn Stone** in The Virginian.

Robert Preston (center) in Idiot's Delight.

STAGE WHISPER:
RICHARD BALDWIN
"On the afternoon of opening night the female lead in The Amazing Dr. Clitterhouse *became ill. Kay Feltus (the lovely woman who married Robert Preston) was rushed into the role by director and male lead, Victor Jory. No one could learn all the lines in the few hours remaining. Jory advised Feltus to let him cover for them. During the performance, Jory either cued her or supplied the critical information needed from her in his next speech. So skillfully did they handle it that few in the audience suspected that the performance was anything other than the usual professional Playhouse production."*

Richard Baldwin relates an ironic prophecy about classmate Will Price. *"Speech teacher Belle Kennedy, exasperated at Price's inability to mouth those round, pear-shaped vowels, told him that he would never get far until he lost his deep-South drawl. But when David Selznick chose Viivian Leigh for the role of Scarlett in* Gone With The Wind, *Price was hired as a voice coach to make the English actress sound authentically Southern."*

VOICES OFF
Alumna **Catherine Feltus Preston**, wife of Robert Preston, remembers a performance of Girl of The Golden West. *"When the villain, Victor Jory, rushes in, Jean Inness must help the injured hero, Preston, up the rungs of a loft ladder. The fringe of Jean's shawl got tangled in Pres's spurs. A seasoned actress, she slipped out of the shawl and tossed it up with Pres, nonchalantly playing out the rest of the scene in her night dress."*

In Appreciation
JULIE & DON HOPF

Diversification

4

T he Pasadena Playhouse can be seen whimsically as Gilmor Brown's treasured toy. He had been collecting the building blocks since he first dreamed of creating his own theatre. And, when it was done, he looked around with great satisfaction and curiosity and wondered how to add on without having the marvelous structure come toppling down. This wasn't child's play. The results were some lasting innovations in experimental theatre, education, radio, and television.

Toys In the Attic

Brown was credited with developing central staging in America. He secured this place in theatrical history almost accidentally when he opened a makeshift stage in his own home. At that time Brown lived at 251 South Fair Oaks Avenue, just south of the Community Playhouse. An artist, the previous owner, had conveniently built a studio which Brown lined with dining room chairs. The year was 1924 and he used this as a clubroom for friends and promising students, never suspecting his pushing furniture against the walls in a horseshoe, half-moon, sandwich or L shape would eventually develop into "theatre-in-the-round."

Intimate theatre was an established European concept by then. Brown had heard of it in his school days. But some suggest this is pure coincidence, that he and his pals were simply performing

plays at home for enjoyment, somewhat like the neighborhood kids doing shows in that Denver basement.

Getting My Act Together and Taking It On the Road

Calling his creation a Playbox, Brown's second theatre-in-the-round was built on Herkimer Street (it later became Union) in 1929. After the city bought this site for a parking lot, the building was moved to 154 North Hudson Street and attached to a house. The original building was then converted to dressing rooms. Brown described this Playbox in a letter to William Saroyan, regarding the August 12, 1940, production of *My Heart's in the Highlands*: "… a small, 'intimate' theatre, just a large room with alcoves on four sides, that seats about forty-five people. There is no stage in the platform sense, no curtain, no footlights, no programs, playbills here." A few years before Brown's death he sold the Hudson property, including the buildings. The living room of his last home at 391 South Madison Avenue became the final Playbox.

Situation Comedy

So-called "drawing room" and "kitchen table" plays were most easily staged. However, the bill of fare at the Playbox was not limited to interior settings. There was a vague correlation to the selections at The Pasadena Playhouse, but the Playbox's offerings were less tra-

***Brown** and **Percy MacKaye**.*

STAGE WHISPER:
LAWRENCE O'SULLIVAN
"We were crammed onto the Separate Tables set. I was seated with an actress, my girl-friend in the play. At a very quiet and dramatic moment, an elderly woman from the audience reached over and grabbed the skirt of her dress. Then this woman commented in a loud voice, 'Oh, it is real silk!'"

STAGE WHISPER:
STUART MARGOLIN
"Once while Gilmor Brown, he must have been almost seventy, was roaming around upstairs in his house during a Playbox production, he stopped the action dead when he screamed, 'Hey! Who didn't flush the damn toilet!'"

ditional. Brown liked poetic dramas. *Pelleas and Melisande* was the second production his first season. *Chanticleer* was the last of his life. *Gaslight's* premiere here led to its Broadway production.

Theatre Arts Monthly, June 1935, reported that "under favorable conditions illusion is heightened rather than dispelled by close proximity to the actors." Brown liked to encourage intimacy between audience and actor. Often this worked, but when it didn't the results provided real-life drama. There are tales of spectators sitting on stage furniture, eating props such as tea sandwiches and mints, pocketing change and carefully placed newspapers. Also, since the Playbox was located in residential areas, passersby often wondered about incessant screaming and shouting. The police were called more than once to break up a choreographed fight scene.

Kept financially separate from The Pasadena Playhouse, the smaller theatre usually did very well. No tickets were available to the general public. Interested persons, an elite group solicited by Brown, including members of civic drama clubs, were able to see the performances by purchasing yearly memberships. Sometimes successful productions from the Playbox had an extended life on the Mainstage.

The Caretaker

Those who worked with Brown closely, both students and faculty, feel that the

Playbox was his real "baby." Brown's use of this then-unorthodox staging visibly changed American theatre. Margo Jones, alumna and founder of a major theatre in Dallas, Texas, wrote Brown three decades later, "You must get a thrill when you see theatres using central staging all over the country and you can remember how the seed was planted in your own living room." Today "theatre-in-the round" is commonplace.

Trouble In the Works

Minimal staging of "plays in progress" was another of Brown's ideas. It was a way to launch new and experimental projects. Relegating the majority of the work to junior directors, Brown produced these untried scripts at Workshops once a month while at the Community Playhouse. After settling into 39 South El Molino, he eventually returned to the practice. The second-floor recital hall became home to the Workshops. It was furnished with a stage in 1927, thanks to donations from the artist Alson Clark, among others.

Broadway Bound

After the tower was finished in 1936, the Workshop space was first converted into the Laboratory Theatre, and then into two small stages for students. Two hundred and fifty plays were done in the Workshop and Laboratory theatres. A story analyst for Paramount has said that he attended the experimental produc-

PASADENA PLAYHOUSE
GILMOR BROWN'S PLAYBOX THEATRE

"TIGER AT THE GATES"
Directed by- Ken Rose

Theatre-in-the-round developed at Gilmor Brown's Playbox.

STAGE WHISPER:
TERRENCE BEASOR

"We were doing The Merchant of Venice. Gilmor Brown, as usual, arrived at the last minute. See, he dressed in a private dressing room concealed behind a door in his office at The Playhouse. His driver brought him over just in time to enter on cue. It was a hot night—you know how hot it can be in Pasadena—and a long show. We were in full dress, wool tights—this was before Spandex—and perspiring heavily. Soon perspiration loosened the spirit gum holding Gilmor's false nose. It began to slip. He had to play hand to nose for almost an hour. I'm sure it's a coincidence, but Gilmor never performed as an actor again."

STAGE WHISPER:
MARY KING BOWDITCH

"I'll never forget the night a man in the audience whipped out a lighter and lit the leading lady's cigarette before the actor who was supposed to do this on stage could strike a match."

VOICES OFF

Alumnus **Richard Vath** writes from Mexico that during a Playbox performance the leading lady was to drop a ball of yarn, which was his entrance cue. However, "one of the Pasadena dears" repeatedly retrieved the ball of yarn and handed it back to the actress, who finally had to hurl it to Vath off stage so the action could continue.

A mishap occurred in another play when a uniformed Western Union boy delivered a telegram to actor Fred Berest on stage. The audience believed this to be part of the show. Vath, also on stage, ad-libbed, "Aren't you going to read it?" It turned out the wire was a congratulatory note from Gilmor Brown.

*South Pasadena coed, **Cheryl Walker**, who went on to become Rose Queen, tried out for Brown and was given a walk-on part.*

Many locals tried out for parts.

tions regularly looking for scripts to buy. In 1938, *Stage* cited the Laboratory Theatre as "foremost among the experimental theatres of this country."

When the first-floor Patio Theatre was added, Brown controlled a total of five stages.

Top Girls

At Brown's bidding the energetic women of The Pasadena Playhouse Association assumed the responsibility of the Workshops. The distinguished screenplay writer, Catherine Turney, later a member of the School of Theatre Arts' first graduating class in 1930, became the managing director and held that position for many years.

Special Offer

Brown remained faithful to his promise to use amateurs in most performances even after the move to the new theatre. Pasadena area residents were invited to audition on Sundays from seven-thirty to midnight. These open readings quickly turned into a "cattle call." The local aristocracy came in droves from as far away as the eastern edge of San Marino. Self-assured husbands escorted buxom wives, anxious mothers chaperoned their lovely young daughters and malleable sons. Proud grandparents dragged boisterous but well-dressed grandchildren. The Pasadena Playhouse developed a central file of over ten thousand viable names. In the late '30s a South Pasadena High School coed, Cheryl Walker (who went on to become Rose Queen), was given a walk-on part and ended up working opposite Victor Mature. Later, while making *Stage Door Canteen* under contract to Paramount, Walker credited Brown with her discovery. Usually, professional actors who lived in town, including Victor Jory and Jean Inness, won the major roles.

In Appreciation
STACY KEACH, JR.

The Young and the Beautiful

The Pasadena Playhouse's School of Theatre Arts (ultimately called the College of Theatre Arts) was one of the most illustrious drama schools in the U.S., at one time second only to The Juilliard School in New York. Toward the end of his life, Brown relied upon the school not only for income, but also for an international reputation. It has been suggested that the celebrated institution was established primarily as a business venture by Charles Prickett—one in which he could dominate—and that Brown's interest in the classrooms was slight. On the other hand, teaching had always been a reliable source of income for Brown.

Basically self-educated, Brown gave elocution lessons off and on, and he continued to do so when he arrived in Pasadena. Prickett's younger brother Oliver, then eleven years old, took a series of them.

The Colony

The school's origins can be traced to board of directors' minutes in 1919, which outline thirty lessons for five dollars starting January, 1920. Additional sessions were planned to bring in extra money during that summer. The Summer Art Colony grew from this series of classes. Brown believed the best way to learn to act was to put on a play, with the side benefit that student productions generated more money.

In Appreciation
JUDY & BOB KILPATRICK

Roderick Richard Deane, aka Richard Smart, Class of 1934, has had a notable career as a musical performer on Broadway and in touring companies.

Set-design was mandatory.

The Colony was popular from the onset. The six-week course offered various classes at fifteen dollars each. Dr. Richard Burton, a former president of the Drama League of America, headed the faculty. The teaching staff was made up of well-known guest lecturers. Classes included dramatic writing, play construction, dramatic interpretation, costume design, dramatic dancing and pantomime, community music, and music drama.

Thirty-four pupils were first enrolled, and the number increased to fifty-six the second year. The young people met in the Community Playhouse on North Fair Oaks and in the old Throop College Building owned by Caltech. By the third year, students received college credits from the University of California, possibly because instructor Dr. Margaret S. Carhart was on the staff of what became UCLA, then on Vermont Avenue.

Credit was given to those who met certain prerequisites. This policy continued after the School of Theatre Arts opened in 1928. Students who entered with two years of previous college experience were able to receive a B.A. in theatre. Those entering directly from high school received only a certificate.

In 1922 the Colony brochure advertised a course for directors.

The Desk Set

After the new theatre opened and was successfully operating, Brown proposed a plan for a full-fledged drama school. It would operate in the winter as an official part of the theatre. Not all board members were enthusiastic, fearing Brown would spread himself too thin. A lengthy discussion ensued. Brown believed he could handle both ventures. He pointed out there was a legitimate need. Several young people who were enrolled at the Marta Oatman School of Dramatics in Los Angeles, where Victor Jory and Joan Crawford were students, could be counted upon to transfer.

Brown went calling on a few of his favorite Pasadena patrons. Soon a donation of five thousand dollars from Mrs. Harriet Hurst specifically for a school arrived in the mail. The abstaining board members were effectively quieted. The school opened on South Los Robles with a qualified faculty of sixteen, many of whom were on the theatre staff as well.

Ads appeared in various national theatre magazines. Twenty-four students of varying backgrounds were enrolled by September 8th. From its inception the school drew well. A financial ledger in 1933 showed a gain of $2,229.01 for the school and a loss of $6,115.75 for the Mainstage.

The Time of Your Life

The curriculum hardly varied in over thirty years. The basic philosophy was Brown's "learn by doing." The stress was on acting. Students took part in scenes, one-acts, and were used whenever possi-

In Appreciation
JAN DIOR KLOKE

ble on Mainstage with professional actors. The school day began at 8:00 a.m. and ended with evening rehearsal. Saturday morning classes were customary, and rehearsals were held on all but a few major holidays until the '60s.

In 1931 post-graduate students were treated like members of a small company. Two years later an arrangement that lasted a short while was made for them to present their plays at the little theatre in Padua Hills, above Claremont, known then for its venue of Mexican folk plays.

Eventually, technical classes were added, nine courses for two hundred dollars. These included instruction in scene design, construction, and painting, as well as stage management. After eighteen months a student could serve as a technical director at Padua Hills.

The Wandering Scholar From Paradise

Along the way an extra-curricular program developed, permitting students to perform in stock companies. One group did playlets between showings of feature films in Palm Springs, and in Riverside at The Golden State theatre. They also toured, playing the prison at Chino, and then service clubs up and down the state, mostly Kiwanis and Rotary. From 1935 on, Brown staged Midsummer Festivals, featuring the work of famous playwrights and recruiting heavily from the ranks of students.

Summer sessions mostly drew drama teachers who lacked technical training.

Cloud Nine

In 1936, the school commandeered the top portion of the new tower building. Large north-facing windows dropped checkerboards of light and shadow onto the gleaming hardwood floors. Classrooms, mirrored dance studios, rehearsal stages, and the cafeteria were fashioned from the lofty space. From the roof a panoramic view took in the purple San Gabriel mountains, and looking west across downtown Los Angeles, Catalina Island seemed anchored at sea. You couldn't quite see the Hollywood sign.

Dreams of Glory

The legend of being discovered at The Pasadena Playhouse enticed students from all over the world to the drama school. Brown placed ads in magazines and gave press interviews stressing the Hollywood bond. "Want to become a move star? Your best bet may be The Pasadena Playhouse." In 1931 ads were headed "Success in Talking Pictures." One brochure boasted, "At almost any Playhouse performance you will find representatives of the great studios 'scouting the show' in search of promising young actors and actresses."

Instant stardom was hinted at, if not almost guaranteed. And in the '30s it was often a fact. Many graduating students signed contracts.

*The late **Yvonne Peattie**, Class of 1936, (shown with **Dana Andrews**) endowed a dressing room which is commemorated with a gold plaque.*

VOICES OFF
*One-time Playhouse instructor **Bea Hassel Rogatz** claims that Gilmor Brown's Siamese cat, Siki, was the resident critic at The Pasadena Playhouse and attended all Mainstage dress rehearsals. "If the cat didn't like the show he screamed his objections loudly as only a Siamese can. But if Siki draped himself over the back of a seat and slept, we knew we had a hit."*

The press usually agreed with Siki.

In Appreciation
DR. & MRS. LEONARD KNAPP

VOICES OFF

Bill Fairchild *moved from an apartment on South El Molino into Miss Hobart's rooming house at 145 North Oakland Avenue in January, 1939, and was soon summoned before the Citizenship Committee for having had continual parties while at the said apartment house. Fairchild countered that the only party worth mentioning was an after-midnight breakfast on Christmas Eve. Six or seven drunks had crashed and were speedily dispatched. This defense was not accepted, and he was to await punishment. Later the same day, the Citizenship Committee retracted their complaint without explanation. Ironically, a short while later, Miss Hobart reported to The Playhouse that she would like to convert her rooming house into a a dorm for young men as polite and mannerly as the handsome Bill Fairchild. "And that's how that dorm came to be."*

A typical dorm near The Pasadena Playhouse.

In Appreciation
MARION M. KUTCHER

Heartbreak House

Out of town students requested housing. Soon spacious old two- and three-story neighborhood homes were converted to dormitories for three hundred women. These were mostly the darkly shingled rambling bungalow-style with large sleeping porches made popular by the Greene brothers' architectural office. The dorms were named for early donors: Mr. and Mrs. Ernest Batchelder, Dr. and Mrs. Robert Millikan, Mr. and Mrs. George Ellery Hale, Mr. and Mrs. Clinton Clarke. A private residence rented to male students became known as "Heartbreak House." Those unlucky young men who lived there nearly always suffered disastrous love affairs.

The School for Scandal

In the following decades, the intriguing campus, an integral part of The Pasadena Playhouse complex, was a scintillating place to be. There's a certain excitement inherent at any college. This holds true as well for any place where theatre happens. Put the two together and it's a dynamic as well as romantic combination. This famous school, the first stop on the way to Hollywood, lured The Girl Next Door and the *femme fatale*, the Pretty Boy and Don Juan. Whether a timid artistic soul or a free spirit, these young people shared a love for the theatre or the silver screen and were brash enough to choose acting or writing or directing over a conventional career,

often bucking parental objections.

Some were naive and exceptionally comely young men and women, away from home-town taboos for the first time. Arriving from all over the globe with abundant *joie de vivre*, they encountered those students who were slightly older, more sophisticated—those who had been around, tried New York or the Armed Forces or marriage or college first. More often than not, sparks flew and drama played out of the classrooms as well as on the various stages.

Conscientious Pasadena-area mothers warned their sons and daughters that "theatre people" weren't to be trusted. The coffee shop, Tops, fronting on Colorado Boulevard across the alley from the stage door, was off-limits to the debutante crowd, as was The Green Lantern country western bar situated in that sleazy section of North Fair Oaks not far from where the Community Playhouse started. Playhouse students with looks to die for were known to drink beer there after curfew. But Cupid has little respect for boundaries, and no doubt there are a few autographed programs tucked away in the locked and musty diaries of one or two Pasadenans who lost more than their hearts when the College of Theatre Arts was in flower.

Lamentably, Brown knew a great deal about theatre and less about Standards Boards, although he employed a rather merciful Citizenship Committee. Unlike his counterpart at any private institution

STAGE WHISPER: **TERRENCE BEASOR**
"For a guy just out of the Navy, The Playhouse was like a candy store. A young lady came to a student production of Hello, Out There, *I think with her grandmother. Anyhow, I guess she liked how I looked in those tight jeans. She came backstage and gave me her phone number, and…Yeah, well, those were the good old days."*

STAGE WHISPER: **STUART MARGOLIN**
"The San Marino mothers wouldn't let us near their daughters, so we went out with their Swedish maids who'd meet us at The Green Lantern. There were some real beauties. Those were fun years. Once I spent all the money my parents sent me on a car. Driving home I ran out of gas. I didn't have enough change to buy one gallon. I had to call a friend to come get me."

The school curriculum was all encompassing.

The school day went from 8:00 a.m. to midnight.

In Appreciation
LLUELLA MOREY MURPHEY FOUNDATION

of higher learning, he relied upon the students to pay their tuition and behave themselves or at least be discreet. Occasional rumors of extremely wild parties shocked the sedate townspeople. When the whispered gossip got out of hand, someone representing The Pasadena Playhouse negotiated a clandestine truce with this person or that, not an easy task if famous names were also involved. Sometimes the police were summoned.

At one point in the late '30s The Pasadena Playhouse formed a basketball team to prove to the community what sports loving All-American youngsters attended the drama school. The Playhouse then challenged various independent teams in the area.

At the very least, those enrolled at The College of Theatre Arts infused the staid community with a sense of dark romance. Some say Pasadena has not been the same since the College of Theatre Arts closed its doors.

Student Prince

Many students came to Pasadena nurturing a dream. They had been told they could act, or sing, or dance, by a small-town drama coach or choir master or ballet instructor, or even a director at some community theatre. These teenagers hoped they had the presence, the voice, or the good looks to make it, usually in motion pictures. So they packed their bags and headed to that mystical place on South El Molino

Avenue; and, if nothing else, they learned a great deal about the theatre.

A few became stars. Some became respected actors and technicians. But most of the graduates of the drama school, accredited in 1961, eventually found employment in the entertainment industry and continue working their craft to this day. The illustrius alumni include: Charles Bronson, Ruth Buzzi, Jamie Farr, Gene Hackman, Dustin Hoffman, David Janssen, Mako, Stuart Margolin, Rue McClanahan, Terry Moore, Barbara Rush, Charlotte Stewart, Sally Struthers, and JoAnne Worley. In the late '50s both "Dusty" Hoffman and Gene Hackman rehearsed in lofty fifth-floor classrooms. The alumni maintain that what was truly taught at The Pasadena Playhouse, disregarding fencing, movement and dialects, was a deep respect for the profession.

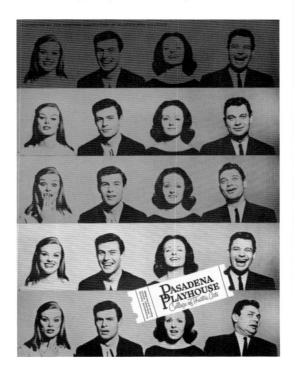

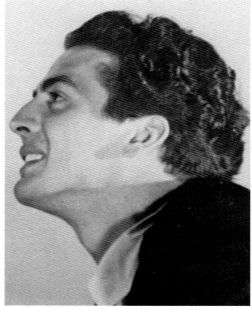

Vic Mature

STAGE WHISPER:
GWEN HORN WILLSON
"Frances Evans and I roomed together at Mrs. Knoop's. One day she came huffing to the door of our room, gingerly dangling a used condom and shouting, 'Who is responsible for this conundrum I found in the garden?' Frances, who used to stop traffic walking down El Molino with Vic Mature and his gorgeous white dog, Duchess, said, 'I have no idea what that is, and besides you don't even know how to pronounce it.'"

Then   *Now*

SUPERIOR COURT JUDGE
ELIZABETH BARON
Some students gave up stardom to play other roles.

In Appreciation
LONGO LEXUS-PENSKE COMPANY

VOICES OFF
In the late '30s The Pasadena Playhouse formed a basketball team to prove to the community what sports loving All-American youngsters attended the drama school. The Playhouse then challenged various independent teams in the area. **Bill Fairchild** *reminisces: "I was puny. My problem was getting the ball high enough to hit the backboard, let alone the basket. But lo and behold Ollie Prickett gave me a uniform. I think the fact that exactly ten of us tried out and he had exactly ten uniforms had something to do with it. My uniform, the smallest available, was about two sizes too large for me."*

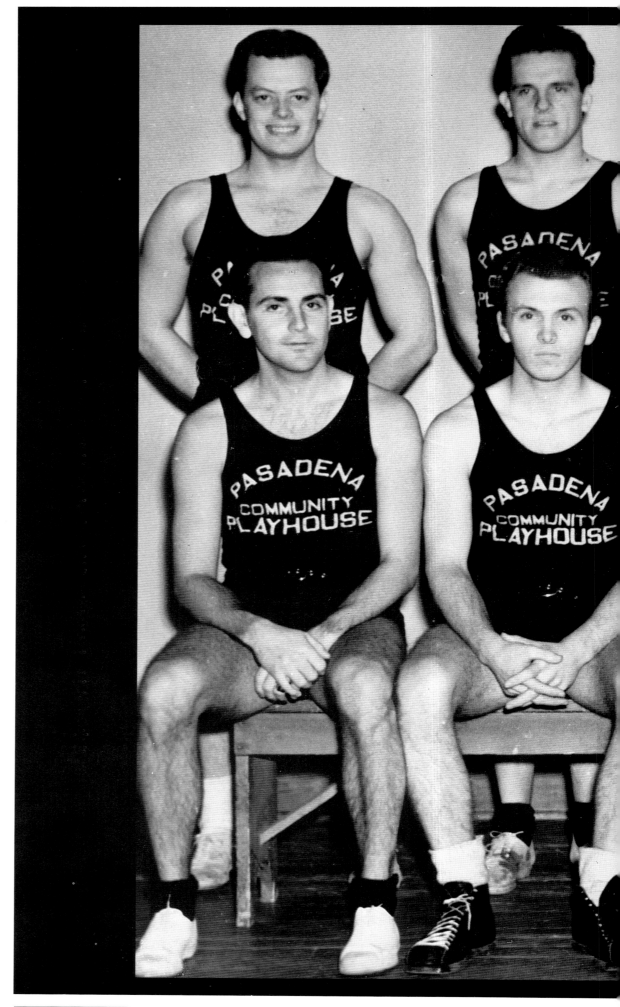

In Appreciation
POST-JORDAN PARTNERS

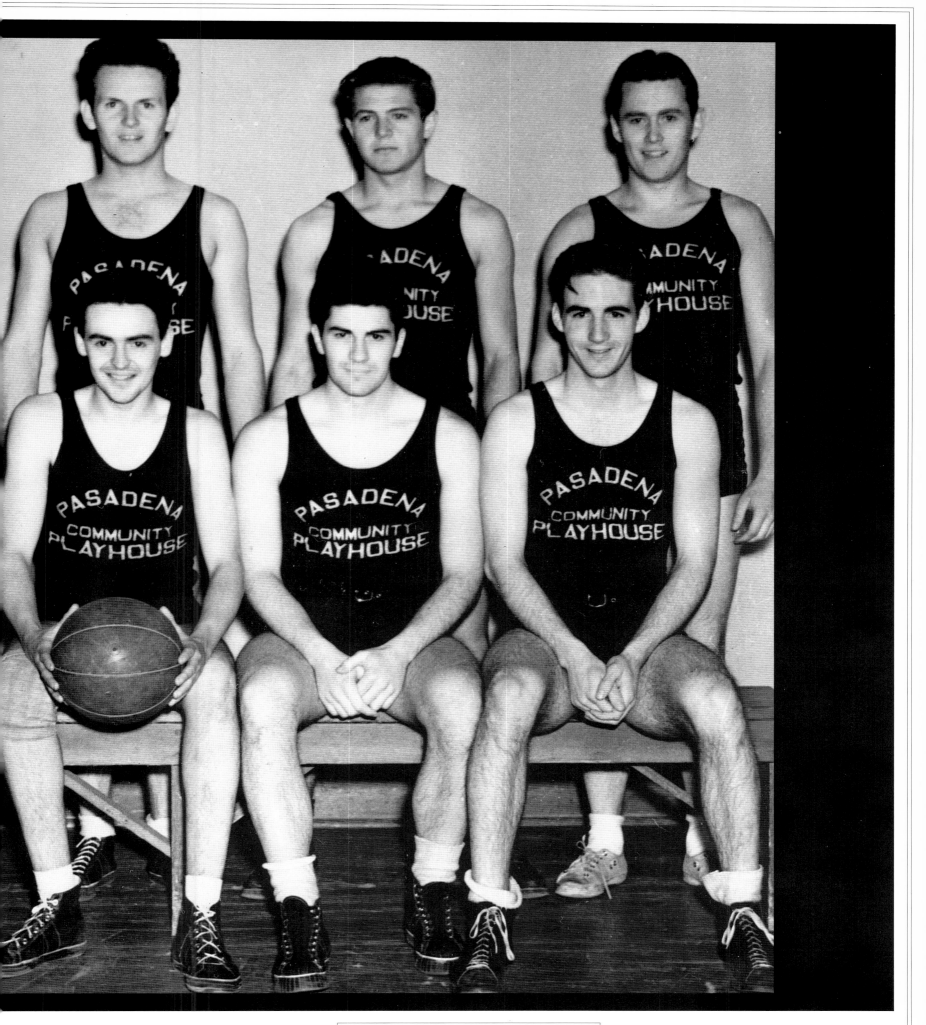

In Appreciation
MR. & MRS. DON LOZE

BACKSTAGE WITH
DUSTIN HOFFMAN

Stellar performer Dustin Hoffman is regarded as an actor's actor, the highest praise. Growing up in Brentwood, he chose the nearby Playhouse as a logical place to begin his training. Of Dustin Hoffman, Ken Rose muses, "He was very eager. When we did Death of a Salesman, he objected to playing one of the sons, Biff, I think. He was a nineteen-year-old kid and determined that he could bring off Willie (the father). Years later he finally did the role on Broadway. The seed for that started at The Pasadena Playhouse. But he always had his eye on New York. It was the late '50s and Hollywood preferred the Tab Hunter look."

A third-year student before becoming a faculty member, Bea Hassel Rogatz comments, "We recognized Dusty's unusual talent and fostered it. I gave him an A grade in a small role in As You Like It."

VOICES OFF
*Director and Playhouse instructor **Ken Rose** remembers that Dustin Hoffman, like most of the male students, lived in chaos. "Dusty's mother, the sweetest woman in the whole world, would drive across L.A. and clean his place. She'd even iron his shirts and throw the moldy lettuce out of his refrigerator."*

STAGE WHISPER: KEN ROSE
"I was in love with this incredibly beautiful woman. She was at my place one night when Dustin Hoffman called and asked her to come read lines with him for a play they were rehearsing. She left, saying she'd be back later. In a jealous rage I followed her, broke through Hoffman's door, and there the two of them sat at either end of his sofa, doing just that, reading lines. I felt like such a fool."

In Appreciation
JOE MANTEGNA

Gene Hackman with Zasu Pitts in The Curious Miss Caraway.

*BACKSTAGE WITH **GENE HACKMAN***
The greatly respected and well-liked film actor, Gene Hackman, earned low marks during his student years. Hackman, after being nominated for a second Academy Award, commented on his Playhouse teachers: "They did their best to discourage me, but I was a slow learner."

*STAGE WHISPER: **GAIL SHOUP***
"I directed Dustin Hoffman in Camino Real. *He had very few lines as The Drunken Bum, but he used every rehearsal to creatively develop the role with his usual care and concern."*

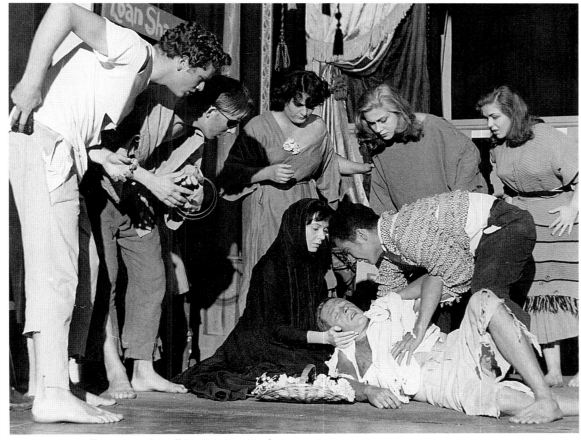

Dustin Hoffman gave his all in Camino Real.

Lenore Shanewise directed Ray Danton in Becket.

In Appreciation
KATHERINE & ALLAN MARTINET

BACKSTAGE WITH **CHARLES BRONSON**

Ken Rose recalls, "He was a roughneck, from a coal mining town, and when he played a tough guy there was a hard-edged honesty. He went right from one role to the next." One day during Bronson's first year, a Hollywood casting agent called the school office wanting a cross between John Garfield and Humphrey Bogart for a World War II comedy. Bronson was sent over and cast in his first of many features, You're in the Navy Now.

Director Bea Hassel Rogatz recalls giving Bronson the lead in a First Year project, Command Decision. The other young men in that particular class were very handsome. "I figured they would have opportunities to play leads that Charles Buchinsky would not. How was I to know he would become Charles Bronson?"

VOICES OFF

Stephen Lord, Playhouse alumnus and screen writer, confronted the then Charles Buchinsky one night after Buchinsky had disrupted a scene Lord was rehearsing. "I'm a Sicilian and we don't run from a fight." Buchinsky ended up apologizing to the 140-pound wanna-be-writer for behaving unprofessionally.

BACKSTAGE WITH **MAKO**

Mako, a familiar face in films, nominated for best supporting actor in The Sand Pebbles, has said that he felt insecure at first because everyone else looked like they'd done theatre. Cast usually as the handsome villain, the evil Communist or menacing Generalissimo, his talent was "startling." Ken Rose recalls seeing him, after graduation, in Rashomon, and being unnerved by Mako's acting ability. "It was incredible, how good he was.

Charles Bronson is remembered as fulfilling his on-screen image.

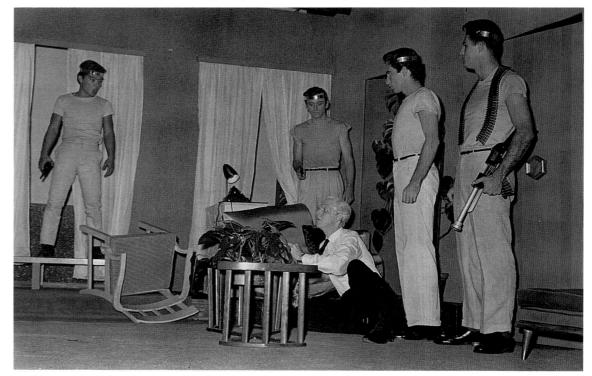

Mako went on to become one of the founders of East West Players in Hollywood, making a great impact on Los Angeles theatre. He recently played on Broadway.

In Appreciation
MARTIN MASSMAN

BACKSTAGE WITH **RUE McCLANAHAN**

Golden Girl Rue McClanahan, recipient of The Pasadena Playhouse Alumni and Associates "Woman of the Year" award in 1985, has accumulated a long list of credits on Broadway, in film and on TV. She arrived at The Pasadena Playhouse, divorced and with a baby, hoping to support herself and her child as an actress. What brought McClanahan to Pasadena? She was staying in Venice Beach with friends and saw an ad in a trade paper for a four-week Talent Finder course at The Pasadena Playhouse and signed on. It was the summer of 1959. After several classes, an instructor asked her to attend the TV show It Could Be You *as an audience member. There, Lee J. Cobb, with cameras rolling, presented the surprised ingenue with a third-year Playhouse scholarship and a set of white Samsonite luggage. McClanahan says gleefully, "I still have the cosmetic case!" Soon cast as Cherie in* Bus Stop, *she was "thrilled" to be on the Mainstage in a part that required her to sing "That Old Black Magic." McClanahan's talent became obvious. Colleagues who knew her then agree, "She was a knock-out. An intense, thin, high-cheek-boned young beauty. And she could act! We were in awe of her."*

Returning to star in House of Blue Leaves, *McClanahan recalls Playhouse instructor Barney Brown's advice from her school days. "Barney told me you have to go out on a limb, be one hundred percent bad before you can be one percent good. It took me awhile to fully comprehend what he meant. But of course that's right. It's what Laurence Olivier said, "You have to give your all. You can't play it safe. You must dive in head first, even if the water is ice cold."*

In Appreciation
KEVIN McCARTHY

BACKSTAGE WITH
STUART MARGOLIN

Stuart Margolin, the definitive working actor, a veteran of feature films and TV, currently starring in a Canadian series as well as directing at home and abroad, played James Garner's sidekick Angel on The Rockford Files. Margolin has fond memories of his days in Pasadena. "Nothing mattered to us then, except the theatre. Well, maybe the last race at Santa Anita. I lost a lot of tuition money at the track." Margolin credits the Pasadena Playhouse with allowing him to hone his art. "I performed sixty-two different roles over a span of three and a half years before paying audiences. It was invaluable, finding out what they (the audience) liked about what you did and what they didn't. I still carry that with me."

STAGE WHISPER: STUART MARGOLIN

"At a performance of Shoemaker's Holiday, director Helmuth Hormann insisted the three-hour show go on despite the fact I had a terrible sore throat, could barely whisper, and there were only two people in the audience. I sent someone out front to ask how much money it would take to get them (audience) to leave. It wasn't much."

In Appreciation
RUE McCLANAHAN

BACKSTAGE WITH **JAMIE FARR**
Jamie Farr, a favorite on the long-running MASH, remembers that while in school, "There were a few old-time character actors who were doing other jobs. They weren't names in the business, but they were occasional working actors, and they lived at the boarding house we lived in and they shared the cabins. I remember seeing this elderly man…that used to come down there and talk about the theatre…who had to do some other job other than acting, and it frightened me to think, my goodness! That's not going to happen to me! I'm an actor! I don't know what's wrong with him, if he's a good actor, he should be working. Little did I know!"

BACKSTAGE WITH **KEVIN TIGHE**
Kevin Tighe grew up in Pasadena and started performing at The Playhouse while still a child. "I loved staying up late and being allowed to eat candy from the candy machines." Respected for his work on stage and in numerous features, including three films of John Sayles (most recently City of Hope), he co-starred in the popular TV series Emergency. By age fourteen, cast by Barney Brown to play newsboy Si Crowell in the 1959 production of Our Town, Tighe recalls, "I was an obnoxious kid and kept bugging Barney for a larger speaking role. This particular night the guy who played Joe Crowell, the older brother, was sick. Barney told me I could go on. So I memorized my part. On stage, I gave about four or five lines and then I stared into the footlights and lost it. I remember responding on cue, just saying anything, and then I ran into the wings and cried. Everyone was nice. They said, 'Don't worry about it. You were fine.' I'll never forget that."

In Appreciation
JUDY & DENIS McDOWELL

BACKSTAGE WITH
CHARLOTTE STEWART
*The dream of being discovered at The
Pasadena Playhouse came true for Charlotte
Stewart. A Playhouse ad featuring Earl
Holliman in* Seventeen *magazine caught the
eye of this fresh-faced girl next door and
changed her destiny. It was 1958 and she
headed south. Playhouse exposure quickly
landed the petite blonde from a walnut farm
in Northern California a job on* The Loretta
Young Show. *Next came an appearance on*
My Three Sons. *A series regular on* Little
House on the Prairie *and a favorite of
David Lynch, she was ultimately written into*
Twin Peaks *and several of his films. Stewart,
a former Miss Yuba City, admits to being
overwhelmed on the first day of class. "When
I actually saw The Pasadena Playhouse, I
was completely awed by the grandeur of the
building, the sense of importance. It was
almost a religious experience, being there.
I learned discipline, and to take acting
seriously."*

Charlotte Stewart and Terry Hall.

Charlotte Stewart today on the Twin Peaks *set
with director/writer David Lynch.*

In Appreciation
DONNA McKECHNIE

A roster of Players who graced The Pasadena Playhouse stages in the past.

Doro Adams	Henry Darrow	Martha Hyer	Douglass Montgomery	Sonia Sorel
Mable Albertson	Francis Dee	Marty Ingle	Michael Moore	Kim Stanley
Louise Allbritton	Don DeFore	Helen Inkster	Terry Moore	Harry Dean Stanton
John Alvin	Agnes de Mille	Jean Inness	Thomas Browne Henry	Onslow Stevens
Rachel Ames	Ward Donovan	David Janssen	Karen Morley	Bob Stevenson
Gwen Anderson	John Doucette	Lois January	Wayne Morris	Houseley Stevenson
Dana Andrews	Bill Erwin	Herbert Johnson	Ben Murphy	Charlotte Stewart
Nancy Andrews	Gene Evans	Carolyn Jones	George Nader	Sally Struthers
Tod Andrews	Judith Evelyn	Victor Jory	Leonard Nimoy	Gloria Stuart
Michael Ansara	Frances Farmer	Cyrus Kendall	David Niven	Joan Taylor
Joseph Anthony	Jamie Farr	John Kennedy	Jeanette Nolan	Robert Taylor
Eve Arden	Frank Ferguson	Werner Klemperer	Lloyd Nolan	William Terry
Russell Arms	Bill Fletcher	Barry Kroeger	Eleanor Parker	Kevin Tighe
Curtis Arnall	Gloria Folland	Hal Landon	Nancy Parsons	John Toler
James Arness	Byron Foulger	Charles Lane	Kenneth Patterson	Robert Totten
Jean Arthur	Jodi Gilbert	Harry Lewis	Charles Pierce	Lurene Tuttle
Lois Austin	William Glenn	Helen Lieberg	Mary Ellen Popel	Joan Valerie
Florence Bates	Martha Graham	Marta Linden	Tyrone Power	Virginia Vincent
Madge Blake	Dabs Greer	Robert Livingston	Mala Powers	Wolfram von Bock
Henry Brandon	William Greer	Congressman	Robert Preston	Fred Warriner
Charles Bronson	Fran Gregory	John Lodge	Maudie Prickett	Maurice Wells
Helen Brooks	Bob Griffen	Arthur Lubin	Oliver Prickett	Michael Whalen
Edgar Buchanan	Gene Hackman	George Lynn	Franklin Provo	Tom Whitney
Charles Buchinsky	Robert Haig	Rita Lynn	George Reeves	Frank Wilcox
Paul Burke	Bruce Hall	Helen Mack	Frances Reid	Robert Willey
Raymond Burr	Ellen Hall	Mako	Craig Reynolds	Mervin Williams
Ruth Buzzi	John Hall	Peter Mamakos	Gene Reynolds	Rush Williams
Richard Carlson	Lois Hall	Stuart Margolin	John Ridgley	Gwen Horn Willson
John Carradine	Kay Hammond	Hugh Marlowe	Patricia Riordan	Robert Wood
Ralph Clanton	Peter Hanson	Kene Martin	John Ritter	JoAnne Worley
Lee J. Cobb	John Hartley	Mary Mason	Robert Rockwell	Mary Wrixon
Chris Connelly	Byron Harvey, Jr.	Victor Mature	Sydney Rome	Meg Wylie
John Conti	Rita Henderson	John Maxwell	Barbara Rush	Murray Yeats
Tommy Cook	William Henry	Marilyn Maxwell	Randolph Scott	Gig Young
Maurice Copeland	Sam Hinds	Elaine May	James Seay	Robert Young
Grace Coppin	Dustin Hoffman	Rue McClanahan	Tom Seidel	Victor Zimmerman
Catherine Craig	William Holden	M'liss McClure	Lucie Shelley	
Laird Cregar	Earl Holliman	Carolyn McWilliams	Nina Shipman	
Donald Curtis	Robert Horton	Muriel Monsell	Max Showalter	
Helmut Dantine	Kim Hunter	Kelly Monteith	Sylvia Sidney	

STAGE WHISPER: **VICTOR QUILES**

"I am so glad The Playhouse has been saved, that (David) Houk made it happen. Being there as students, it is hard to explain. Those were the glory years for us. We talked theatre non-stop and philosophy. Nobody had any money. My father and mother owned a market in East L.A., and they would send beans and rice over in a pickup to guys who were living on Ritz crackers and mustard."

STAGE WHISPER: **CONCETTA MARLO**

"Scholarship students paid no tuition. We worked twelve months for fifteen dollars a month and then started going to school. Who else but Charles Prickett would have thought of the idea of having us do almost all the secretarial work and cleaning. The hours those boys spent scrubbing bathrooms, sweeping floors and manning the box office. The girls worked in the library and as office clerks. Oh, the scripts, the sides, we typed! Also, I operated the switchboard. With my Texas drawl! But we were just glad to be there."

Charles Prickett, 1937.

In Appreciation
DONALD & KATIE NACK

THE CHILDREN'S HOUR
Children's Theatre sponsored by the Junior League was coordinated with local schools' curriculum. When Sally Struthers starred in Tom Edison and the Wonderful Why, *thousands of school children studying electricity were bused in.*

BACKSTAGE WITH SALLY STRUTHERS
The popular actress who came to the country's attention on All In The Family has been a staunch supporter of her alma mater. She has said that, "The Playhouse accepted me and Pasadena was the farthest from Portland, Oregon, that I could get. I was an art major and never had a burning desire to be an actress."

In Appreciation
PASADENA JUNIOR CHAMBER OF COMMERCE

Talk Radio

Commercial radio was just beginning in the early '20s. Brown liked the idea of mass entertainment and became involved while still at the Community Playhouse. In 1923, he recruited actors who radiocast a one-act play, *The Bank Account,* over KHJ. This proved so successful that a group organized into the Community Broadcasters of Pasadena. Comprised of three women and six men, including Brown himself, they presented *The Merchant of Venice* the next year, again on KHJ. This was the first time Shakespeare was done on radio.

As radios became an increasingly popular fixture in most family living rooms, The Lone Ranger, Fred Allen, Jack Benny, and Amos and Andy were as familiar to the American public as their president. By 1939 Brown seriously considered turning a portion of The Pasadena Playhouse into a radio station; the tower was on a direct line to Mt. Wilson. But a vague mistrust of the media—theatre was to be seen as well as heard—held him back, even though by now there was an official radio agent for The Pasadena Playhouse Association. The agent's first major project was arranging to have The Pasadena Playhouse host the popular Edgar Bergen and Charlie McCarthy shows which were broadcast nationwide from the Mainstage. Radio classes became a part of the school when Edgar Bergen's production staff left behind surplus transmitting equipment. Students put

Edgar Bergen broadcasted from the Mainstage.

In Appreciation
PEGGY PHELPS

KTTV utilized the third-floor studio at The Pasadena Playhouse.

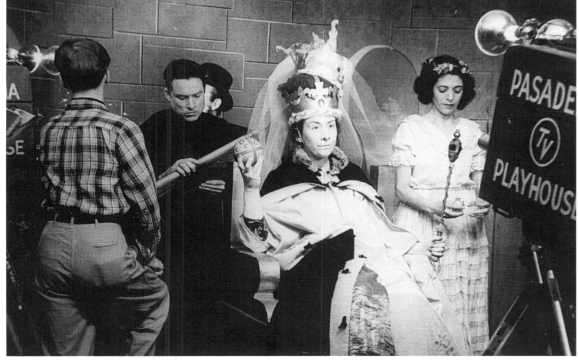

Playhouse star Maudie Prickett appeared on camera.

Pasadena on the airwaves several times a week on KXLA and KWKW.

The Glimpse of Reality

The Pasadena Playhouse experimented with television as well. Brown suspected that TV was here to stay and wanted to be the first to teach this untested theatre art. He formed a relationship with Times Mirror Company, which was eager to become involved with electronic media. There was talk of money being loaned to The Pasadena Playhouse to build a 10-foot tower which would then be leased back to Times-Mirror Company, but it ultimately wasn't feasible. In 1945, David Crandell was hired by Times Television as program director to help obtain the FCC license, which he did. This newly created station, KTTV, channel 11, installed a pilot facility on the south side of the third-floor tower at The Pasadena Playhouse. The Times people paid for the equipment and brought in trained engineers to operate a closed-circuit studio which sent pictures down to the Student Union. Meanwhile, continuing to work for Times, the very knowledgeable Crandell became head of the TV department at the College of Theatre Arts.

The pioneering station moved to Hollywood after three years and for a time was operated by CBS, pending a sale to Metromedia. The TV department and the crude equipment remained behind. The technical students who

Times' television staff: **David Crandell**, *Program Director.*

In Appreciation
MRS. CHARLES PLUMMER

learned their craft on those cameras are mostly still working that side of the business today. Some drama students who scoffed at running a camera eventually ended up at the networks doing just that.

The Playbox, the school, radio, TV—there didn't seem to be anything Brown couldn't do with his beloved plaything, The Pasadena Playhouse.

ALUMNI: TV OR NOT TV

John Mantley, nephew of Mary Pickford, became the producer of Gun Smoke.

Jim Hobson produced and directed The Lawrence Welk Show.

Tom Hatten hosted L.A.'s Matinee Theatre for fourteen years.

Jack Scott graduated from The Pasadena Playhouse to KTTV and has just retired.

Don Remacle works as set designer on ABC's series Coach.

VOICES OFF
Albert McCleery, an executive in the '50s at NBC and later artistic director at The Pasadena Playhouse, believed The Pasadena Playhouse had "an active, aggressive TV department that made real contributions to the industry."

STAGE WHISPER: **TED SAMUEL**
"*Victor Jory* (far left) and his wife, **Jean Inness**, starred in this TV rendition of Macbeth. **Leo Matranga** was murderer number one and I was murderer number two. Well, during rehearsal, every time we crouched at Jory's feet listening to Macbeth's plan to kill Banquo and Fleance, Leo would do something to make me laugh. Finally, Jory bent over, grabbed us by our throats, and in a very menacing voice said if we couldn't keep quiet he'd slit our throats. That silenced us, and we weren't bad in the performance. Still, the reviews said the scenes varied from the very fine banquet scene to that of the two murderers who acted like soda jerks. Oh, my, that hurt so much!"

VOICES OFF
In 1957 NBC's **Robert W. Sarnoff** wrote Brown: "Broadcasting, as well as the theatre and motion pictures, is richer for the talent discovered and developed by your (radio) project. Your graduates are seen everywhere in our industry and they, themselves, are your most loyal boosters."

VOICES OFF
Award-winning documentary film maker and playwright **Lawrence O'Sullivan** remembers, "We were serious actors then. We couldn't be bothered with the technical side. Why should we learn the mechanics of running a camera? We went directly from Pasadena to New York. Then, eventually, most of us made our way back to Hollywood and ultimately the other side of the camera."

Gilmor Brown in Dickens' Cricket on the
Hearth *which Brown adapted for the stage.*

Decline and Fall: 1937 to 1969

5

The Pasadena Playhouse's "rags to riches" story could have been concocted in Hollywood: set it in upscale Pasadena, give Gilmor Brown the lead, add celebrity cameo parts and an agreeable-looking cast of thousands. The theatre's fall from grace was possibly a more difficult concept to pitch or even to understand.

There's no proof that any community theatre could have survived the next two decades in Southern California. Nor is there a single reason why The Pasadena Playhouse curtain slowly began to fall. The deaths of both Charles Prickett and Gilmor Brown certainly ended an era, but the demise of dynamic leadership didn't necessarily have to be a lethal blow to the theatre.

Lion In Winter

To those around him during his later years, Brown seemed to decline before their eyes. Once a persuasive man of great magnetism and force, he became a revered but frail figurehead. Toward the end of his life, weak after an automobile accident and confined to a wheelchair, Brown became something of a recluse.

Tea and Sympathy

Brown's society matrons were a dying breed. There were fewer invitations to intimate teas and *tete-a-tetes*, gatherings he truly enjoyed, and from which he usually exited gracefully with a check for the theatre. These patrons of the arts

were quietly passing away, leaving their fortunes to executors.

Loves Labours Lost

Problems with the labor unions began in 1938 when Actors' Equity forced the issue of paying actors living wages for their work. Under a great deal of pressure to comply, The Pasadena Playhouse finally signed a union contract in 1942 and thus became a commercial house with professional status. This went against the basic philosophy of "community theatre" upon which Brown had based his dream, an episodic drama for which Pasadenans had continued to pay.

The unionizing of the Mainstage may have caused a break from the community and its generosity. It definitely meant a loss of control for Brown. The theatre game had new rules and officials to enforce them. Yet, the configuration of the community—the population increased twenty-five percent in ten years—changed so drastically after World War II that blaming Actors' Equity for The Pasadena Playhouse's losing amateur status, and therefore local support, is economically and sociologically naive.

Born Yesterday

A local growth explosion, partially due to continued expansion of the aircraft industries, caused a housing shortage as well as pollution and traffic congestion in downtown Pasadena. The City could no longer afford to be an idyllic resort for

In Appreciation
IBM CORPORATION

VOICES OFF
*Jack hammers blasted throughout rehearsals for Peer Gynt as the old rows of seats were ripped out and replaced in the continental style with no center aisles. Alumnus **David Banks**, who was stage manager for Lowell Lees, recalls, "There were sixty extras on stage, mostly students from the school, supposedly climbing this mountain. They were trying desperately to listen to the director who basically was like a traffic cop during rush hour traffic attempting to organize this crowd. But no one could hear a thing. It was really quite comical, if it hadn't been so sad."*

the rich. The once small town, with grand residential streets so resembling wealthy sections of the East and Midwest that it was a favorite Hollywood location, was faced with a new reality: a middle class technological society with a zeal for mass consumption and democracy.

Our Town

To meet the demands for new homes, the mansions on Orange Grove Avenue, so admired by Brown when he first arrived, were hacked up into apartments. Over on Raymond Hill the acres of flower gardens that had belonged to The Raymond Hotel were plowed under, and affordable one- and two-bedroom housing units sprouted like weeds. Hastings Ranch became a tract development.

Estate lots were split in half to make room for new houses. New construction overtook Linda Vista and San Rafael. Eventually, down in South Pasadena, bulldozers attacked the remaining acres of virgin land where sheep still grazed in the federally financed Monterey Hills project.

Ballad of a City

Pasadena, inundated with the problems of going from a quiet refuge to an urbanized city, had scant time for the arts. The city struggled to improve its strained school and transportation systems and to deal with integration and survival in the shadow of neighboring Los Angeles.

In Appreciation
MR. & MRS. RICK POWELL

The Rivalry

The newfangled invention television didn't help motion picture theatres or The Pasadena Playhouse. By the late '50s there were tens of millions of cumbersome black and white sets in American homes, mesmerizing the occupants. Ed Sullivan brought stars right into the living room, and few could resist seeing Uncle Miltie wearing a dress, or Jackie Gleason's *Honeymooners*, or the antics of Lucille Ball, or quiz shows. It has been said that when the *Sixty-four Thousand Dollar Question* was on, a bowling ball could be rolled down any American street without hitting a soul. TV was fierce competition, and it was free.

The Impossible Years

Meanwhile, back on South El Molino, The Pasadena Playhouse faced escalating labor and production costs and a decrease in ticket sales. Audiences were seduced, in part, by the opening of the downtown Music Center. The Mainstage began to slide dangerously into the red. There had always been money problems, but Charles Prickett's death in 1954 prevented another miraculous return to the black.

Those who still sought cultural recreation suddenly seemed to prefer the sophistication of Los Angeles. Pasadena was referred to as a "bedroom community." It was no longer *chic*. Long-time theatregoers let their season tickets lapse. A San Marino matron who is once again a Playhouse subscriber remembers that, "We had L.A. Philharmonic tickets and when the Music Center opened our tickets transferred there, and it was easy to also buy theatre tickets. We just forgot about The Pasadena Playhouse, I guess. Started going to the Dorothy Chandler, The Ahmanson, and the Mark Taper instead."

The School of Theatre Arts, usually a reliable source of tuition income, lost students to the recently formed drama departments at USC and UCLA. Parents didn't object quite so strenuously to a child's majoring in theatre if he or she could graduate with a university degree. The great numbers of those attending The Pasadena Playhouse on the GI bill, following both World War II and the Korean War, dropped off when the government stopped paying.

Accent On Youth

The male students who were enrolled at The Pasadena Playhouse during the late '50s and early '60s became dissatisfied with classical training. The films of Marlon Brando had made an indelible impression upon them. Seemingly overnight they objected to what was being taught. Nicknamed "the mumblers" by the staff, the young men imitated Marlon Brando and James Dean, impatient to learn the new style of acting. A few of the instructors tried to teach "method," but it was not The Pasadena Playhouse's strong suit. Many of the neo-

In Appreciation
JOHN RAITT

Gilmor Brown *passed away on a bleak January day in 1960.*

phyte actors took off for New York—including Gene Hackman and Dustin Hoffman.

The Hollywood film industry, with problems of its own, no longer kept a stable of stars under contract. Film directors stopped using Brown Prep, as it was called, as a feeder-school.

Death Knocks

Brown's demise in 1960 was a severe blow to The Pasadena Playhouse. A dark gray sky shrouded Pasadena the January day of his memorial service, which was held on the eerily lit Mainstage. It attracted hundreds of somberly dressed mourners. Friends and admirers, theatre professionals and numerous celebrities, came from New York and Europe.

Raymond Burr called out, "Good night, sweet prince!" and silent voices echoed the farewell. Students from the College of Theatre Arts, given a holiday to attend the funeral, plucked souvenir roses from the flower-draped coffin and felt the uneasiness of mortality.

It was as if a great leader or elder statesman had passed on. With no heir apparent, there was whispered concern about the future of The Pasadena Playhouse. Could the show still go on without the eulogized Great God Brown? With Prickett also buried, the old guard was felled.

In Appreciation
KAY & BOB REHME

The Temptest

Brown may have been merely a figure-head in his later years, but the board of directors remained deferential. Afterwards, policy differences that had been buried over the years erupted. Board members couldn't agree upon management issues, and there was also no longer any meaningful dialogue between the "money men" and "the artists."

Crimes of the Heart

While the members of the board squabbled among themselves, idealistic Lowell Lees, a professor from the University of Utah who served as artistic director during the mid-'60s, had free reign. He encouraged the Junior League to back the Children's Theatre, which ran successfully for four years. Lees also formed a resident company, which he saw as a theatrical baseball team for whom the community could root. But baseball teams bring in a great deal of money. The theatre did not. There were no funds to pay these actors' salaries.

An amiable man, Lees managed to rally some support. His weighty but interesting productions of classical works, including *Richard the III* and *Peer Gynt*, lacked popular appeal. He lacked a fiscal sense, and with no one to stop him, spent fifty thousand dollars tearing out the existing auditorium seats to put in eighteen rows of continental seating—without center aisles. The arches that originally opened to the center aisles, remnants of better days, remain in the lobby.

Financially a disastrous period, The Pasadena Playhouse sank $265,000 into the hole. Money that couldn't realistically be paid back was borrowed from the bank. In addition, around $30,000 worth of withholding tax money was spent, which riled the Internal Revenue.

Desperate Hours

Agents from the IRS unceremoniously trooped in, right out of a melodramatic play, and gave the staff twenty minutes to retrieve their belongings. The Children's Theatre was sold out that summer, but that was beside the point. The IRS men padlocked The Pasadena Playhouse doors for non-payment of withholding taxes.

Current Community Relations Director Peggy Ebright commented, "The IRS money was a band-aid. There had always been tremendous financial problems that Charles Prickett just kept solving somehow!"

The Threepenney Opera

The *Star News* started a "Save The Pasadena Playhouse" campaign and raised more than $17,000 in contributions. The City granted The Pasadena Playhouse $10,000, and The Pasadena Playhouse Association raised $4,000 in advance ticket sales for a Fiftieth Anniversary Benefit which ultimately contributed another $6,000.

*The ever-smiling **Peggy Ebright** forged ahead.*

In Appreciation
LLOYD RIGLER

Raymond Burr

*STAGE WHISPER: **GAIL SHOUP***
*"I gave **Raymond Burr** an honorary doctor-ate degree at the school's last graduation cere-mony, so at least we went out respectably."*

Master of Ceremonies Victor Jory kissed the proscenium arch. Charlton Heston movingly read Robert Frost, "I have miles to go before I sleep." Larry Storch, Marilyn Maxwwell, Lloyd Nolan, and Leon Ames gave their all. When the show was broadcast on TV with the added appearances of Milton Berle, Bette Davis, and alumna Carolyn Jones, anoth-er seven thousand dollars was received. The government removed the padlocks when the taxes were repaid, but the bills didn't go away.

Serious Bizness

Next Albert McCleery, a disciple of Gilmor Brown and a network executive, assumed the role of artistic director, determined to do professional theatre. It was 1966. McCleery staged several popu-lar shows, including Shaw's *Captain Brassbound's Conversion* and *The Decent Thing* with Jane Wyatt and Karen Black. Playing the father, Leon Ames scored a big hit with the popular *Life with Father*. In 1967, O'Neill's *Ah, Wilderness* featured Sally Struthers. *The Caine Mutiny Court Martial*, *I Remember Mama* and *Cat on a Hot Tin Roof* rounded out a successful season. But only *I Remember Mama* broke even. A professional house that seats seven hundred can't make money back quickly. Rave reviews were worthless at the bank. The debt remained.

The Mainstage was losing $50,000 to $100,000 a year, on top of the other debts.

Measure for Measure

One measure after another was tried to raise money, and the theatre earned the nickname The Pasadena Poorhouse. An endowment fund would have helped, but over the years none was established. There was hesitation on the part of the board to accept large donations that would obligate them to a certain philosophy.

There was still some spirited commu-nity support for The Pasadena Playhouse, but the trendy new and sleekly modern Pasadena Art Museum with a world-class collection of paintings and sculpture siphoned money away.

The Fantasticks

The school was still self-supporting, but on shaky financial ground. The teachers were not paid the last month. During the summer, Midwestern Secur-ities Corporation seemed to come to the rescue, agreeing to subsidize the faculty for another year, and offering $500,000 for The Pasadena Playhouse.

The school opened tentatively the fol-lowing fall with one hundred students enrolled. Cash was to change hands on November 19th when Midwestern Secur-ities closed escrow. But escrow never closed, although Midwestern paid the teachers' salaries until May, when the deal completely fell apart. This made it two years running that the teachers worked their last month for free.

That the College of Theatre Arts remained open through graduation of

In Appreciation
RICHARD & KATHY ARNTZEN ROAT

1969 was due solely to the devotion and dedication of the teaching staff.

Tiger at the Gates

John Sears then appeared from a Dunn and Bradstreet ranked construction company in Washington. He wanted to buy the property, lease it back to The Pasadena Playhouse and build himself an office. The bank patiently agreed to withhold foreclosure on The Pasadena Playhouse. Then Sears became deathly ill and stopped returning phone calls.

Bankruptcy was the only way out. The Pasadena Playhouse filed for bankruptcy on December 23, 1969. Dealing with a very understanding Bank of America, the board of directors hoped that when the property came up for sale the bank would be the only interested bidder and might be induced to turn it back, since B of A had no interest in running a theatre. But there was no guarantee, even free of debt, that the board of directors could turn The Pasadena Playhouse around.

Subsequently, Bank of America, The Pasadena Playhouse's biggest creditor, took the property into receivership for $285,000, which was $315,000 less than its appraised value in 1936. It was August of 1970 as the final curtain fell on this agonizing last act.

In Appreciation
JERRY ROBIN - J. ROBIN & ASSOCIATES

Ollie Prickett

Dark Days: 1969-1979

Peggy Ebright's intricate diary pages fit together like large pieces of a complicated puzzle. Once in place, the detailed written record of cliff-hanging deals that almost rescued The Pasadena Playhouse from its receivership presents a dizzy pattern colored by hope, despite the repeated entry, "Time is running out." The record of this period, carefully delineated in notes typed single-spaced on two sides of ruled notebook paper, reveals Ebright's determined optimism. "It was impossible to believe we wouldn't actually go on. We'd always managed before."

Alice in Wonderland

A private corporation was formed immediately following bankruptcy. The Pasadena Theatre Academy legally retained title of The Pasadena Playhouse. Ebright was elected their president. She had been involved at the theatre for years. As Community Vice President of the Junior League, she had sat on local boards of the organizations to whom the League gave financial support, including The Pasadena Playhouse.

Strange Bedfellows

For five years diverse buyers came and went, attracted to the idea of owning a legendary theatre. The newly formed Pasadena Theatre Academy board, under Ebright's sunny leadership, concocted its own survival techniques.

Bell, Book and Candle

Meanwhile, the bankruptcy court insisted that personal property be auctioned. On an appropriately stormy afternoon in November of 1970, over fifty years' worth of historic and expensive theatrical goods—including stage equipment—was lost to the highest bidders. The theatre was a madhouse. An auctioneer, continually sidestepping as water leaked onto his head from a gaping hole in the roof, tried to maintain order from the Mainstage. Droves of adults and children alike squabbled over boxes of lavish costumes. For a dollar or two you could buy an outfit fit for a king or queen, bride or soldier, pirate or princess. The following Halloween the streets of Pasadena were populated with well-dressed Trick-or-Treaters courtesy of The Pasadena Playhouse.

Salvaged by the board for less than $2,000 were the commemorative bell that summoned the audience back at intermission, the Gilmor Brown Room, photos and scrapbooks, portraits, and school files. Fire extinguishers sold for $10 each. A Tiffany lamp shade brought $70. A painting of Josephine Dillon, the first Mrs. Clark Gable, went for $45. A portrait of Sarah Bernhardt as Portia was bought for $37.50.

Catch as Catch Can

The Pasadena Playhouse library was worth a fortune in itself. Over the years many wealthy Pasadenans had donated

VOICES OFF
C. Bernard Jackson, *Executive Director of Inner City Cultural Center and the Ivar Theatre in Hollywood, attended The Pasadena Playhouse auction. Jackson bought fifty-six folding chairs and an addressograph system. This antiquated machine cranked out all of Inner City Cultural Center's mailing labels until they advanced to the computer age. Jackson woefully recalls that stormy day. "There was tangible unhappiness in that auditorium. I was desperately trying to keep Inner City going and here this great institution was failing. It was incredibly depressing. It almost didn't seem right to participate in the auction. We really didn't need what I bought. I think I just wanted to somehow feel I was helping The Playhouse."*

In Appreciation
PAMELA & BRUCE ROSE

their personal libraries to the collection. A concerned citizen who had been contributing money to The Pasadena Playhouse for years, Herbert Rempel, purchased the library for $13,500 with the help of a professional bidder. He planned to return it intact after The Pasadena Playhouse reopened. But as time went on and storage costs rose—there were 209 boxes—he eventually decided to sell to Cal State Long Beach, which had bid against him originally. Rempel lost a thousand dollars in the transaction. The rare book collection was later traded by Cal State Long Beach to Xanadu Galleries in Glendale. The owner was pleased to find a priceless copy of *Old Drury Lane*, a history of the famous English theatre, and an equally scarce acting version of *Romeo and Juliet*. The rest of the rare books were ultimately retrieved by The Pasadena Playhouse Alumni and Associates for $2,500.

After the Fall

The Pasadena Playhouse, suffering many indignities bravely, waited to be rescued like a damsel in distress. The foul odor of neglect replaced the smell of grease paint. Vandals scribbled graffiti on the walls. Vagrants moved in and burned manuscripts and furniture to keep warm. Rain water poured through broken windows and holes in the roof, forming deep stagnant pools on the carpet. Birds nested in the tower, leaving behind their mess. And only a handful of people seemed to care.

Raymond Burr, a loyal friend to The Pasadena Playhouse, brought in the prestigious University of the Pacific to consider the property and buildings for a satellite graduate facility. University of the Pacific's president died before the deal could be consummated.

Other People's Money

Suddenly, the ominous For Sale sign disappeared, replaced by "now leasing." William Converse Jones had proposed to sublet the theatre space and make a mini mall out of the remaining property, bringing in shops and restaurants. Auspicious negotiations began with the Bank of America.

Jones had became intrigued with the project when Ebright presented him with a package deal that included a long-term lease from Henry Fonda and Martha Scott, co-founders of the Plumstead Playhouse. Usually the group performed at the Huntington Hartford. But they were looking for a permanent space and tentatively agreed to pay a percentage of their Mainstage gross, and to serve as the professional umbrella organization under which a variety of other rentals could be made. Ebright, acting for the board, also wooed The American Academy of Dramatic Arts as a proposed tenant, as she knew the Academy wished to open a West Coast branch. She suggested they utilize the empty fourth and fifth floors of the tower building. The American

Academy of Dramatic Arts backed out when Jones extended the escrow, and no restoration seemed imminent. Two years later, with the economy sinking around him, Jones tried to keep his escrow from doing likewise.

The Miracle Worker

Inadvertently, Pasadena architects who were working on plans for a United States Colleges International campus in Laguna Niguel mentioned The Pasadena Playhouse property to evangelist David Ghent. Ghent, the leader of the religious school, quickly toured the Pasadena facility and then made a $310,000 cash offer to Bank of America with a sixty-day escrow and the right to renovate the theatre during this period. Jones had no recourse but to abandon his negotiations. With this unforeseen change of plans, The Plumstead Playhouse settled elsewhere.

Ghent, a self-proclaimed savior, promised to save The Pasadena Playhouse. But as fate would have it, he vanished before escrow closed and the awaited resurrection never happened.

One for the Money

Refusing to give up, Ebright worked to have the theatre become listed on the National Registry of Historic Places, a lengthy and tedious process. The first step was state recognition. She filled out the necessary applications with the help of South Pasadena architect Ray

Girvighian, who later was the consultant for the restoration of the capitol building. They managed to convince the appropriate bureaucrats of the theatre's unique architecture and history. After becoming a state landmark, The Pasadena Playhouse was eligible to apply for national status and grants.

Chapter Two

Next Armen Sarafian, a member of The Pasadena Playhouse board as well as president of Pasadena City College, envisioned the community college as the prime renter of the theatre. His school's drama department would move over from classrooms on Colorado Boulevard and the Mainstage could still be rented out to various groups. Sarafian also proposed to use the tower building to expand PCC's radio and TV departments.

Ebright advised the city to buy The Pasadena Playhouse with PCC as the major tenant. The Coleman Concerts and the Pasadena Ballet Company expressed interest in possible leases as well.

All the Way Home

So, in the summer of 1975, contingent on Jones' failing to close escrow after three years, Mayor Don Yokaitis announced that the city wished to buy The Pasadena Playhouse property from Bank of America for $325,000. Assistant City Manager Don Pollard represented the city in this deal.

*BACKSTAGE WITH **RAYMOND BURR***
Raymond Burr, better known as detective Perry Mason—a role he made famous on TV—or as the star of Ironsides, *writes in the introduction to Lenore Shanewise's* Oral History, *"A week before the opening of the play* Quiet Wedding *(November 1942), Lenore Shanewise lost her leading man. Leta Bonynge and Russell Gold, who were cast members, knew I was in town and very interested in pursuing a career in the theatre. They suggested to Miss Shanewise that I might be suited in the role. She called me, I auditioned, I got the part. That began our friendship and professional relationship. Ultimately I, too, was added to the faculty of The Pasadena Playhouse and have been associated with it, Gilmor Brown, Lenore Shanewise, in one degree or another ever since."*

In Appreciation
BARBARA RUSH

*STAGE WHISPER: **DAVID HOUK***
"I know that theatres are one of the few uses of real estate where location is not material. With appropriate product on the stage, theatres can draw people out of their way to an urban area, changing traffic patterns and providing a very good tool to make cities work better."

Meanwhile, back at PCC, Sarafian resigned, taking his liberal ideas with him, and the city lost the community college as a tenant.

Magic Time

Suddenly, Milt Larsen pulled a rabbit out of a hat. Larsen, one-time Pasadena resident and owner of the Mayfair Music Hall in Santa Monica and the Magic Castle, a private magicians' club in Hollywood, expressed interest in buying the property or operating The Pasadena Playhouse. He planned to put legitimate theatre back on the Mainstage by showing American musical comedies. He envisioned a restaurant, a roof garden, cabaret theatre, a museum, a players' tavern, and patio dining. After endless negotiations, Larson decided instead to buy the space that is now the Variety Arts Theatre.

The Last Mile

Next, five major proposals came in, accompanied by ten thousand dollars each. The first, Voynow Investment Company, was basically a real estate investment. Next, Frank Biggin wanted to base small schools in the existing buildings. Then, the American National Opera Foundation considered the Mainstage as a home. At one point, The Studio Theatre Playhouse, which operates the Studio Theatre on Riverside Drive in LA, seemed a viable option. These and other offers were dangling

when an Economic Development Administration grant for $1.3 million came in, thanks to the newly acquired landmark designation.

The grant had to be matched by an equal amount.

The Decent Thing

Enter David Houk, Theatre Corporation of America, and a group of private investors with interests in real estate and the restoration of legitimate theatres who were in other development projects in Los Angeles, including the legendary Philharmonic Auditorium.

David Houk made an offer in 1978 to develop a complex plan to allow the theatre to operate. The plan continued to evolve over the years. Houk's company agreed to ensure full rehabilitation of the buildings and to provide the private matching dollars necessary to do the job.

The Deal

The agreement reached in 1981 allowed David Houk to buy the property and then lease the Mainstage Theatre to the City of Pasadena for twenty years with four twenty-year options. The Pasadena Playhouse would be owned by Historical Restoration Associates and Pasadena Playhouse State Theatre of California, Inc., a non-profit organization. Theatre Corporation of America would handle the day-to-day management of The Pasadena Playhouse. The non-profit organization would form a community board of directors.

The property was divided into three sections: the original structure to be immediately renovated, the old school tower to be restored at a later date, and the parking lot directly behind the theatre which could be incorporated into the project in the future.

Camelot

In the early '80s Pasadena had respected art museums, and a first-rate symphony orchestra; but with the Pasadena Playhouse dark, there was no legitimate professional theatre. Gilmor Brown, no doubt, smiled down on Houk's plans.

Endgame

With The Pasadena Playhouse being operated as a theatre for six highly professional plays and musicals each year, Houk saw its restoration as a catalyst for the re-development of what has become known as "the Playhouse District" in mid-town Pasadena.

There was to be an upbeat Hollywood ending after all.

Restoration Drama: 1979-1986

Pasadena had breathlessly watched The Pasadena Playhouse melodrama for a decade as each suspenseful rescue attempt played out. This latest installment seemed almost too true to be good. The community, slightly jaded and suspicious, applauded hero Houk with some skeptical reservation.

The Homecoming

The restoration drama began with a star-studded press conference. Reporters and celebrities, many former Playhouse students, gathered in the patio to hear the long-awaited news. Enthusiastic Stephen Rothman, the newly appointed artistic director, his old friend Ed Asner at his side, delivered visionary gospel with missionary zeal.

Action

To facilitate the restoration Houk relied on his theatre management company, the predecessor of Theatre Corporation of America, to represent community interest. A non-profit corporation would integrate local citizens and business leaders appointed by the city with three members appointed by Houk.

The Cocktail Hour

Things began to happen. On November 3, 1979, The Pasadena Playhouse doors opened for the first time in ten years with a frenzied Builders' Bash that brought in unruly crowds and forty thousand dollars in seed money.

By 8:00 p.m. hundreds were waiting in a line extending clear to Colorado Boulevard to mingle with Lloyd Nolan and ninety other celebrities.

Fiddler on the Roof

Sally Struthers, co-chairperson of the Builders' Bash, signed autographs as continuous entertainment played on four different stages. There was music, there were roving entertainers; and of the four thousand attendees, a good time was had by at least two hundred who were able to reach the food tables on the third floor.

Pilgrim's Progress

Richard McCann became the architect for the restoration. The cause was advanced in 1981 when the city approved bids and reconstruction planning got under way. The entire federal grant was ultimately used for the theatre restoration; Houk's funding sources and donations provided for the remaining two thirds of the rehabilitation. For only twenty-five dollars (later one hundred dollars), individuals became a permanent part of the theatre by having a personalized name tile on the Wall of Support. Corporate money was sought for other projects.

Sally Struthers, *co-chairperson of the Builders' Bash.*

In Appreciation
FRANK J. SHERWOOD

Uncommon Women and Others

Gilmor Brown had originally chosen Pasadena because he believed in the generosity and willingness of this community to support a theatre. Pasadenans proved worthy one more time. Support groups suddenly blossomed like the potted jade trees in the patio. From a small article in the *Star News*, eighty recruits appeared ready to work. Most of them had never been to a show at The Pasadena Playhouse. These volunteers attacked the building and courtyard with brooms and paint brushes. More than one hundred of them worked one thousand hours to clean up a place which had endured ten years of neglect. Local Girl Scouts swept the patio where the wrought-iron fixtures were repaired to light the way for the Patio Theatre, which was chosen as the first stage to reopen.

The inaugural show at the re-christened fifty-three-seat Interim Theatre, *Echoes*, opened almost twenty years after Brown's death. Working in a waiver situation allowed by Actors' Equity for a house with less than one hundred seats, this theatre operated during the restoration.

The second play was *Robert Frost Fire and Ice*. *Room Service* followed. Because of unprecedented ticket demands, it was obvious a larger space was needed.

The $100,000 restoration of the Balcony Theatre provided an additional theatre with expanded seating. *El Grande*

In Appreciation
CLARE & JOHN SLEETER

The damage due to neglect and vandalism was extensive.

In Appreciation
RICHARD SMART

VOICES OFF
Professor of Ideas at nearby Occidental
College and long-time Pasadena resident
Dr. Robert Winter, *the ultimate architectural*
authority, waxes poetic about the restoration.
"It's such a lovely surprise to turn down El
Molino and come unexpectedly to that wonder-
ful oasis of the past. The renovation comes as
close as possible to the original as any I've ever
seen. There were no liberties taken. Everything
is picturesque and authentic—even if it is a bit
phony. That's what's so magnificent about
Spanish Colonial Revival, the pretentiousness."

In need of a face lift.

In Appreciation
GREGG SMITH

De Coca Cola opened the fully equipped ninety-nine-seat Balcony Theatre in May, 1982. The critically acclaimed *The Gin Game* played simultaneously in the Interim Theatre, setting box office records. A special edition of *The Subject Was Roses* and *Dames at Sea* were next on the agenda in the Balcony Theatre.

It was time for the volunteers to devise an overall strategy. Ultimately, The Friends evolved. Three hundred members provided staff positions from ushering to cooking dinner for the cast to costume repair.

Steadfast, The Pasadena Playhouse Alumni and Associates, composed of former students and faculty of the College of Theatre Arts and non-students who had performed routinely at The Pasadena Playhouse, voted to present several annual achievement awards at their yearly brunch and thus generate additional press and membership interest.

Many individuals interested in the theatre's success, demonstrated support with financial contributions.

Noises Off

Construction was determined by a strong sense of the past. The renewal program sought to upgrade the theatre to meet contemporary standards while preserving the historical integrity of the structure.

Plain and Fancy

The facade of the theatre was technically given to the Pasadena Historical Society, whose members acted as advisors during the restoration.

Care was taken to replace only those roof tiles which were damaged and could not be renovated. By laying new tiles similar in color and texture to what existed, roofers and designers were able to retain the historic integrity of The Pasadena Playhouse. The leaking roof over the lobby was mostly replaced.

The carved oak doors to the lobby and woodwork around the box office and the library windows were carefully refinished.

A new handicap access ramp was built to blend with the flagstone in the courtyard. The former student center metamorphosed into an expanded contemporary box office, and a cashier's office was added. When a new coat of plaster was applied it merged with the original structure.

Tomorrow and Tomorrow

McCann did not attempt an exact replica. The '20s interiors resembled a

VOICES OFF
Believing that "any theatre that can be adapted for present-day use is an investment in the community and the future of the performing arts," **Richard McCann**, *the architect for the restoration, installed state-of-the-art lighting and scenery systems. He mused early on, "People ask where the money goes because it's not always easily seen. It gets spent inside the walls and above the ceiling."*

In Appreciation
STITZEL COMPANY

rainbow of bright hues. Practically every room was different. He chose to unify and seemingly expand the space with a simplified color scheme. Still, by using eye-witness accounts, scraping down to bare plaster, and learning old-fashioned techniques of layering paint and varnish, the grandeur was brought back. Even frayed edges of the ceiling's burlap veneer were carefully mended.

Time Remembered

Improvements were made for both comfort and preservation. Initial acoustical design called for the installation of cork on the floor. Today plush carpeting provides a more luxurious solution. An air conditioning and heating system was installed with a high-tech 100-ton air condenser unit hoisted to the roof by crane. But the plaster grates that once covered the air vents in the auditorium were lovingly reconstructed. New molds were created from sections of existing grates to reproduce the archetypes. Public restrooms were enlarged and modernized, with an eye to authenticity.

To build a seismic support wall, a second wall of concrete block running the width of the theatre on both orchestra and balcony levels, workers had to cut through and then carefully replace several of the existing arches along the back wall of the balcony.

In Appreciation
ANGELA TEEK

VIPs gathered to celebrate the re-opening.
Ruth Buzzi and Fritz Feld were there.

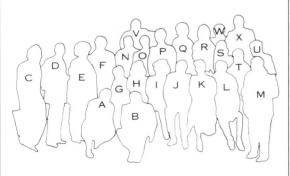

PASADENA PLAYHOUSE RESTORATION GROUND
BREAKING SEPTEMBER 20, 1982
(A) Tom Hatten (B) Anthony Caruso (C) Alan Shearman
(D) Oliver Prickett (E) Virginia Capers (F) Peter Hansen
(G) Peggy Converse (H) Julie Adams (I) Ruta Lee
(J) Werner Klemperer (K) Francis Reid (L) Dana Andrews
(M) Fritz Feld (N) Don Porter (O) Bob Cummings
(P) Buddy Ebsen (Q) Sue Ane Langdon (R) Ruth Buzzi
(S) Bill Daily (T) Norma Ransom (U) Arthur Peterson
(V) Stephen Rothman (W) Caroline Kearney
(X) Noel Desuza

M is for the Million

It became obvious at this point that in order to reopen the Mainstage, operating and start-up funds were needed. David Houk sold one-half interest in the building to raise the money. Houk's partnership donated the much needed one million dollars to the non-profit organization. The following year Theatre Corporation of America made an additional donation in the form of cancelling out the $1.2 million in debt owed by the non-profit organization.

Something for Everyone

In 1984 the renovation of the Mainstage was completed. The Pasadena Playhouse was officially placed on the National Register of Historical Places.

Jessica Myerson was named artistic director early in 1985. Rothman had moved on the previous December. The first Mainstage season featured *Arms and the Man*, *Look Homeward Angel* and *Spokesong*.

In November 1986, Susan Dietz came aboard espousing her personal three E's: "Entertain, enrich and enlighten." Add energetic and electric for her high-voltage personality. Steve Rothman returned. The two were to function as producing directors for the second Mainstage season. James Whitmore was appointed honorary chairperson of The Pasadena Playhouse's Actors Advisory Board. (Currently, the artistic director is Paul Lazarus.)

In Appreciation
DR. & MRS. PAUL TOFFEL

VOICES OFF

Ken Ott, the busy director of development, passed along a lovely tidbit of hearsay about the selection of the current interior paint color in the lobby and auditorium. "People were arguing that the lobby had been blue or green or whatever, so someone said let's take down the furnace grill and see what color's underneath. It was sort of—I guess you'd call it persimmon. The issue was settled. The walls were painted. Later, it was supposedly learned the room had been ivory and that rusty color was nothing but layers of age-old tar and nicotine from when smoking was permissible inside during intermission."

In Appreciation
TIMES MIRROR FOUNDATION

LA TIENDA: A RARE GIFT SHOP

La Tienda brings in about fifty thousand dollars a year. At first volunteers sold concessions in the lobby from behind the confiscated counter that had served as the reservations desk in Room Service. Eventually, volunteers were selling excess cast tee shirts from a decorated cart that was rolled into the patio. Now La Tienda is located off the patio in space originally intended as a shop. The cash register sits on the the same counter, and the cart is used to display sequined sweaters. An interesting place to browse pre-show or intermission, the store offers speciality gift items, theatre books, scripts, posters, prints, watercolors, tee shirts, mugs, jewelry, dolls, clowns, tapes, masks, and fanciful handcrafted art.

An Old-Fashioned Gentleman

When Rothman departed the second time, congenial Lars Hansen (a California native) came aboard as Executive Director. Hansen, back from three years on the East Coast, brought years of expertise and level-headed verve. His experience included the premiere season of the prestigious American Music Theatre Festival in Philadelphia, and business management from the highly distinguished Playwrights Horizons in New York City.

The Pasadena Playhouse had come back in glory.

It's Only a Play

Refurbished and in its sixth season, The Pasadena Playhouse has the smug look of a dowager come into her inheritance at last. It's commonplace once again on mild evenings to see tastefully attired playgoers filling the courtyard. Their graceful movements seem choreographed: the gentlemen in summer suits, the ladies clad elegantly in soft floral silks and pastel linens. They wander past a dozen arching palms toward the outside bar and their footsteps on the flagstone almost drown out a faint rustling of ghostly memories.

Friends serve up dinner and hospitality.

The newly installed patio bar offers refreshments.

In Appreciation
LILY TOMLIN

STAGE WHISPER: **LARS HANSEN**
"The board, comprised of prominent citizens who love the theatre, are not mired in the day-to-day decision making, nor are they responsible for shouldering any financial burden."

The Pasadena Playhouse is big in the numbers racket; to date it has attracted more than 950,000 playgoers since reopening in 1986. In cityspeak that's ten Rose Bowl games. Twenty-four thousand subscribers currently attend from 327 zip codes in Southern California; fourteen percent of those subscribers come from the City of Pasadena with the rest coming from all over the Southland. About six hundred to seven hundred persons nightly attend the theatre at each of the eight performances per week. The theatre now schedules 310 event days per year. With time out to change over the stage from one play to the next, the building is operating at capacity. According to a standard economic multiplier of 3.2 for arts and cultural events, the thirteen million dollars in revenue since 1986 translated to an economic impact of forty-one million to date for the City of Pasadena.

VOICES OFF

David Crandell, head of the early TV department at The Pasadena Playhouse's College of Theatre Arts and twice president of The Pasadena Playhouse Alumni and Associates, received the Gilmor Brown Award from this group at their annual brunch in 1991. Crandell is still enthusiastic after forty years of devoted service. "If Brown's ghost does not truly stalk the hallowed halls in dark of night, his spirit, his inspiration and his dream live on in both that historic edifice and in the hearts and minds of all of us who are the talented theatre-folk known as The Pasadena Playhouse Alumni and Associates."

Ross Eastty (left) served The Pasadena Playhouse Alumni and Associates as president for twenty years. Helen Shaw, in her nineties, has given many decades of her life to acting. She still makes commericals.

In Appreciation
COLLEEN & JOSEPH UNTERREINER

Area residents **Cindy** and **Kevin Costner** pose for the camera
with Lars Hansen at a recent opening. "We are selective about the
organizations with which we become involved, but we both feel
that The Pasadena Playhouse is a tremendous asset for the entire
Los Angeles community."

STAGE WHISPER: **LARS HANSEN**
"Audiences remember that the productions
are exceptional, and their specific memory is
simply the pleasure of being at The Pasadena
Playhouse."

In Appreciation
FRIENDS OF THE PASADENA PLAYHOUSE

The Pasadena Playhouse and all that it entails, the property, the buildings, the shows, have come back in style.

*David and Mickey Houk found a moment
to enjoy the historic courtyard fountain.*

Portrait of an Entrepreneur

Thanks to a happy ending provided by David Houk, the saga of The Pasadena Playhouse's seventy-five years can read today like a cherished fairy tale.

Man and Superman

David G. Houk assumed the responsibility of restoring and reopening The Pasadena Playhouse, along with the original guarantors Michael Sharp and Sam and Betty Behar, after many dark years. Houk, with many others, achieved what at the time appeared nearly impossible. A few of the "key" people who helped him accomplish his mission were: first and foremost, his beautiful wife Mickey; his friend and partner Donald Loze, a brilliant attorney and strategist; Stephen Rothman, the first producer for the theatre; Bob Siner, the first executive director of the theatre; Jessica Myerson, the first artistic director, followed by Stephen Rothman and Susan Dietz as co-producing directors; and Lars Hansen, who joined the team. There were also the financial partners who pledged their support, and of course the dedicated and loyal staff of the theatre. All, working together, created the success of The Pasadena Playhouse.

This lengthy interview takes place in the comfortable living room of David and Mickey Houk's European-style home, shrouded by old oaks on a quiet street in the Linda Vista area of Pasadena. Morning sun spills through French doors onto the gleaming wood floors and leaves a streak of jewel colors on the Oriental rug. Antiques collected by the Houks fill the room, and large framed photographs taken in the patio at The Pasadena Playhouse hang above a lustrous black grand piano. Azalea bushes explode with vivid pink blossoms on the other side of leaded glass. The view through the north-facing bay window is of the lush side garden. Here, a child's yellow swing and basketball hoop seem delightfully incongruous, looking perhaps like bright man-made talismans.

QUESTION: *Let's start with a short bio. You basically grew up in Glendale?*

HOUK: I was born in Ohio, moved to Pennsylvania a year later and to Glendale in the eighth grade. From there I went to Westmount College (in Montecito) on a track scholarship with aspirations of trying out for the Olympics. A slipped disc curtailed those aspirations.

QUESTION: *What led to your becoming an entrepreneur?*

HOUK: Before I learned what entrepreneur meant, I saw my father, who is a Presbyterian minister—as was his father—suffer at the hands of those who held the purse strings. I realized that you need money to finance dreams. I became an entrepreneur to get myself in a situation wherein I would be able to finance my dreams. I was raised to believe it is possible to change the world through the church. I became disillusioned with the

Alumna **Rue McClanahan** *returned to raves in* The House of Blue Leaves.

The world premiere of Mail *was delivered first class and then expressed to Broadway.*

Forever Plaid *revived the music and spirit of the '50s.*

*Area resident **Ray Bradbury** took time out from his usual science fiction to try his hand at writing for the stage and bought* The Wonderful Ice Cream Suit *to life with music by **Jose Feliciano**.*

The stunning Cole Porter revival You Never Know *based on the play* By Candlelight *delighted playgoers.*

Other People's Money broke box office records, later became a motion picture.

church as a means to encourage man getting along with man at an early age. The other options seemed to be business. I chose business.

QUESTION: *What attracts you to the theatre?*

HOUK: Theatre is an effective instrument of city planning. It's a very logical combination. I know for a fact that theatre changes neighborhoods.

QUESTION: *Could you be more explicit?*

HOUK: You bring people into an area to the theatre and enhance the area. If you want to effect change, then that makes for a natural alignment with theatre. And conversely, theatre has always been a place where social change is advocated. The end result either way ultimately is a better city, state, world. That's my ultimate goal. It's what I heard my father preaching.

QUESTION: *Now let's be even more specific and talk about your involvement with The Pasadena Playhouse. You must have been ecstatic back in 1986, when The Pasadena Playhouse finally reopened after six or more years of your time and effort. How did you feel that night?*

HOUK: That moment felt anti-climactic. My greatest joy during that long transaction came at a different point.

QUESTION: *When was that?*

HOUK: At the beginning I had this intangible idea—this vision for The Pasadena Playhouse—but it didn't seem real then. Later, it was 1979, I was speaking about the proposed restoration at the annual Pasadena Playhouse Alumni and Associates brunch and I encountered four hundred to five hundred people all of whom were so full of emotion for the theatre. It truly touched me. All the care and love this distinguished group of people have for The Pasadena Playhouse. I was overwhelmed. For the second time in my life I choked. I still do when I talk about it. I tried to speak, but no words came out.

QUESTION: *When was the first time?*

HOUK: At Mickey's and my wedding. My father married us at the Presbyterian Church in Glendale. During the rehearsal I was fine and Mickey was very emotional. She could barely talk; so I said, "Mickey, come on, it's not that hard, just do it." (CHOKING UP) Well, the next day she was just wonderful, came bounding down the aisle looking beautiful, and my dad performed great and I opened my mouth to speak and nothing came out.

QUESTION: *That's a lovely story. You're driven by emotion then?*

HOUK: Emotion and a fascination with making a difference in the world.

QUESTION: *Do you see parallels between yourself and Gilmor Brown?*

HOUK: The similarities are that Gilmor and I both started with a dream and a vision and no money.

QUESTION: *Yes! The differences?*

HOUK: My dream is to ultimately contribute to the place where we come together as a community—the theatre. It's not from the point of view of the action

In Appreciation
WARREN PRINTING & MAILING

upon the stage. It's centered on seeing the theatre as part of a larger picture.

QUESTION: *What will the development of the property surrounding The Pasadena Playhouse mean to the theatre, and to Pasadena?*

HOUK: I'm working toward a certain synergy of community that results in a positive kind of communication which will improve the neighborhood, and the city. I think this can occur when actors, writers, and audience mingle. I want to provide a place to do that.

QUESTION: *Brown believed the community was best served by establishing intimacy between the actors and society as well.*

HOUK: It allows for respect and understanding to go both ways. I like to think I'm in the city animation business. We put life back into cities using theatre.

QUESTION: *You are planning to renovate the area bounded by Green Street, Colorado Boulevard, Madison Avenue, El Molino Avenue?*

HOUK: Yes.

QUESTION: *Will the area be like a plaza with The Pasadena Playhouse in the middle?*

HOUK: Somewhat. The architecture will match the theatre. We're planning a second theatre with 1,500 seats adjacent to the existing stage which will allow us to produce larger productions, big plays, more musicals.

QUESTION: *A new theatre? What else?*

HOUK: We're working with the American Academy of Dramatic Arts to build them a new campus for their West Coast branch. It's exciting for students to be involved with the professional theatre. Talk to any of The Pasadena Playhouse College of Theatre Arts alumni. Also, there will be a small fifty- to seventy-room European-style inn. And a residential component for artists, students, and theatre people. Restaurants. A theatre club.

QUESTION: *A private club for theatre lovers?*

HOUK: A private club that has theatre privileges.

QUESTION: *What is the time frame?*

HOUK: Our goal is two to three years.

QUESTION: *Where will you be ten years from now?*

HOUK: Here, I hope. Operating fifty theatres across the country. The Pasadena Playhouse can serve as a source of American plays and musicals. When you think of country music you think of the Grand Ol' Opry in Nashville. I'd like The Pasadena Playhouse to be the equivalent of that in regards to new plays and musicals.

QUESTION: *Do you see your overriding goals for animating cities serving as a blueprint for other regions of the country?*

HOUK: Yes.

QUESTION: *What is the future of The Pasadena Playhouse?*

HOUK: Because of the theatre's reputation we can take work from Pasadena anywhere in the world. I intend to restore and operate theatres wherever the oppor-

Born Yesterday *delighted Pasadena audiences whose grandparents were shocked the first time around.*

Robert Harling's Steel Magnolias *turned the fledging playwright into an overnight success.*

Accomplice *by award-winning playwright* **Rupert Holmes** *headed east to Broadway.*

In Appreciation
DONNA GALE WASHBURN

Stacy Keach, Jr. wowed audiences with his one-man show Solitary Confinement, *a multi-media piece again by* **Rupert Holmes.**

The very popular Lend Me A Tenor *sold out and left them laughing.*

Conrad Bain *in a revival of* **Paul Osborn's** *gentle '30s script,* On Borrowed Time, *proved to be a tear-jerker.*

tunity presents itself. We're leasing theatres in North San Diego County, Santa Barbara, and other areas of Southern California. After that we'll expand geographically.

QUESTION: *Do you have a long-term goal?*

HOUK: I have a three-pronged plan: entertainment, city planning, and transit. Number one includes the restoration of theatres. Number two is hiring the brightest minds there are to work on city planning using a theatre as the focal point. And number three gets into urban transit.

QUESTION: *Lars Hansen insists you'll put theatre on the moon.*

HOUK: People first. But he's absolutely right. We're just beginning. There's a big world out there. But there will always be The Pasadena Playhouse. We're designing our future around it.

QUESTION: *What do you want your legacy to be?*

HOUK: My favorite quote from Shakespeare is, "All the world's a stage." I want to change that stage into a global community.

QUESTION: *Anything else?*

HOUK: I hope to leave behind an established institution to carry on my dreams. I want to show my son that one person can make a difference. When Geoffrey was born I didn't pass out cigars. I passed out small brandy bottles with a card attached that gave the following toast to my son: "May you have the wisdom to know what you want to do, and the courage to do it."

Pasadena makes the same toast to David G. Houk.

In Appreciation
CHLOE WEBB

*In downtown Santa Barbara the 680-seat historic **Lobero Theatre**, built in 1924, will be the home of productions from The Pasadena Playhouse starting in the fall of 1992.*

*The 815-seat **Poway Center for the Performing Arts** opened in 1990 to serve the entire San Diego area. This, too, will be home to The Pasadena Playhouse season of plays and musicals starting in the fall of 1992.*

In Appreciation
WEINGART FOUNDATION

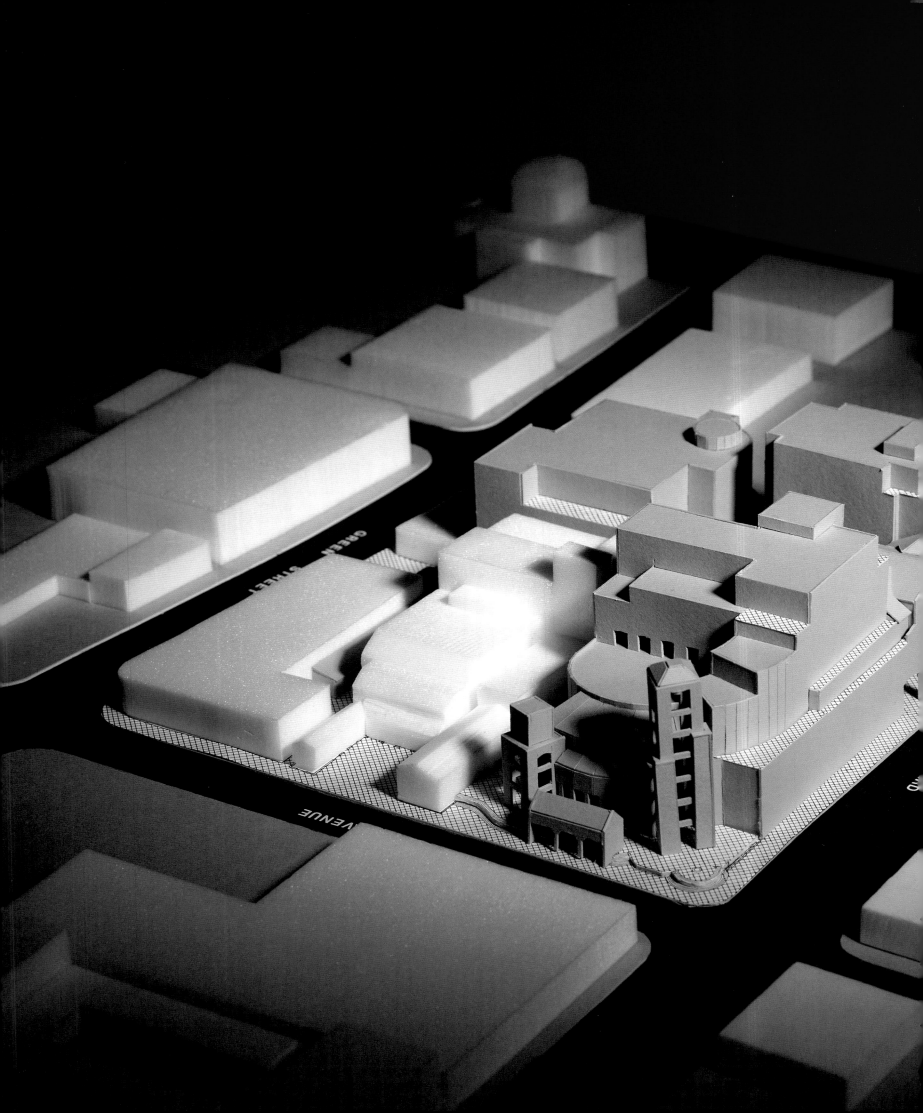

Coming Soon: A Blockbuster Attraction

Future plans earn rave reviews. The property surrounding The Pasadena Playhouse—an area bounded by Colorado Boulevard to the north, Madison to the west, and Green to the south—will soon become an enchanting Pasadena classic-style plaza. "The Block" will be developed by Theatre Corporation of America.

The Master Builder

It's an impressive undertaking. There will probably be more theatres, a small European-style inn, apartments for students, restaurants, a cabaret, and a private club. An effort is underway to incorporate a new permanent home for the West Coast branch of The American Academy of Dramatic Arts.

The Pasadena Playhouse will sit in the physical center of the project, continuing to reign, proud and confident.

Closer Than Ever

Gilmor Brown turned Pasadena into a real theatre town. David Houk has even higher hopes. He envisions a global communtiy using theatre as a positive source for change. The seventy-five-year-old-dream goes on.

In Appreciation
THE VONS COMPANIES

STAGE WHISPER: **LARS HANSEN**

"David Houk figured out a way to blend public and private resources for the benefit of a cultural institution. The development of the other businesses on the property will aid The Pasadena Playhouse, financially."

In Appreciation
VROMAN'S

In Appreciation
ANTHONY J. AMENDOLA, ESQ.

STAGE WHISPER:
KEN OTT, Director of Development
"The American Theatre of the future will have to develop a spirit of entrepreneurship and work toward a goal of self sufficiency. We see our proposed expansions as private/public partnerships that can preserve and nurture cultural institutions.

"I am excited about forthcoming plans for 39 South El Molino. We will be building a second larger theatre, club/restaurants, a European-style inn and a drama school. The Pasadena Playhouse will remain as the 'jewel-in-the-crown.' These additions should have an aesthetic as well as a positive financial impact upon Pasadena."

Gretchen Wyler, Joe Mantegna, Ken Ott and Kevin McCarthy at a fundraising gala.

In Appreciation
LARS HANSEN

In Appreciation
JAMES WHITMORE

1993 TOURNAMENT OF ROSES PARADE FLOAT
The Vons Company along with The Pasadena Playhouse will enter a dazzling replica of
The Pasadena Playhouse in the 1993 Tournament of Roses Parade. According to Lars Hansen,
"It is our way of sharing the 75th Anniversary Diamond Jubilee celebration with the hundreds
of millions of people around the world who view the parade on television."

In Appreciation
GRETCHEN WYLER

The Pasadena Playhouse History

1917 A theatre was founded by actor/director Gilmor Brown in an old burlesque space called The Savoy.

1922 The Savoy was declared a fire hazard. The recently formed Community Playhouse Association of Pasadena collected funds door-to-door for a grandiose new theatre.

1923 Land was purchased on South El Molino.

1924 On May 31st, the cornerstone for The Pasadena Playhouse structure was laid.

1925 On May 18th, The Pasadena Playhouse opened with *The Amethyst.*

1928 The Pasadena Playhouse's School of Theatre was founded and the first class enrolled. Famous alumni include Gene Hackman, Robert Preston, Carolyn Jones, Barbara Rush, Charles Bronson, Ruth Buzzi, and many more.

The world premiere of Eugene O'Neill's *Lazarus Laughed* was staged.

1930 The first class of the School of Theatre graduated.

The entire building debt of $150,000 was paid off through a donation by Mrs. Fannie Morrison.

1935-55 The Midsummer Festivals occurred, each featuring works of a famous playwright. The first two seasons were Shakespeare.

The policy of presenting both premiere performances of works by leading playwrights and plays by new dramatists made The Pasadena Playhouse an active force in local theatre, and it was considered by *Stage* Magazine to be "The most prolific drama-producing organization in the United States." Every year, several hundred actors appeared on its stages in more than sixty plays.

1936 The Pasadena Playhouse was the first American theatre to present all thirty-seven of Shakespeare's plays in their entirety.

1937 The Pasadena Playhouse was declared the State Theatre of California by an unanimous vote of the State Legislature.

1937 The Playbox was established in Gilmor Brown's home.

1960 Gilmor Brown died.

1966 The IRS padlocked the front doors of The Pasadena Playhouse due to more than $30,000 of indebtedness.

1968 Dire financial circumstances forced The Pasadena Playhouse to close its doors.

1969 The Pasadena Playhouse declared bankruptcy. The contents of The Pasadena Playhouse were sold in an auction.

The Pasadena Playhouse was designated as a Historical Monument. It was subsequently granted recognition by the National Register of Historic Places.

1970 The Pasadena Playhouse was purchased by Bank of America for $285,000.

1975 The Pasadena Playhouse was acquired by the City of Pasadena for $325,000.

1979 David Houk negotiated with the City of Pasadena to restore The Pasadena Playhouse. Stephen Rothman was named executive director.

On November 3rd, The Pasadena Playhouse doors reopened for the first time in ten years with the fund-raising Builders' Bash. Over two thousand people filled the theatre complex to view entertainers, both on and off stage.

1980 The fifty-three-seat Interim Theatre was remodeled with volunteer help.

In May, the theatre opened with the production of *Echoes* by N. Richard Nash.

1981 The city signed a contract with David Houk.

Robert Frost Fire and Ice opened in April as the first world premiere in The Pasadena Playhouse Interim Theatre.

1981 Due to an unprecedented ticket demand for the production of *Room Service* in the Interim Theatre, it became apparent that a larger equity-waiver space was necessary.

In Appreciation
MOLLY & RALPH WOLVECK

1981 The fully equipped ninety-nine-seat Balcony Theatre was remodeled.

In May, the theatre opened with *El Grande De Coca Cola*, featuring the original Low Moan Spectacular. With the critically acclaimed *The Gin Game* playing simultaneously in the Interim Theatre, a six thousand-member subscriber base was laid for The Pasadena Playhouse.

In November, ground was broken on the restoration of the seven hundred-seat Mainstage of The Pasadena Playhouse.

1983 A special edition of Frank D. Gilroy's *The Subject was Roses* and *Dames at Sea* were produced in the Balcony Theatre.

1984 In November, the renovation of the Mainstage of The Pasadena Playhouse was completed.

Stephen Rothman left The Pasadena Playhouse.

1985 Jessica Myerson was named artistic director.

1986 The first Mainstage season opened following a $4.5 million restoration. The season included *Arms and the Man, Look Homeward Angel* and *Spokesong*.

1986 The Pasadena Playhouse placed on National Register of Historical Places.

In November, Susan Dietz and Stephen Rothman were named co-producing directors for The Pasadena Playhouse's second Mainstage season. James Whitmore was appointed Honorary Chairperson of The Pasadena Playhouse's Actors Advisory Board.

1988 The Balcony Theatre reopened after being transformed into a ninety-nine-seat professional theatre.

Mail, a new musical originally produced by The Pasadena Playhouse in 1987, opened on Broadway.

1988 The La Tienda gift shop opened on the courtyard.

1990 The Pasadena Playhouse Partners support group was launched. Cindy and Kevin Costner served as honorary chairs.

1992 Theatre Corporation of America signed leases with the Lobero Theatre in Santa Barbara and The Poway Center for the Performing Arts in North San Diego County for the purpose of presenting all future productions throughout the Southland.

Peggy Ebright's mural, depicting seventy-five years of Pasadena Playhouse history, will eventually decorate the patio arcade.

In Appreciation
LIZARDI COMMUNICATIONS

List of Mainstage Plays

In its heyday, The Pasadena Playhouse produced 500 new scripts—claiming 23 American and 477 World premieres. Among these: Noel Coward's *Cavalcade*, and F. Scott Fitzgerald's *An American Jazz Comedy: The Vegetable*. Brown befriended a timid, obscure playwright named Tennessee Williams, who tried out several plays on somewhat shocked Pasadena audiences. All thirty-seven Shakespeare plays were staged in their entirety. During the first twenty-five years, The Pasadena Playhouse produced 1,348 plays, an average of over fifty plays a year with more than six hundred mounted on the mainstage. (By the 1960s this figure exceeded one thousand.)

NO.	PLAY	AUTHOR	DATE	DIRECTOR
	(Shakespeare Club House)			
1	The Song of Lady Lotus Eyes	B.A.Purrington	Nov. 20-23, 1917	Gilmor Brown
2	The Critics	St. John Ervine	Nov. 20-23, 1917	Gilmor Brown
3	The Neighbors	Zona Gale	Nov. 20-23, 1917	Gilmor Brown
4	Pierre Patelin	Anonymous	Nov. 20-23, 1917	Gilmor Brown
5	The Man from Home	Booth Tarkington	Nov. 27-Dec. 1, 1917	Gilmor Brown
	(Savoy)			
6	An Old Fashioned Gentleman	(from the old French)	Dec. 6-8, 1917	Gilmor Brown
7	Lady Windermere's Fan	Oscar Wilde	Dec. 10-15, 1917	Gilmor Brown
8*	Tommy Imagines	Alfred Brand	Dec. 17-22, 1917	Gilmor Brown
9*	Cinderella	Mrs. Torrey Everett	Dec. 17-22, 1917	Gilmor Brown
10	The Neighbors	Zona Gale	Dec. 17-22, 1917	Gilmor Brown
11	Wanted, A Wife	Anonymous	Dec. 24-29, 1917	Gilmor Brown
12	A Lesson in Diplomacy	Anonymous	Dec. 31-Jan. 5, 1918	Gilmor Brown
13	Twelfth Night	Wm. Shakespeare	Jan. 7-19, 1918	Gilmor Brown
14	The Tribulations of Jimmie	Anonymous	Jan. 21-26, 1918	Gilmor Brown
15	Board and Lodging	Anonymous	Jan. 28-Feb. 2, 1918	Gilmor Brown
16	Oliver Twist	Charles Dickens	Feb. 4-9, 1918	Gilmor Brown
17	The Taming of the Shrew	Wm. Shakespeare	Feb. 11-16, 1918	Gilmor Brown
18*	The Infernal Masculine	Alfred Brand	Feb. 18-23, 1918	Gilmor Brown
19*	The Only Son	Marjorie Sinclair	Feb. 18-23, 1918	Gilmor Brown
20	Washington's First Defeat	C. F. Nirdlinger	Feb. 18-23,1918	Gilmor Brown
21	The Bear	Anton Tchekoff	Feb. 18-23, 1918	Gilmor Brown
22	A Night at the Play	Baker Version	Feb. 25-Mar.1, 1918	Gilmor Brown
23	Betsy Ross	Anonymous	Mar. 3, 1918	Gilmor Brown
24	Rip Van Winkle	Washington Irving	Mar. 4-8, 1918	Gilmor Brown
25	Have You a Little Burglar in Your Home?	F. W. Sidney	Mar. 11-15, 1918	Gilmor Brown
26*	A Case of Eviction	Mrs. W. A. Boadway	Mar. 18-22,1918	Gilmor Brown
27	The Hour Glass	Wm. Butler Yeats	Mar. 18-22, 1918	Gilmor Brown
28	Spreading the News	Lady Gregory	Mar. 18-22, 1918	Gilmor Brown
29	Niobe	Anonymous	Mar. 25-29, 1918	Gilmor Brown
30	The School for Scandal	R. B. Sheridan	Apr. 2-6, 1918	Gilmor Brown
31	College Chums	Anonymous	Apr. 9-13, 1918	Gilmor Brown
32*	Family Pride	Mrs. W. M. Boadway	Apr. 16-20, 1918	Gilmor Brown
33	Alice in Wonderland	Lewis Carroll	Apr. 16-20, 1918	Gilmor Brown
34	The Marriage of Kitty	C. Gordon-Lennox	Apr. 23-27, 1918	Gilmor Brown
35	Mrs.Wiggs of the Cabbage Patch	Alice Rice	Apr. 30-May 11, 1918	Gilmor Brown
36	The Gentle Honeymoon	Mrs. E. K. Covey	May 14-18, 1918	Gilmor Brown
37*	Just Mammy	Sybil E. Jones	May 21-25, 1918	Gilmor Brown
38	Pygmalion and Galatea	W. S. Gilbert	May 21-25, 1918	Gilmor Brown
39	The Gentle Honeymoon	Mrs. E. K. Covey	May 27-June 1, 1918	Gilmor Brown
40	The Would-Be Nobleman	Molière	June 3-8, 1918	Gilmor Brown
	(In Cruickshank Garden)			
41	A Midsummer Night's Dream	Wm. Shakespeare	Aug. 8-10, 1918	Gilmor Brown
	(At Broadoaks School Garden)			
42	The Tyranny of Tears	Haddon Chambers	Sept. 5-6, 1918	Gilmor Brown
	(Savoy)			
43	Mrs.Wiggs of the Cabbage Patch	Alice Rice	Nov. 18-22, 1918	Gilmor Brown
44	Hekna's Husband	Philip Moeller	Dec. 26-31, 1918	Gilmor Brown
45	Two Crooks and a Lady	Eugene Pilot	Dec. 26-31, 1918	Gilmor Brown
46	Food	Wm. C. DeMilk	Dec. 26-31, 1918	Gilmor Brown
47	The Pierrot of the Minute	E. Dowson	Jan. 2-4, 1919	Gilmor Brown
48	Abraham and Isaac	Anonymous	Jan. 2-4, 1919	Gilmor Brown
49	Joint Owners in Spain	Alice Brown	Jan. 2-4, 1919	Gilmor Brown
50	The Yellow Jacket	G. C. Hazelton J. H. Benrimo	Feb. 3-13, 1919	Gilmor Brown
51	The Rejuvenation of Aunt Mary	Anne Warner	Feb. 24-Mar. 8, 1919	Gilmor Brown

NO.	PLAY	AUTHOR	DATE	DIRECTOR
52	Much Ado About Nothing	Wm. Shakespeare	Mar. 24-29, 1919	Gilmor Brown
53	The Passing of the Third Floor Back	Jerome K. Jerome	Apr. 21-May 7, 1919	Gilmor Brown
54*	Did It Really Happen?	Alfred Brand	May 8-10, 1919	Gilmor Brown
55*	The Song with Wings	Marjorie Driscoll	May 8-10, 1919	Gilmor Brown
56*	Thirty	Anna Nissen	May 8-10, 1919	Gilmor Brown
57	You Never Can Tell	G. B. Shaw	May 19-24, 1919	Gilmor Brown
58	The Stepmother	Arnold Bennett	May 29-31, 1919	Cloyd Dalzell
59	Ashes of Roses	Constance D. MacKay	May 29-31, 1919	Cloyd Dalzell
60	Addio	Stark Young	May 29-31, 1919	Cloyd Dalzell
61	Maiden Over the Wall	Bertram Bloch	May 29-31, 1919	Cloyd Dalzell
62	The Scarecrow	Percy MacKaye	June 9-14, 1919	Gilmor Brown
63	The Fortune Hunter	Winchell Smith	Sept. 29-Oct.4, 1919	Gilmor Brown
64	The Rivals	R.B.Sheridan	Oct. 27-Nov. 1, 1919	Gilmor Brown
65	The Little Princess	Frances H.Burnett	Nov. 24-Dec.6, 1919	Gilmor Brown
66	A Message from Mars	Richard Ganthony	Dec. 29-Jan.3, 1920	Gilmor Brown
67	The Tempest	Wm. Shakespeare	Jan. 26-Feb.7, 1920	Gilmor Brown
68	Trelawney of the Wells	Arthur W. Pinero	Feb. 23-Mar.6, 1920	Gilmor Brown
69*	The Master of Shadows	Sybil E. Jones	Apr. 5-17, 1920	Gilmor Brown
70	In Walked Jimmie	Mrs. Ronie H.Jaffa	Apr. 26-May 8, 1920	Gilmor Brown
71*	Redleaf	Alice Garwood	May 18, 1920	Gilmor Brown
72	Bunty Pulls the Strings	Graham Moffat	May 24-June 2, 1920	Gilmor Brown
73	Tartuffe	Moliere	June 21-26, 1920	Gilmor Brown
	(At Brookside Park)			
74	The Merry Wives of Windsor	Wm. Shakespeare	July 28-31, 1920	Gilmor Brown
75	The Fisherman and His Soul	Oscar Wilde Dickson Morgan	Aug. 5-7, 1920	Cloyd Dalzell
	(At Brookside Park)			
76	The Piper	Josephine P. Peabody	Aug. 30-Sept. 4, 1920	Gilmor Brown
77	Rip Van Winkle	Washington Irving	Sept. 20-25, 1920	Garnet Holme
78	Rebecca of Sunnybrook Farm	Kate D. Wiggin	Oct. 21-30, 1920	Gilmor Brown
79	She Stoops to Conquer	Oliver Goldsmith	Nov. 18-27, 1920	Gilmor Brown
80	Alice Sit-by-the-Fire	James M. Barrie	Dec. 15-25, 1920	Gilmor Brown
81	The Comedy of Errors	Wm. Shakespeare	Jan. 13-22, 1921	Gilmor Brown
82	The Passing of the Third Floor Back	Jerome K. Jerome	Feb. 1-5, 1921	Gilmor Brown
83	An Enemy of the People	Henrik Ibsen	Feb. 17-26, 1921	Gilmor Brown
84	The Palace of Truth	W. S. Gilbert	Mar. 17-29, 1921	Gilmor Brown
85*	Peter	Marion Wightman	Apr. l4-30, 1921	Gilmor Brown
86	Androcles and the Lion	G. B. Shaw	May 12-21, 1921	Gilmor Brown
87	Where Shall Adelaide Go?	F. M. Livingston	May 12-21, 1921	Gilmor Brown
88	Potash and Perlmutter	Montague Glass	June 9-25, 1921	Gilmor Brown
	(At Brookside Park)			
89	Pilgrim's Progress	John Bunyan	July 13-16, 1921	Gilmor Brown
90	The Knight of the Burning Pestle	Beaumont and Fletcher	Aug. 3-6, 1921	Frayne Williams
	(At Brookside Park)			
91	Pomander Walk	Louis N. Parker	Aug. 10-13, 1921	Gilmor Brown
92	Seven Keys to Baldpate	Earl D. Biggers	Sept. 15-24, 1921	Eloise Sterling
93	Little Women	Louisa M. Alcott	Oct. 13-29, 1921	Eloise Sterling
94	The Dawn of a Tomorrow	Frances H. Burnett	Nov. 17-26, 1921	Gilmor Brown
95*	Will o'Bishopsgate	Alfred Brand	Dec. 5-10,1921	Gilmor Brown
96	The Things that Count	Laurence Eyre	Dec. 29-Jan.7, 1922	Eloise Sterling
97	His House in Order	Arthur W. Pinero	Jan. 16-21, 1922	Eloise Sterling
98	King Lear	Wm. Shakespeare	Jan. 26-Feb.4, 1922	Gilmor Brown
99	Too Many Cooks	Frank Craven	Feb. 13-18, 1922	Eloise Sterling
100	Good Gracious, Annabelle	Clare Kummer	Feb. 23-Mar. 4, 1922	Gilmor Brown
101	The Yellow Jacket	G. C. Hazelton J. H. Benrimo	Mar. 13-18, 1922	Gilmor Brown

NO.	PLAY	AUTHOR	DATE	DIRECTOR
102	Strife	John Galsworthy	Mar. 23-Apr. 1, 1922	Gilmor Brown
103	The Traveling Man	Lady Gregory	Apr. 10-15, 1922	Cloyd Dalzell / Ruth Bolgiano
104	Sister Beatrice	M. Maeterlinck	Apr.10-15,1922	Cloyd Dalzell / Ruth Bolgiano
105*	The Mandarin Coat	Alice C. D. Riley	Apr. 19-22, 1922	Eloise Sterling
106	My Lady	Fanny B. McLane	Apr. 19-22, 1922	Eloise Sterling
107	Other People's Husbands	Margaret Penney	Apr. 19-22, 1922	Eloise Sterling
108	The Great Divide	Wm. Vaughn Moody	Apr. 27-May 6, 1922	Eloise Sterling
109	Ruddigore	Gilbert & Sullivan	May 15-20, 1922	Ruth Bolgiano
110	The Charm School	Alice D. Miller	June l-10, 1922	Eloise Sterling
111	The Rejuvenation of Aunt Mary	Anne Warner	June 22-July l, 1922	Gilmor Brown
112	The Importance of Being Earnest	Oscar Wilde	July 10-15, 1922	Gilmor Brown
113*	The Boy (At Friendship Forum-Brookside Park)	Bess J. Crary	July 24-29, 1922	Eloise Sterling
114	As You Like It	Wm. Shakespeare	Aug. 2-5, 1922	Gilmor Brown
115	The Private Secretary	Charles Hawtrey	Aug. 7-19, 1922	Eloise Sterling
116	A Pair of Sixes	Edward Peple	Aug. 29-Sept. 2, 1922	Eloise Sterling
117	Green Stockings	A. E. W. Mason	Sept. 18-23, 1922	Eloise Sterling
118	Polly With a Past	G. Middleton G.Bolton	Oct. 2-7, 1922	Eloise Sterling
119	Arms and the Man	G. B. Shaw	Oct. 16-29, 1922	Gilmor Brown
120	Sherlock Holmes	Wm. Gillette	Nov. 6-11, 1922	Gilmor Brown
121	The Pirates of Penzance	Gilbert & Sullivan	Nov. 20-Dec.2, 1922	Gilmor Brown
122	Mary Goes First	H.A.Jones	Dec. 11-16, 1922	Eloise Sterling
123*	The Cricket on the Hearth	Charles Dickens Gilmor Brown	Dec. 25-30, 1922	Gilmor Brown
124	The School for Scandal	R. B. Sheridan	Jan. 8-13, 1923	Gilmor Brown
125	Just Folks	A. E. Rouverol	Jan. 15-16, 1923	Eloise Sterling
126*	Elusive Cynthia	Margaret Penney	Jan. 22-27, 1923	Gilmor Brown
127	My Lady's Dress	Edward Knoblock	Feb. 5-10, 1923	Gilmor Brown
128	Love's Labours Lost	Wm. Shakespeare	Feb. 19-24, 1923	Gilmor Brown
129	Wedding Bells	Salisbury Field	Mar. 5-17, 1923	Gilmor Brown
130	The Copperhead	Augustus Thomas	Mar. 26-31, 1923	Gilmor Brown
131	Mrs. Bumpstead-Leigh	Harry James Smith	Apr. 9-21,1923	Eloise Sterling
132*	Boy o'Dreams	Claudia L.Harris	Apr. 30-May 5, 1923	Gilmor Brown
133*	The Follies of Pasadena	Alfred Brand	May 14-26,1923	Gilmor Brown
134*	Wooden Shoes	Omar Barker	May 30-June 2, 1923	Gilmor Brown
135*	Suicide	Conrad Seiler	May 30-June 2, 1923	Gilmor Brown
136*	The Wind	Agnes E.Peterson	May 30-June 2, 1923	Gilmor Brown
137*	Himself	Alice Garwood	May 30-June 2, 1923	Gilmor Brown
138*	The Altar of Innocence	S. M. Ilsley	June 11-16, 1923	Gilmor Brown
139	His Majesty, Bunker Bean	Lee Wilson Dodd	July 2-7, 1923	Maurice Wells
140	Fanny and the Servant Problem	Jerome K. Jerome	July 11-14, 1923	Gilmor Brown
141	Twelfth Night	Wm. Shakespeare	July 18-21, 1923	Gilmor Brown
142**	Lucky Pehr	August Strindberg	July 30-Aug.4, 1923	Gilmor Brown
143	The Critic	R. B. Sheridan	Aug. 6-8, 1923	Maurice Wells
144	Girls	Clyde Fitch	Aug. 13-18, 1923	Gilmor Brown
145	Candida	G.B. Shaw	Aug. 27-Sept. 1, 1923	Gilmor Brown
146	Old Lady 31	Rachel Crothers	Oct. 15-20, 1923	Lenore Shanewise
147	Rollo's Wild Oat	Clare Kummer	Oct. 29-Nov. 3, 1923	Maurice Wells
148**	Melloney Holtspur	John Masefield	Nov. 12-25, 1923	Lenore Shanewise
149	The Merchant of Venice	Wm. Shakespeare	Nov. 29-Dec. 8, 1923	Gilmor Brown
150*	Sing a Song of Sleepy Head	James W. Foley	Dec. 17-22, 1923	Lenore Shanewise
151	At the Sign of the Greedy Pig (Five in Repertory)	Chas. S. Brooks	Dec. 17-22, 1923	Lenore Shanewise
152	The Romancers	Edmond Rostand	Dec.25 / 26 / Jan.4, 1923	Maurice Wells
153	The Importance of Being Earnest	Oscar Wilde	Dec.27 / 23 / Jan. 3, 1924	Lenore Shanewise
154	Twelfth Night	Wm. Shakespeare	Dec.29 / Jan. 2, 1924	Gilmor Brown
155	Candida	G. B. Shaw	Dec.31 / Jan. 1-5, 1924	Gilmor Brown
156	The Merchant of Venice	Wm. Shakespeare	Jan. 7, 1924	Gilmor Brown
157	The Torch Bearers	George Kelly	Jan. 21-Feb. 9, 1924	Lenore Shanewise
158	The Thief	Henri Bernstein	Feb. 18-23, 1924	Gilmor Brown
159	The New York Idea	Langdon Mitchell	Mar. 3-15, 1924	Lenore Shanewise
160	Liliom	Franz Molnar	Mar. 24-Apr. 12, 1924	Lenore Shanewise
161	The Seven Keys to Baldpate (Four Prize Plays)	Earl D. Biggers	Apr. 21-26, 1924	Gilmor Brown
162*	The Sponge	Alice C. D. Riley	May 5-10, 1924	Lenore Shanewise
163*	Boots	Ransom Rideout	May 5-10, 1924	Gilmor Brown
164*	The Duchess and the Dancer	Alice W. Alden	May 5-10, 1924	Lenore Shanewise
165*	It Couldn't Happen to Us	Nancy B.Cox	May 5-10, 1924	Gilmor Brown
166	David Garrick	T. W. Robertson	May 12-17, 1924	Gilmor Brown
167	Jane Clegg	St. John Ervine	May 20-28, 1924	Lenore Shanewise
168	Follies of Pasadena	Alfred Brand	June 5-21, 1924	Gilmor Brown
169	Lady Windermere's Fan	Oscar Wilde	June 30-July 5, 1924	Lenore Shanewise

Little Women

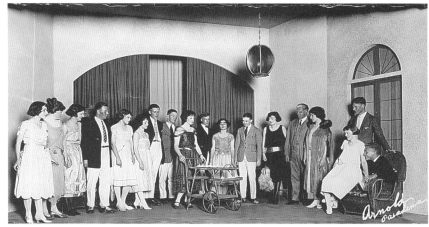

Hoyt Martin in *The Boy*

A Pair of Sixes

Douglass Montgomery and Lurene Tuttle in *The Playboy of the Western World*

NO.	PLAY	AUTHOR	DATE	DIRECTOR	NO.	PLAY	AUTHOR	DATE	DIRECTOR
170	A Night Out	Robert M. Baker	July 14-19,1924	Maurice Wells	240	Her Own Way (1903)	Clyde Fitch	Mar. 28-Apr. 2, 1927	Ralph Freud
171	Engaged	W. S. Gilbert	July 28-Aug.2, 1924	Ralph Freud					Maurice Wells
172	The Dover Road	A. A. Milne	Aug. 4-5, 1924	Maurice Wells	241	The Show-Off (1926)	George Kelly	Apr. 4-9, 1927	Ralph Freud
173	The Servant in the House	Charles R. Kennedy	Aug. 11-16, 1924	Maurice Wells					Maurice Wells
174	A Midsummer Night's Dream	Wm. Shakespeare	Aug. 18-23, 1924	Gilmor Brown	242	Cyrano de Bergerac	Edmond Rostand	Apr. 18-30, 1927	Gilmor Brown
175	Seventeen	Booth Tarkington	Aug. 28-Sept. 6, 1924	Maurice Wells	243	The Wisdom Tooth	Marc Connelly	May 5-14, 1927	Maurice Wells
176	Mary the Third	Rachel Crothers	Oct. 6-11, 1924	Lenore Shanewise	244	The Haunted House	Owen Davis	May 19-28, 1927	Ralph Freud
177	Fashion	Anna C. Mowatt	Oct. 20-Nov.1, 1924	LenoreShanewise		(In Repertory)			
178	He Who Gets Slapped	Leonid Andreyev	Nov. 10-22, 1924	Lenore Shanewise	245	Misalliance	G. B. Shaw	June 1 / 4/ 10 / 18 /	Maurice Wells
179	The Way of the World	Wm.Congreve	Dec. 1-6, 1924	Lenore Shanewise				21 / 22 / 23, 1927	
180	Little Women	Louisa M. Alcott	Dec. 15-27, 1924	Lenore Shanewise	246	Two Gentlemen of Verona	Wm. Shakespeare	June 2 / 3 / 11 / 24 /	Maurice Wells
181	Kempy	J.C. / E. Nugent	Dec. 29-Jan.10, 1925	Maurice Wells				July 8, 1927	
182*	If Everybody Had A Window in His House Like This	Marion C. Wentworth	Jan. 19-31, 1925	Gilmor Brown	247	Justice	John Galsworthy	June 7 / 8 / 9, 1927	Maurice Wells
					248	They Called Him Babbitt	Irving Brant	June 14 / 15 / 17 26, 1927	Lenore Shanewise
183	The Intimate Strangers	Booth Tarkington	Feb. 5-14, 1925	Lenore Shanewise	249**	The Duenna	R. B. Sheridan	June 28-July 2 / 5 7, 1927	Lenore Shanewise
184	The Enchanted Cottage	Arthur W. Pinero	Feb. 23-28, 1925	Gilmor Brown					
185	On the Hiring Line	H. O'Higgins Harriet Ford	Mar. 5-14, 1925	Maurice Wells	250	Easy Virtue	Noel Coward	July 12-23, 1927	Maurice Wells
					251*	The Black Flamingo	Sam Janney	July 26-Aug. 6, 1927	Maurice Wells
186*	Heritage	Bosworth Crocker	Mar. 19-28, 1925	Gilmor Brown					Ralph Freud
187*	Desire	Willard Robertson	Apr. 13-18, 1925	Gilmor Brown	252	Cake	Witter Bynner	Aug. 9-13, 1927	Gilmor Brown
188	Expressing Willie (The New Playhouse)	Rachel Crothers	Apr. 20-May2, 1925	Lenore Shanewise	253	The Sunken Bell	Gerhart Hauptmann	Aug. 16/ 17, Sept. 27-30, Oct. 1, 1927	Lenore Shanewise
189*	The Amethyst	Victor Mapes	May 18-30, 1925	Lenore Shanewise	254	The Dover Road	A. A. Milne	Aug. 18-20, 1927	Maurice Wells
190*	The Lady of the Lamp	Earl Carroll	June 4-15, 1925	Lenore Shanewise	255	Grumpy	H. Hodges W. Percyval	Aug. 23-27 / Sept. 20-24, 1927	Ralph Freud
191	To the Ladies	Kaufman and Connelly	June 18-27, 1925	Maurice Wells					
192	Peer Gynt	Henrik Ibsen	July 2-11, 1925	Irving Pichel	256	The Devil's Den	Sam Janney	Aug. 30/31, - Sept. 1 / 2 / 31 3 / 6 / 10, 1927	Maurice Wells
193	Tweedles	Booth Tarkington	July 16-25, 1925	Maurice Wells					
194	The Green Goddess	Wm. Archer	July 30-Aug.8, 1925	Gilmor Brown	257	The Illustrious Departed	J. Magnussen P. Sarauw	Sept. 13-17, 1927	Lenore Shanewise
195	The Swan	Franz Molnar	Aug. 13-22, 1925	Maurice Wells					
196	You Never Can Tell	G.B. Shaw	Aug. 27-Sept. 5, 1925	Maurice Wells	258	Anthony and Anna	St. John Ervine	Oct. 4-8 / 11-15, 1927	Ralph Freud
197	The Show Shop	James Forbes	Oct. 1-10, 1925	Lenore Shanewise	259	Red Bird	Wm. E. Leonard	Oct. 18-22 / 25-29, 1927	Lenore Shanewise
198**	Pharaoh's Daughter	Dr. / Mrs.Allison Gaw	Oct. 15-24, 1925	Lenore Shanewise	260	The Admirable Crichton	James M. Barrie	Nov. 1-5 / 8-12, 1927	Maurice Wells
199*	The Main Thing	N. N. Yevreynov	Oct. 29-Nov.7, 1925	Maurice Wells	261	Yellow Sands	E. & A. Phillpotts	Nov. 15-19 / 22-26, 1927	Lenore Shanewise
200*	The Devil in the Cheese	Tom Cushing	Nov. 12-21, 1925	Lenore Shanewise					
201	You and I	Philip Barry	Nov. 26-Dec.5, 1925	Maurice Wells	262	A Royal Family	Robert Marshall	Nov. 29 / Dec.3 / 6 / 10, 1927	Maurice Wells
202	Treasure Island	R. L. Stevenson	Dec. 10-19, 1925	Lenore Shanewise					
203	The Prince Chap	Edward Peple	Dec. 24-Jan.2, 1926	Maurice Wells	263	The Old Homestead	Denman Thompson	Dec.13-17 / 20-24, 1927	Ralph Freud
205	The Merry Wives of Windsor	Wm. Shakespeare	Jan. 7-16, 1926	Gilmor Brown	264	Aren't We All?	Frederick Lonsdale	Dec. 26-31 / Jan.2-7, 1928	Lenore Shanewise
206	Major Barbara	G. B. Shaw	Jan. 21-30, 1926	Maurice Wells					
207*	Head Acres	Colin C. Cooper	Feb. 4-13, 1926	Gilmor Brown	265	White Wings	Philip Barry	Jan. 10-21, 1928	Maurice Wells
208	The Makropoulos Secret (Four in Repertory)	Karel Capek	Feb.18-27, 1926	Lenore Shanewise	266	Miss Lulu Bett	Zona Gale	Jan. 24-Feb. 4, 1928	Lenore Shanewise
					267	Getting Married	G. B. Shaw	Feb. 7-18, 1928	Gilmor Brown
209	March Hares	Harry W. Gribble	Mar.4 / 5 /10 /15 / 20 / 23 / 26, 1926	Maurice Wells					Maurice Wells
					268	Iris	Arthur W. Pinero	Feb. 21-Mar.3, 1928	Lenore Shanewise
210	Hedda Gabler	Henrik Ibsen	Mar. 6 / 12/ 17-24, 1926	Lenore Shanewise	269	The Lilies of the Field	John H. Turner	Mar. 6-17, 1928	Maurice Wells
211	Outward Bound	Sutton Vane	Mar.8 / 9 / 16 / 18 19 / 22 / 27, 1926	Lenore Shanewise	270	The Wild Duck	Henrik Ibsen	Mar. 20-31,1928	Maurice Wells
					271*	Lazarus Laughed	Eugene O'Neill	Apr. 9-May 12, 1928	Gilmor Brown
212	The Two Virtues	Alfred Sutro	Mar. 11 / 13 /25, 1926	Gilmor Brown	272	Quinney's	Horace A. Vachell	May 15-26,1928	Ralph Freud
213	Hassan	James E. Flecker	Apr. 5-17, 1926	Gilmor Brown Lenore Shanewise	273	Just Suppose	Albert E. Thomas	May 29-June 9, 1928	Maurice Wells
					274	The Jest	Sam Benelli	June 12-23, 1928	Victor Jory Maurice Wells
214	Hay Fever	Noel Coward	Apr. 22-May 1, 1926	MauriceWells					
215*	Amaranth	Conly Keeney	May 3-8, 1926	Agnes de Mille	275	Right You Are (If You Think So)	Luigi Pirandello	June 26-July 7, 1928	Gilmor Brown
216	A Soul for Mary Jane	Dunsany / Brown	May 3-8, 1926	Agnes de Mille	276	Mr. Pim Passes By	A. A. Milne	July 10-21, 1928	Maurice Wells
217	The Potters	J.P. McEvoy	May 13-29, 1926	Maurice Wells	277	Dear Brutus	James M. Barrie	July 24-Aug.4, 1928	Lenore Shanewise
218	Why Marry?	Jesse L.Williams	June 3-12, 1926	Maurice Wells	278	Pomeroy's Past	Clare Kummer	Aug. 7-18, 1928	Maurice Wells
219	Minick	G. S. Kaufman E. Ferber	June 17-26, 1926	Lenore Shanewise	279	East Lynne	Mrs. Henry Wood	Aug. 21-Sept. l, 1928	Ralph Freud
					280	Puppy Love	A. Mathews M. Stanley	Sept. 4-15, 1928	Ralph Freud
220	In The Next Room	E. Robson / H. Ford	July 1-10, 1926	Maurice Wells					
221	The Youngest	Philip Barry	July 15-24, 1926	Maurice Wells	281	The Devil's Disciple	G. B. Shaw	Sept. 18-29, 1928	Irving Pichel
222	Caesar and Cleopatra	G. B. Shaw	July 29-Aug.7, 1926	Irving Pichel	282*	Street of a Thousand Shadows	E.Wadsworth K. B. Miller	Oct. 2-13, 1928	Lenore Shanewise
223	The Great God Brown	Eugene O'Neill	Aug. 12-21, 1926	Irving Pichel					
224	Pygmalion	G. B. Shaw	July 29-Aug.7, 1926	Irving Pichel	283	The Great Broxopp	A. A. Milne	Oct. 16-27, 1928	Cyril Armbrister
225*	Skidding	A. E. Rouverol	Sept. 9-18, 1926	Lenore Shanewise	284**	The Wolves	Romain Rolland	Oct. 30-Nov. 10, 1928	Gilmor Brown
226	Dulcy	G. S. Kaufman Marc Connelly	Oct. 7-16, 1926	Lenore Shanewise	285	Hobson's Choice	Harold Brighouse	Nov. 13-24, 1928	Lenore Shanewise
					286	The Living Corpse	Leo Tolstoy	Nov. 27-Dec.8, 1928	Irving Pichel
227	The Farmer's Wife	Eden Phillpotts	Oct. 21-30, 1926	Ralph Freud	287	The Torch Bearers	George Kelly	Dec. 11-22, 1928	Lenore Shanewise
228	In a Garden	Philip Barry	Nov. 4-13, 1926	Maurice Wells	288	A Kiss for Cinderella	James M. Barrie	Dec.25-Jan. 5, 1929	Cyril Armbrister
229	The Mask and the Face	C. B .Fernald	Nov. 18-27, 1926	Lenore Shanewise	289	The New Morality	Harold Chapin	Jan. 8-19, 1929	Ralph Freud
230*	Amber	Dudley S .Corlett	Dec. 2-11, 1926	Maurice Wells / Ralph Freud	290	The Good Fellow	H. Mankiewicz G. S. Kaufman	Jan. 22-Feb. 2, 1929	Ralph Freud
231	The Goose Hangs High	Lewis Beach	Dec. 16-25, 1926	Gilmor Brown					
232	Captain Applejack	Walter Hackett	Dec. 30-Jan. 8, 1927	Ralph Freud	291	The Dybbuk	S. Ansky	Feb. 5-Mar. 2, 1929	Nahum Zemach
233	Turandot	Carlo Gozzi	Jan. 13-22, 1927	Lenore Shanewise	292	Ten Nights in a Bar-Room	Wm. W. Pratt	Mar. 5-23, 1929	Ralph Freud
234	The Doctor's Dilemma	G. B. Shaw	Jan. 27-Feb. 5, 1927	Maurice Wells	293	Lazarus Laughed	Eugene O'Neill	Apr. 1-13, 1929	Gilmor Brown
235	The Lady of Belmont	St. John Ervine	Feb. 10-19, 1927	Lenore Shanewise	294	Eva the Fifth Golden	K. Nicholson / John	Apr. 16-27, 1929	Richard Menefee
236	The Angel in the House	E. Phillpotts B.M.Hastings (The American Series)	Feb. 24-Mar. 5, 1927	Maurice Wells	295	No. 17	J. Jefferson Farjeon	Apr. 30-May 11, 1929	Lenore Shanewise
					296	The High Road	Frederick Lonsdale	May 14-25, 1929	Cyril Armbrister
237	The Contrast (1787)	Royall Tyler	Mar. 7-12, 1927	Lenore Shanewise	297	An Enemy of the People	Henrik Ibsen	May 28-June 8, 1929	Gilmor Brown
238	Uncle Tom's Cabin (1852)	Harriet B.Stowe	Mar. 14-19, 1927	Ralph Freud	298	Under Cover	Roi C. Megrue	June 11-22, 1929	Cyril Armbrister
239	Aristocracy (1892)	Bronson Howard	Mar. 21-26, 1927	Ralph Freud Maurice Wells	299	Why Not?	Jesse L. Williams	June 25-July 6, 1929	Gilmor Brown
					300*	Gentlemen, Be Seated	Anonymous	July 9-27, 1929	Lenore Shanewise

In Appreciation
JACOB MAARSE

NO.	PLAY	AUTHOR	DATE	DIRECTOR
301	Enchanted April	Kane Campbell	July 30-Aug. 10,	Cyril Armbrister
302	Trilby	George DuMaurier	Aug. 13-25, 1929	Chas. Levison
303	Commencement Days	Margaret Mayo	Aug. 27-Sept.7, 1929	Ralph Freud
		Virginia Frame		
304*	The Plutocrat	Booth Tarkington	Sept. 10-21, 1929	Chas. Coburn
				Ralph Freud
305	Mary, Mary Quite Contrary	St. John Ervine	Sept. 24-0ct.5, 1929	Lenore Shanewise
306	Nellie, the Beautiful Cloak	Owen Davis	Oct. 8-19, 1929	Gilmor Brown
307	Julius Caesar	Wm. Shakespeare	Oct. 22-Nov.2, 1929	Gilmor Brown
308	Man and Superman	G. B. Shaw	Nov. 7-23-1929	Ralph Freud
				Gilmor Brown / Harrison Ford
309	Atta Boy, Oscar	Hazel C. MacDonald	Nov. 28-Dec.7, 1929	Chas. Levison
310*	Fear of Houses	Virginia Church	Dec. 9-14, 1929	Eugart Yerian
311	The Blue Bird	Maurice Maeterlinck	Dec.19-Jan.4, 1930	Lenore Shanewise
312	Jack Straw	W. S. Maugham	Jan. 9-25, 1930	Stuart Buchanan
313*	The Armoured Train	Vsevold Ivanov	Jan. 30-Feb. 15, 1930	Gilmor Brown
314**	Lavender Ladies	Daisy Fisher	Feb. 20-Mar. 1, 1930	Lenore Shanewise
315	Our American Cousin	Tom Taylor	Mar. 6-22, 1930	Chas. Levison
316*	Spindrift	Martin Flavin	Mar. 27-Apr. 5, 1930	Stuart Buchanan
317*	They Had to See Paris	Mae S. Croy	Apr. 10-19, 1930	Lenore Shanewise
318*	To What Red Hell	Percy Robinson	Apr. 24-May 3,1930	Lucille La Verne
				Gilmor Brown
319	Candida	G. B. Shaw	May 8-17, 1930	Gilmor Brown
320	Wings Over Europe	R. Nichols / M. Browne	May 22-31, 1930	Gilmor Brown
321	The Queen's Husband	Robert E. Sherwood	June 5-14, 1930	Chas. Levison
322	Marco Millions	Eugene O'Neill	June 19-28, 1930	Gilmor Brown
323	The Second Man	S. N. Behrman	July 3-12, 1930	Maurice Wells
324	Merton of the Movies	G. S. Kaufman	July 17-26, 1930	Lenore Shanewise
		Marc Connelly		
325*	The Man Saul (This One Man)	Sidney R. Buchman	July 31-Aug. 9, 1930	Arthur Lubin
326	Dracula	Hamilton Deane	Aug. 14-23, 1930	Chas. Levison
		J .Balderston		
327	The Importance of Being Earnest	Oscar Wilde	Aug. 28-Sept.6, 1930	Lenore Shanewise
328	Doctor Knock	Jules Romains	Sept. 11-20,1930	Chas. Levison
329*	Dancing Days	Martin Flavin	Oct. 2-11, 1930	Lenore Shanewise
330	If	Lord Dunsany	Oct. 16-25,1930	Morris Ankrum
331	The Poor Little Rich Girl	Eleanor Gates	Oct. 30-Nov. 8, 1930	Addison Richards
332	Othello	Wm. Shakespeare	Nov. 13-22, 1930	Morris Ankrum
333	Shore Acres	James A. Herne	Nov. 27-Dec. 6, 1930	Morris Ankrum
334*	Spring Song	Bella Spewack	Dec. 11-20, 1930	Lenore Shanewise
335	Cock Robin	Elmer Rice / Philip Barry	Jan. 8-17, 1931	Morris Ankrum
336	Her Shop	Aimee / Philip Stuart	Jan. 22-31, 1931	Lenore Shanewise
337	What Every Woman Knows	James M. Barrie	Feb. 5-28, 1931	Addison Richards
338	Richelieu	Bulwer-Lytton	Mar. 5-14, 1931	Morris Ankrum
339	June Moon	Ring Lardner	Mar. 19-28, 1931	Lenore Shanewise
		G. S. Kaufman		
340	No More Frontier	Talbot Jennings	Apr. 2-11, 1931	Morris Ankrum
341	The Perfect Alibi	A. A. Milne	Apr. 16-25, 1931	Addison Richards
342	Death Takes a Holiday	Walter Ferris	Apr. 30-May 9, 1931	Lenore Shanewise
343*	The Watched Pot	H. H. Munro (Saki)	May 14-23, 1931	Ralph Freud
344*	Green Fire	Glenn Hughes	May 28-June 6, 1931	Addison Richards
345	Many Waters	Monckton Hoffe	June 11-20, 1931	Morris Ankrum
346	Broken Dishes	Martin Flavin	June 25-July 4, 1931	Gilmor Brown
347	Overruled	G. B. Shaw	July 9-18, 1931	Gilmor Brown
348	A Pair of Spectacles	Sydney Grundy	July 9-18, 1931	Gilmor Brown
349	The Three Musketeers	Charles Rice	July 23-Aug. l, 1931	Morris Ankrum
350	Saturday's Children	Maxwell Anderson	Aug. 6-15, 1931	Lenore Shanewise
351	The Marriage of Kitty	C. Gordon-Lennox	Aug. 20-29, 1931	Addison Richards
352	The Speckled Band	Arthur Conan Doyle	Sept. 3-12, 1931	Morris Ankrum
353	The Constant Nymph	Margaret Kennedy	Sept. 17-26, 1931	Marion Gering
354	Young Woodley	John Van Druten	Oct. l-10, 1931	Lenore Shanewise
355	The Play's the Thing	Ferenc Molnar	Oct. 15-Nov.7, 1931	Guy Bates Pcst
356	The Apple Cart	G. B. Shaw	Nov. 12-21, 1931	Addison Richards
357**	Passing Brompton Road	Jevan Brandon Thomas	Nov. 26-Dec. 5, 1931	Morris Ankrim
358	Twelfth Night	Wm. Shakespeare	Dec. 10-19, 1931	John Craig
359	Canaries Sometimes Sing	Frederick Lonsdale	Dec. 24-Jan. 2, 1932	Harrison Ford
360	The Blue Bird	Maurice Maeterlinck	Dec. 28-Jan. 1, 1932	Lenore Shanewise
361	Berkeley Square	John L. Balderston	Jan. 7-16, 1932	Addison Richards
362	Once in a Lifetime	G. S. Kaufman	Jan. 21-30, 1932	Morris Ankrum
		Moss Hart		
363	The Music Master	Charles Klein	Feb. 4-13, 1932	Ralph Freud
364*	Censored	Conrad Seiler	Feb. 15-27, 1932	Robert Chapin
365	When Knighthood was in Flower	Paul Kester	Mar. 3-12, 1932	Lenore Shanewise
366	The Young Idea	Noel Coward	Mar. 17-26, 1932	Addison Richard
367	What Might Happen	H. F. Maltby	Mar. 28-Apr. 9, 1932	Ralph Freud
368*	Episode	Gilbert Emery	Apr. 14-23, 1932	Gilbert Emery
369	I Love an Actress	Laszlo Fodor	Apr. 28-May 7, 1932	Addison Richards
370	A Murder Has Been Arranged	Emlyn Williams	May 12-21, 1932	Frederick Stover
371	Around the World in Eighty Days	Jules Verne	May 26-June 4, 1932	Lenore Shanewise

Robert Preston in *Montezuma*

Margaret O'Brian and John Barrymore, Jr. in *Romeo and Juliet*

A Midsummer Night's Dream

The Livewire

NO.	PLAY	AUTHOR	DATE	DIRECTOR
372*	Hullabaloo	H. Hecht / P.G. Smith	June 9-25, 1932	Herold Hecht / Paul G. Smith
373	Green Grow the Lilacs	Lynn Riggs	June 28-July 9, 1932	Morris Anluum
374*	A Plain Man and his Wife (Big Hearted Herbert)	Sophie Kerr	July 12-23, 1932	Lenore Shanewise
375	Peer Gynt	Henrik Ibsen	July 26-Aug.13, 1932	Morris Anluum
376	The Butter and Egg Mara	G. S. Kaufman	Aug. 16-27, 1932	John W.Young
377	Captain Brassbound's Conversion	G. B. Shaw	Aug. 30-Sept. 10, 1932	James Fagan
378	Louder, Please	Norman Krasna	Sept. 13-24, 1932	Monty Collins
379	Lightnin'	Winchell Smith / Frank Bacon	Sept. 27-Oct.1, 1932	T.B.Henry
380	These Few Ashes	Leonard Ide	Oct.4-15, 1932	Lenore Shanewise
381*	Mr. Mary Sawyer	E. Treacy / J .Puker	Oct. 18-22, 1932	Morris Ankrum
382	The First Mrs. Fraser	St. John Ervine	Oct. 25-Nov. 5, 1932	Addison Richards
383	The Man with a Load of Mischief	Ashley Dukes	Nov. 8-12, 1932	T. B. Henry
384	Brief Moment	S. N. Behrman	Nov. 15-26, 1932	Harrison Ford
385	Henry VIII	Wm. Shakespeare	Nov. 29-Dec.17, 1932	Morris Ankrum
386	The Cricket on the Hearth	Chas.Dickens	Dec.20-24, 1932	Gilmor Brovrn / Gilmor Brown
387	Alice in Wonderland	Lewis Carroll	Dec. 26-Jan.7, 1933	Lenore Shanewise
388	The Devil Passes	Benn W. Levy	Jan. 10-21, 1933	Addison Richards
389	The Cricket on the Hearth	Chas.Dickens	Jan. 24-29, 1933	T.B.Henry / Gilmor Brown
390	Louder, Please	Norman Krasna	Jan. 31-Feb.4, 1933	Morris Ankrum
391	Mr. Faithful	Lord Dunsany	Feb. 7-11, 1933	Morris Ankrum
392	Alison's House	Susan Glaspell	Feb. 14-25, 1933	Addison Richards
393	Liliom	Ferenc Molnar	Feb. 28-Mar. 11, 1933	Frank Reicher
394	Too True to be Good	G. B. Shaw	Mar. 14-25, 1933	Morris Ankrum
395	Hamlet	Wm. Shakespeare	Mar. 28-Apr. 8, 1933	Lenore Shanewise
396	Maria Marten	H. J. Byron	Apr. 11-15, 1933	Gilmor Brown
397	The Crime At Blossoms	Mordaunt Shairp	Apr. 19-24, 1933	Lenore Shanewise
398*	Fidelity Insured	Constance Bridges	Apr. 27-May 6, 1933	Ralph Freud
399	Petticoat Influence	Neil Grant	May 9-13, 1933	Morris Ankrum
400	Low and Behold	Leonard Sillman	May 16-June 3, 1933	Leonard Sillman
401	Volpone	Stefan Zweig	June 6-24, 1933	Morris Ankrum
402	Foolscap	G. M. Curci / E. Ciannelli	June 27-July 1, 1933	Addison Richards
403	Uncle Tom's Cabin	Harriet B. Stowe	July 4-15, 1933	Morris Ankrum
404	The Lover	Martinez Sierra	July 18-29, 1933	Addison Richard
405*	A Lion in Her Lap	D. S. Fairchild	July 18-29, 1933	Addison Richard
406*	Man of Wax	J. Thompson / W. Hasenclever	Aug. 1-19, 1933	Lenore Shanewise
407*	Growing Pains	Aurania Rouverol	Aug. 22-Sept. 9, 1933	Addison Richards
408	Inspector General	Nikolai Gogol	Sept. 12-23, 1933	Leonid Snegoff
409	Enter Madame	G. Varesi / D. Byrne	Sept. 26-39, 1933	Albert Lovejoy
410	An Attic in Paris	Zoe Akins	Oct. 3-14, 1933	Lenore Shanewise
411	Alien Corn	Sidney Howard	Oct. 17-28, 1933	Lenore Shanewise
412*	Best Sellers	D. Bennett / E. Bourdet	Oct. 31-Nov. 11, 1933	T. B. Henry
413	The Spider	F. Ousler / L. Brentano	Nov. 14-25, 1933	Byron Foulger
414*	The Master Thief	G. B. Williams / F. Tipton	Nov. 28-Dec. 9, 1933	Robert Chapin
415*	The Moon and Sixpence	W. S. Maugham	Dec. 12-22, 1933	Byron Foulger
416	Mr. Pickwick	Dickens / C. Hamilton / F. C. Reilly	Dec. 25-Jan. 6, 1934	T. B. Henry
417	Dangerous Corner	J. B. Priestley	Jan. 9-13, 1934	Lenore Shanewise
418	A Night Off	F. / P. Shoenthan	Jan. 15-20, 1934	Gilmor Brown
419	Camille At Roaring Camp	Thomas Wood	Jan. 23-27, 1934	Paul Huston Stevens
420	A Night Off	F. / P.Shoenthan	Jan. 29-Feb. 3, 1934	Gilmor Brown
421	MacBeth	Wm. Shakespeare	Feb. 6-17, 1934	Byron Foulger / Benyamin Zemach
422*	The Terrible Turk	B. Blackmar / B. Gould	Feb. 20-Mar. 3, 1934	Seymour Robinson
423*	An Affair of State	Maurice Anthoni	Mar. 6-17, 1934	T. B. Henry
424*	Let's Be Civilized	G. Logan / C. Seiler	Mar. 20-24, 1934	Gwendolen Logan
425	The Passing of the Third Floor Back	Jerome K. Jerome	Mar. 27-31, 1934	Lenore Shanewise
426	Salome	Oscar Wilde	Apr. 3-7, 1934	Benyamin Zemach
427	The Lady in the Sack	Conrad Seiler	Apr. 3-7, 1934	Wallace Dow
428	She Passed Through Lorraine	Lionel Hale	Apr. 10-14, 1934	May Gleason
429*	Stolen Summer	Ramon Romero / C. Grayson	Apr. 18-21, 1934	T. B. Henry
430	The Late Christopher Bean	Sidney Howard	Apr. 24-28, 1934	Lenore Shanewise
431	The Little Minister	James M. Barrie	May 1-12, 1934	Byron Foulger
432	Saint Joan	G. B. Shaw	May 15-19, 1934	Irving Pichel
433	Balcony Scene from Romeo and Juliet	Wm. Shakespeare	May 22-June 3, 1934	Byron Foulger
434	Moonlight at the Crossroads	Neil Fitzgerald	May 22-June 3, 1934	Zwayne Griffin
435	The Playboy of the Western World	J. M. Synge	May 22-June 3, 1934	Byron Foulger
436**	Cavalcade	Noel Coward	June 6-23, 1934	Morris Ankrum
437*	Finder's Luck	Alice H. Baskin	June 26-30, 1934	Jerome Coray
438*	Boulevard Stop	M. Monroe Ward	July 3-14, 1934	T. B. Henry
439	The Virginian	Owen Wister	July 17-29, 1934	Byron Foulger
440	Paid in Full	Eugene Walters	July 31-Aug. 4, 1934	Gilmor Brown
441	Anna Christie	Eugene O'Neill	Aug. 7-18, 1934	Victor Jory
442	Within the Law	Bayard Veiller	Aug. 21-26, 1934	Hardie Albright
443	The Enchanted Cottage	Arthur W. Pinero	Aug. 28-Sept. 1, 1934	Benyamin Zemach
444	Jesse James	Anonymous	Sept. 4-9, 1934	T. B. Henry
445	The Prisoner of Zenda	Edward Rose	Sept. 11-23, 1934	Byron Foulger
446	By Candle-Light	P. G. Wodehouse	Sept. 25-Oct. 13, 1934	Lenore Shanewise
447	The Brothers Karamazov	F. Dostoievesky	Oct. 16-27, 1934	Reginald Pole
448	Nobody Much	Margaret Echard	Oct. 30-Nov.3, 1934	Byron Foulger
449	The Joyous Season	Philip Barry	Nov. 6-10, 1934	Lenore Shanewise
450	The Return of Peter Grimm	David Belasco	Nov. 13-17, 1934	Byron Foulger
451	She Stoops to Conquer	Oliver Goldsmith	Nov. 20-Dec. 1, 1934	T. B. Henry
452	A Texas Steer	Charles A. Hoyt	Dec. 4-8, 1934	Byron Foulger
453	Both Your Houses	Maxwell Anderson	Dec. 11-22, 1934	Byron Foulger
454	The Shopkeeper Turned Gentleman	Moliere	Dec. 25-29, 1934	T. B. Henry
455	The Distaff Side	John Van Druten	Dec. 31-Jan. 12, 1935	Lenore Shanewise
456	Girls in Uniform (The Ibsen Series)	Christa Winslow	Jan. 15-19, 1935	Lillian Rivers
457	A Doll's House	Henrik Ibsen	Jan. 21-22, 1935	Jean Inness
458	Ghosts	Henrik Ibsen	Jan. 23, 1935	Jerome Coray
459	Hedda Gabler	Henrik Ibsen	Jan. 24, 1935	Jerome Coray
460	Love's Comedy	Henrik Ibsen	Jan. 25-26, 1935	Jerome Coray
461	Old Heidelberg	Meyer Foerster	Jan. 30-Feb. 16, 1935	Hans von Twardowski
462	Gallows Glorious	Ronald Gow	Feb. 19-Mar. 2, 1935	Byron Foulger
463*	The Mystery of Boardwalk Asylum	C. E. Reynolds / Robert Chapin	Mar. 5-23, 1935	Gilmor Brown
464	Judgment Day	Elmer Rice	Mar. 19-Apr. 20, 1935	Victor Jory
465*	Achilles Had a Heel	Martin Flavin	Apr. 23-May 4, 1935	Byron Foulger
466*	Wedding	Judith Kandel	May 7-18, 1935	Henry Dunn
467*	Amaco	Martin Flavin	May 21-25, 1935	Edward Gering
468	Roadside	Lynn Riggs	May 28-June 8, 1935	Morris Ankrum
469*	The World Is My Onion	Elliot / J. C. Nugent	June 11-22, 1935	T. B. Henry
470*	Smoke Screen (Blind Alley)	James Warwick	June 25-29, 1935	Lorin Raker

FIRST MIDSUMMER FESTIVAL (Shakespeare's Chronicle Plays)

NO.	PLAY	AUTHOR	DATE	DIRECTOR
471	King John	Wm. Shakespeare	July 1-3, 1935	Byron Foulger
472	King Richard II	Wm. Shakespeare	July 4-6, 1935	Morris Ankrum
473	King Henry IV, Part 1	Wm. Shakespeare	July 8-13, 1935	Gilmor Brown
474	King Henry IV, Part 2	Wm. Shakespeare	July 15-20, 1935	Gilmor Brown
475	King Henry V	Wm. Shakespeare	July 22-24, 1935	T. B. Henry
476	King Henry VI, Part 1	Wm. Shakespeare	July 25-27, 1935	T. B. Henry
477	King Henry VI, Part 2	Wm. Shakespeare	July 29-31, 1935	Byron Foulger / Lenore Shanewise
478	King Henry VI, Part 3	Wm. Shakespeare	Aug. 1-3, 1935	Lenore Shanewise / Byron Foulger
479	King Richard III	Wm. Shakespeare	Aug. 5-7, 1935	Morris Ankrum
480	King Henry VIII	Wm. Shakcspeare	Aug. 8-10, 1935	Morris Ankrum
481	Squaring the Circle	Valentine Katayev	Aug. 13-17, 1935	Henry Dunn
482*	Sunday (Just Around the Corner)	Martin Flavin	Aug. 20-24, 1935	Robert Chapin
483*	I am Laughing	Edwin J. Mayer	Aug. 27-Sept. 1, 1935	Victor Jory / Jean Inness
484*	Doc Lincoln	L. A. Levy / H. Daniels	Sept. 10-15, 1935	Henry Kolker / Clarence Muse
485	The Tavern	George M. Cohan	Sept. 17-22, 1935	Byron Foulger
486*	Rhythm Madness	M. L. Kisell	Sept. 24-Oct. 5, 1935	Maurice Kusell
487	Judgment Day	Elmer Rice	Oct. 8-19, 1935	T. B. Henry
488	Fly Away Home	D. Bennett / I. White	Oct. 22-Nov. 11, 1935	Lenore Shanewise
489	The Cherry Orchard	Anton Chekhov	Nov. 5-16, 1935	Leo Bulgakov
490	Bird in Hand	John Drinkwater	Nov. 19-30, 1935	Byron Foulger
491	The Guardsman	Ferenc Molnar	Dec. 3-14, 1935	Ilia Motyleff
492	Rose and the Ring	W. M. Thackeray	Dec. 17-28, 1935	T. B. Henry
493	Noah	Andre Obey	Dec. 30-Jan. 11, 1936	Gilmor Brown
494	Yellow Jack	Sidney Howard	Jan. 14-25, 1936	Morris Ankrum
495*	Royal Street	Lee Freeman	Jan. 28-Feb. 8, 1936	T. B. Henry
496	A Glass of Water	Eugene Scribe / DeWitt Bodeen	Feb. 11-22, 1936	Lenore Shanewise
497**	Not for Children	Elmer Rice	Feb. 25-Mar. 7, 1936	T. B. Henry
498	Laburnum Grove	J. B. Priestley	Mar. 10-21, 1936	Lenore Shanewise
499	Hollywood Holiday	Benn Levy / J. Van Druten	Mar. 24-Apr. 4, 1936	Morris Ankrum
500	Queen Victoria	D. Carb / W. P. Eaton	Apr. 7-18, 1936	Byron Foulger
501*	Stalemate	James Warwick	Apr. 21-May 2, 1936	John K.Ford
502	The Dominant Sex	Michael Egan	May 5-16, 1936	Lenore Shanewise
503	Tess of the D'Urbervilles	Thomas Hardy	May 19-30, 1936	John K. Ford

NO.	PLAY	AUTHOR	DATE	DIRECTOR
504	Rain from Heaven	S. N. Behrman	June 2-13, 1936	Morris Ankrum

SECOND MIDSUMMER FESTIVAL (Shakespeare's Greco-Roman Plays)

NO.	PLAY	AUTHOR	DATE	DIRECTOR
505	Troilus and Cressida	Wm. Shakespeare	June 15-20, 1936	T. B. Henry
506	Timon of Athens	Wm. Shakespeare	June 22-27, 1936	Lenore Shanewise
507**	Pericles	Wm. Shakespeare	June 29-July 4, 1936	Byron Foulger
508	Coriolanus	Wm. Shakespeare	July 6-11, 1936	Morris Ankrum
509	Julius Caesar	Wm. Shakespeare	July 13-18, 1936	Gilmor Brown
510	Antony & Cleopatra	Wm. Shakespeare	July 20-25, 1936	Reginald Pole T. B. Henry
511	Cymbeline	Wm. Shakespeare	July 27-Aug. l, 1936	Morris Ankrum
512	The Wind and the Rain	Merton Hodge	Oct. 5-17, 1936	Lenore Shanewise
513*	Deadline	R. P. White G. Burtnett	Oct.20-31, 1936	T. B. Henry
514*	The Empress	E. Carrington F. P. Walkup	Nov. 2-14, 1936	Byron Foulger
515	Paths of Glory	Sidney Howard	Nov. 17-28, 1936	Frank Fowler
516	The Bishop Misbehaves	Frederick Jackson	Dec. 1-12, 1936	Lenore Shanewise
517	A Christmas Carol	Chas. Dickens Gilmor Brown	Dec. 15-26, 1936	Ralph Urmy
518	The Chalk Circle	Klabund	Dec. 28-Jan. 9, 1937	T. B. Henry
519*	Money	Aurania Rouverol	Jan. 12-23, 1937	Barbara Vajda
520*	We Dress for Dinner	Aben Kandel	Jan. 26-29, 1937	Maxwell Sholes
521*	Beach House	Robert Chapin	Jan. 30-Feb. 6, 1937	Robert Chapin
522	Murder in the Cathedral	T. S. Eliot	Feb. 9-20, 1937	T .B. Henry
523*	Emma	Jane Austin DeWitt Bodeen	Feb. 23-Mar.6, 1937	Phililp Van Dyke
524	Lost Horizons	John Hayden	Mar. 9-20, 1937	Ralph Urmy
525**	Tobias and the Angel	James Bridie	Mar. 23-Apr. 3, 1937	Frederick Blanchard
526**	Periphery	Frantisak Langner	Apr. 6-17, 1937	Barbara Vajda
527*	God Save the Queen	Frederick Jackson	Apr. 20-May 1, 1937	Lenore Shanewise
528	Ethan Frome	Owen / Donald Davis	May 4-15, 1937	Hale McKeen
529	Madame Sans-Gene	Sardou / Moreau	May 18-29, 1937	T .B. Henry
530	Nude with Pineapple	Oursler / Kennedy	June 1-12, 1937	Maxwell Sholes
531	Libel	Edward Wooll	June 15-26, 1937	Ralph Urmy

THIRD MIDSUMMER FESTIVAL (Story of the Great Southwest)

NO.	PLAY	AUTHOR	DATE	DIRECTOR
532	Montezuma	Gerhart Hauptmann	June 28-July 3, 1937	Philip Van Dyke Onslow Stevens
533*	Miracle of the Swallows	Ramon Romero	July 5-10, 1937	Wm. Williams
534	Night over Taos	Maxwell Anderson	July 12-17, 1937	Hale McKeen
535	Juarez & Maximilian	Franz Werfel	July 19-24, 1937	Ralph Urmy
536	The Girl of the Golden West	David Belasco	July 26-31, 1937	Victor Jory
537	The Rose of the Rancho	Belasco & Tully	Aug. 2-7, 1937	T. B. Henry
538*	Miner's Gold	Agnes Peterson	Aug. 9-14, 1937	Maxwell Sholes
539	The Amazing Dr. Clitterhouse	Barre Lyndon	Oct. 4-16, 1937	Victor Jory
540	Accent on Youth	Samson Raphaelson	Oct. 19-30, 1937	T. B. Henry
541	The Old Maid	Zoe Akins	Nov. 2-13, 1937	Lenore Shanewise
542*	Sing, Sweet Angels	Belford Forrest	Nov. 16-20, 1937	Ralph Urmy
543	The Winter's Tale	Wm.Shakespeare	Nov.22-23, 1937	Frederick Blanchard
544	Measure for Measure	Wm. Shakespeare	Nov. 24-25, 1937	Hale McKeen
545	All's Well That Ends Well	Wm. Shakespeare	Nov. 26-27, 1937	Maxwell Sholes
546	Titus Andronicus	Wm. Shakespeare	Nov. 29-Dec. l, 1937	T. B. Henry
547	Romeo and Juliet	Wm. Shakespeare	Dec. 24, 1937	Lenore Shanewise
548	Fresh Fields	Ivor Novello	Dec. 7-18, 1937	Wm. Williams
549	The Blue Bird	Maurice Maeterlinck	Dec. 21-Jan. l, 1938	Frank Ferguson
550	Three Men on a Horse	Holm / Abbott	Jan. 4-15, 1938	Victor Jory
551	First Lady	Dayton / Kaufman	Jan. 18-28, 1938	Moroni Olsen
552	Idiot's Delight	R. E. Sherwood	Feb. 1-12, 1938	Hale McKeen
553	Pride and Prejudice	Helen Jerome	Feb. 12-26, 1938	Lenore Shanewise
554*	Knights of Song	Glendon Allvine	Mar. 1-19, 1938	Wm. Williams
555	The Bread-Winner	W. S. Maugham	Mar. 23-Apr. 2, 1938	Ralph Urmy
556	High Tor	Maxwell Anderson	Apr. 5-16, 1938	T. B. Henry
557	The Case of the Frightened Lady	Edgar Wallace	Apr. 19-30, 1938	Maxwell Sholes
558	Merrily We Roll Along	Kaufman / Hart	May 3-14, 1938	Moroni Olsen
559	George and Margaret	Gerald Savory	May 17-18, 1938	T. B. Henry
560*	Star of Navarre	Victor Victor	May 31-June 11, 1938	Victor Jory Maxwell Sholes
561	Tonight at 8:30	Noel Coward	June 13-25, 1938	Hale McKeen

FOURTH MIDSUMMER FESTIVAL (G. B. Shaw Plays)

NO.	PLAY	AUTHOR	DATE	DIRECTOR
562	Arms and the Man	G. B. Shaw	June 27-July 2, 1938	Ralph Urmy
563	Major Barbara	G. B. Shaw	July 4-9, 1938	Maxwell Sholes
564	Heartbreak House	G. B. Shaw	July 11-16, 1938	Hale McKeen
565	On the Rocks	G. B. Shaw	July 18-23, 1938	T. B. Henry
566	Back to Methuselah (Part l)	G. B. Shaw	July 25-30, 1938	Frank Ferguson
567	Back to Methuselah (Part 2)	G. B. Shaw	Aug. 1-6, 1938	Maxwell Sholes
568	Back to Methuselah (Part 3)	G. B. Shaw	Aug. 8-13, 1938	Frederick Blanchard
569	Autumn Crocus	C. L. Anthony	Sept. 26-Oct. 8, 1938	Ralph Urmy
570	O Evening Star	Zoe Akins	Oct. 11-22, 1938	Maxwell Sholes

Ollie Prickett in *Pigeons and People*

Carolyn Jones in *Cricket on the Hearth*

The Reluctant Debutante

Reginald Denny in *Visit to a Small Planet*

In Appreciation
MARILYN & KEN OTT

NO.	PLAY	AUTHOR	DATE	DIRECTOR
571	Tovarich	Jacques Duval	Oct. 25-Nov. 5, 1938	Hale McKeen
572	And Stars Remain	J. J. / P. G. Epstein	Nov. 8-19, 1938	Frank Ferguson
573*	Paradise Plantation	Shirland Quinn	Nov. 22-Dec. 3, 1938	T. B. Henry
574	Yes, My Darling Daughter	Mark Reed	Dec. 6-17, 1938	Lenore Shanewise
575**	The Boy David	James M. Barrie	Dec. 20-Jan. 7, 1939	Herschel Daugherty
576	You Can't Take It With You	Hart / Kaufman	Jan. 10-21, 1939	T. B. Henry
577	Ah, Wilderness	Eugene O'Neill	Jan. 24-Feb. 4, 1939	Maxwell Sholes
578	Stage Door	Ferber / Kaufman	Feb. 7-18, 1939	Ralph Urmy
579*	Where the Blue Begins	Christopher Morley	Feb. 21-Mar. 4, 1939	Eva M. Fry
580	Brother Rat	Monks / Finklehoff	Mar. 7-18, 1939	Victor Jory
581	Olympia	Ferenc Molnar	Mar. 22-Apr. 1, 1939	Barbara Vajda
582	The Unguarded Hour	Bernard Merivale	Apr. 4-15, 1939	Hale McKeen
583	To Quito and Back	Ben Hecht	Apr. 18-29, 1939	Maxwell Sholes
584*	The Great American Family	Lee Shippey	May 2-June 10, 1939	Frank Ferguson

FIFTH MIDSUMMER FESTIVAL (Maxwell Anderson Plays)

NO.	PLAY	AUTHOR	DATE	DIRECTOR
585	Elizabeth the Queen	Maxwell Anderson	June 26-July 1, 1939	T. B. Henry
586	Valley Forge	Maxwell Anderson	July 3-8, 1939	Maxwell Sholes
587	The Wingless Victory	Maxwell Anderson	July 10-15, 1939	Lenore Shanewise
588	The Masque of Kings	Maxwell Anderson	July 17-22, 1939	Hale McKeen
589	Both Your Houses	Maxwell Anderson	July 24-29, 1939	Ralph Urmy
590	Gods of the Lightning	Maxwell Anderson	July 31-Aug. 5, 1939	Victor Jory
591	Winterset	Maxwell Anderson	Aug. 7-12, 1939	Frank Ferguson
592	The Star-Wagon	Maxwell Anderson	Aug. 14-19, 1939	Hale McKeen
593	Dear Octopus	Dodie Smith	Oct. 2-14, 1939	T. B. Henry
594	The Morning Glory	Zoe Akins	Oct. 17-28, 1939	Ralph Urmy
595	Our Town	Thornton Wilder	Oct. 31-Nov. 11, 1939	Frank Ferguson
596	Kiss the Boys Goodbye	Clare Boothe	Nov. 14-25, 1939	Lenore Shanewise
597*	David Harum	Westcott R. / M .W. Hitchcock	Nov. 28-Dec. 9, 1939	Maxwell Sholes
598*	Young April	A. / W. S. Rouverol	Dec. 12-23, 1939	T. B. Henry
599	The Cricket on the Hearth	Dickens Gilmor Brown	Dec. 25-Jan. 6, 1940	Frederick Blanchard
600	She Loves Me Not	Howard Lindsay	Jan. 9-20, 1940	Herschel Daugherty
601	Father Malachy's Miracle	Brian Doherty	Jan. 23-Feb. 3, 1940	Ralph Urmy
602	The Comedy of Errors	Wm. Shakespeare	Feb. 6-17, 1940	T. B. Henry
603	Susan and God	Rachel Crothers	Feb. 20-Mar. 2, 1940	Lenore Shanewise
604*	Pancho	Lowell Barrington	Mar. 5-16, 1940	Maxwell Sholes
605	Room Service	Murray / Boreu	Mar. 19-30, 1940	Victor Jory
606	The Texas Nightingale	Zoe Akins	Apr. 2-13, 1940	Frank Ferguson
607	What a Life	Clifford Goldsmith	Apr. 17-27, 1940	Herschel Daugherty
608*	Heritage of the Desert	Zane Grey	Apr. 30-May 11, 1940	Ralph Urmy
609*	The Dictator's Boots	B. H. Orkow	May 14-25, 1940	T. B. Henry
610	Rocket to the Moon	Clifford Odas	May 28-June 8, 1940	Maxwell Sholes
611**	Glorious Morning	Norman Macowan	June 11-15, 1940	T. B. Henry
612	The Queen was in the Parlor	Noel Coward	June 18-22, 1940	Ralph Urmy

SIXTH MIDSUMMER FESTIVAL (James M. Barrie Plays)

NO.	PLAY	AUTHOR	DATE	DIRECTOR
613	Quality Street	James M. Barrie	June 24-29, 1940	Lenore Shanewise
614	The Professor's Love Story	James M. Barrie	July 1-6, 1940	Maxwell Sholes
615	Dear Brutus	James M. Barrie	July 8-13, 1940	T .B. Henry
616	The Little Minister	James M. Barrie	July 15-20, 1940	Ralph Urmy
617	Mary Rose	James M. Barrie	July 20-27, 1940	Lenore Shanewise
618	A Kiss for Cinderella	James M. Barrie	July 29-Aug. 3, 1940	Herschel Daugherty
619	The Admirable Crichton	James M. Barrie	Aug. 5-10, 1940	Frank Ferguson
620	What Every Woman Knows	James M. Barrie	Aug. 12-17, 1940	Ralph Urmy
621	The Merchant of Yonkers	Thornton Wilder	Sept. 30-Oct. 12, 1940	T. B. Henry
622	A Slight Case of Murder	Runyon / Lindsay	Oct. 15-26, 1940	Herschel Daugherty
623	Two on an Island	Elmer Rice	Oct. 29-Nov. 9, 1940	Frank Ferguson
624	Morning's at Seven	Paul Osborn	Nov. 12-23, 1940	Ralph Urmy
625	Of Mice and Men	John Steinbeck	Nov. 26-Dec. 7, 1940	Onslow Stevens
626	See My Lawyer	Maibaum / Clork	Dec. 10-21, 1940	Maxwell Sholes
627	Knickerbocker Holiday	Maxwell Anderson	Dec. 24-Jan. 11, 1941	Herschel Daughtery
628	I Killed the Count	Alec Coppel	Jan. 14-25, 1941	Lenore Shanewise
629	All the Comforts of Home	Wm. Gillette	Jan. 27-Feb. 8, 1941	Ralph Urmy
630*	Across the Board on Tomorrow Morning	Wm. Saroyan	Feb. 11-22, 1941	Frank Ferguson
631	Margin for Error	Clare Boothe	Feb. 25-Mar. 8, 1941	T. B. Henry
632	Design for Living	Noel Coward	Mar. 11-22, 1941	Lenore Shanewise
633	The Merchant of Venice	Wm. Shakespeare	Mar. 25-Apr.5, 1941	Onslow Stevens
634	The Lady of Belmont (sequel to Merchant of Venice)	St. John Ervine	Apr. 7-12, 1941	Onslow Stevens
635	The Front Page	Hecht / MacArthur	Apr. 15-26, 1941	Ralph Urmy
636	Topaze	Pagnol / Levy	Apr. 29-May 10, 1941	Barbara Vajda
637*	A-Lovin' an' A-Feudin'	Richardson / Barnouw	May 13-24, 1941	Herschel Daugherty
638	Strictly Dishonorable	Preston Sturges	May 27-June 7, 1941	Morris Ankrum
639*	Whistling for a Wind	DeWitt Bodeen	June 10-14, 1941	Maxwell Sholes
640**	Mañana is Another Day	Apstein / Morris	June 17-21, 1941	T. B. Henry

SEVENTH MIDSUMMER FESTIVAL (George S. Kaufman Plays)

NO.	PLAY	AUTHOR	DATE	DIRECTOR
641	Beggar on Horseback	Kaufman / Connelly	June 23-28, 1941	Frank Ferguson
642	George Washington Slept Here	Kaufman / Hart	June 30-July 5, 1941	Ralph Urmy
643	Dinner at Eight	Kaufman / Ferber	July 7-12, 1941	Lenore Shanewise
644	Minick	Kaufman / Ferber	July 14-19, 1941	Frederick Blanchard
645	Once in a Lifetime	Kaufman / Hart	July 21-26, 1941	Herschel Daugherty
646	You Can't Take it with You	Kaufman / Hart	July 28-Aug. 2, 1941	T .B. Henry
647	The Royal Family	Kaufman / Ferber	Aug. 4-9, 1941	Maxwell Sholes
648	Skylark	Samson Raphaelson	Sept. 29-Oct. 11, 1941	Victor Jory
649	Ladies in Retirement	Edward Percy Reginald Denham	Oct. 14-25, 1941	Onslow Stevens
650	Flight to the West	Elmer Rice	Oct. 28-Nov. 8, 1941	Herschel Daugherty
651	A Riddle for Mr. Twiddle	Madison L. Goff	Nov. 11-22, 1941	T. B. Henry
652	Jim Dandy	Wm. Saroyan	Nov. 25-Dec. 6, 1941	Onslow Stevens
653*	Escape to Autumn	DeWitt Bodeen	Dec. 9-20, 1941	George Phelps
654	The Great American Family	Lee Shippey	Dec. 23-Jan. 10, 1942	Frank Ferguson
655	The Little Foxes	Lillian Hellman	Jan. 13-24, 1942	Lenore Shanewise
656	The Male Animal	James Thurber Elliott Nugent	Jan. 27-Feb. 7, 1942	Herschel Daugherty
657	The Far-Off Hills	Lennox Robinson	Feb. 10-21, 1942	T. B. Henry
658	The Yellow Jacket	Hazelton / Benrimo	Feb. 24-Mar. 7, 1942	Onslow Stevens
659	The Philadelphia Story	Philip Barry	Mar. 10-21, 1942	Lenore Shanewise
660	Much Ado About Nothing	Wm. Shakespeare	Mar. 24-Apr. 4, 1942	George Phelps
661	One Sunday Afternoon	James Hagan	Apr. 7-18, 1942	Stacy Keach
662	Out of the Frying Pan	Francis Swann	Apr. 21-May 2, 1942	T. B. Henry
663*	Lovely Miss Linley	Belle Kennedy Lee Gilmore	May 5-16, 1942	Herschel Daugherty
664	Mr. and Mrs. North	Owen Davis	May 19-30, 1942	Onslow Stevens
665**	Home from Home	Muriel / Sidney Box	June 2-13, 1942	Lenore Shanewise
666	Food	Wm. C. deMille	June 16-20, 1942	Onslow Stevens
667	Ladies in Waiting	Cyril Campion	June 16-20, 1942	Onslow Stevens

EIGHTH MIDSUMMER FESTIVAL (50 Yrs. of American Comedy)

NO.	PLAY	AUTHOR	DATE	DIRECTOR
668	The Fortune Hunter	Winchell Smith	June 22-25, 1942	George Phelps
669	Because She Loved Him So	Wm. Gillette	June 29-July 4, 1942	T .B .Henry
670	The College Widow	George Ade	July 6-11, 1942	Herschel Daugherty
671	Captain Jinks of the Horse Marines	Clyde Fitch	July 13-18, 1942	Lenore Shanewise
672	Good Gracious, Annabelle	Clare Kummer	July 20-25, 1942	George Phelps
673	Clarence	Booth Tarkington	July 27-Aug. 1, 1942	Onslow Stevens
674	The Baby Cyclone	George M. Cohan	Aug. 3-5, 1942	Onslow Stevens
675	Abie's Irish Rose	Anne Nichols	Aug. 10-29, 1942	T. B. Henry
676	The Eve of St. Mark	Maxwell Anderson	Sept. 28-Oct. 11, 1942	Onslow Stevens
677*	Very Unusual Weather	Stone / Robinson	Oct. 14-25, 1942	George Phelps
678	The Moment is Now	Hallie F. Davis	Oct. 28-Nov. 8, 1942	Morris Ankrum
679**	Quiet Wedding	Esther McCracken	Nov. 11-22, 1942	Lenore Shanewise
680	Cuckoos on the Hearth	Parker Fennelly	Nov. 28-Dec. 6, 1942	Stacy Keach
681	The Women	Clare Boothe	Dec. 9-20, 1942	Hale McKeen
682	Charley's Aunt	Brandon Thomas	Dec. 23-Jan. 10, 1943	George Phelps
683	Heaven Can Wait	Harry Segall	Jan. 13-24, 1943	Victor Jory
684*	The Return of Ulysses	Emil Ludwig	Jan. 27-Fcb. 7, 1943	Onslow Stevens
685	Arsenic and Old Lace	Joseph Kesselring	Feb. 10-Mar. 7, 1943	George Phelps
686	The Lights of Duxbury	Clare Kummer	Mar. 10-21, 1943	Lenore Shanewise
687	Jason	Samson Raphaelson	Mar. 24-Apr. 4, 1943	Onslow Stevens
688	Watch on the Rhine	Lillian Hellman	Apr. 7-18, 1943	Hale McKeen
689	Family Portrait	Coffee / Cowen	Apr. 21-May 2, 1943	George Phelps
690	Boy Meets Girl	Bella / Samuel Spewack	May 5-16, 1943	Hale McKeen
691	Papa is All	Patterson Greene	May 19-30, 1943	Onslow Stevens
692	Cry Havoc	Allan Kenward	June 2-20, 1943	Victor Jory

NINTH MIDSUMMER FESTIVAL (Booth Tarkington Plays)

NO.	PLAY	AUTHOR	DATE	DIRECTOR
693	The Man from Home	Tarkington / Wilson	June 22-27, 1943	Onslow Stevens
694	The Intimate Strangers	Booth Tarkington	June 29-July 4, 1943	Lenore Shanewise
695	Colonel Satan	Booth Tarkington	July 6-11, 1943	Hale McKeen
696	The Country Cousin	Booth Tarkington	July 13-18, 1943	George Phelps
697	Mister Antonio	Booth Tarkington	July 20-25, 1943	Howard Graham
698	Your Humble Servant	Booth Tarkington	July 27-Aug. 1, 1943	Onslow Stevens
699	Monsieur Beaucaire	Booth Tarkington	Aug. 3-8, 1943	Hale McKeen
700	Seventeen	Booth Tarkington	Aug. 10-29, 1943	George Phelps
701	Othello	Wm. Shakespeare	Sept. 27-Oct. 3, 1943	John Carradine
702	The Merchant of Venice	Wm. Shakespeare	Oct. 5-10, 1943	John Carradine
703	Hamlet	Wm. Shakespeare	Oct. 12-17, 1943	John Carardine
704	Personal Appearance	Lawrence Riley	Oct. 20-31, 1943	Lenore Shanewise
705	Rebecca	Daphne du Maurier	Nov. 3-21, 1943	Onslow Stevens
706	Dark Eyes	Miramova Leontovich	Nov. 24-Dec. 12, 1943	Hale McKeen
707	A Christmas Carol	Chas. Dickens Gilmor Brown	Dec. 15-26, 1943	Ralph Mead
708	Claudia	Rose Frankne	Dec. 29-Jan. 9, 1944	Howard Graham
709	The Damask Cheek	Van Druten Horse	Jan. 12-23, 1944	Hale McKeen
710	A Decent Birth, A Happy Funeral	Wm. Saroyan	Jan. 26-Feb. 6, 1944	Gilmor Brown
711	The Pursuit of Happiness	L. / A. M. Langner	Feb. 9-20, 1944	George Phelps
712**	Quiet Week-End	Esther McCracken	Feb. 23-Mar. 5, 1944	Lenore Shanewise

In Appreciation
R. F. McCANN & ASSOCIATES

NO.	PLAY	AUTHOR	DATE	DIRECTOR
713	Rope's End	Patrick Hamilton	Mar. 8-19, 1944	Hale McKeen
714	Ladies of the Jury	Fred Ballard	Mar. 22-Apr. 9, 1944	Onslow Stevens
715	My Sister Eileen	Fields / Chodorov	Apr. 12-30, 1944	Howard Graham
716*	Young Man of Today	Aurania Rouverol	May 3-14, 1944	George Phelps
717	It's A Wise Child	Larry E. Johnson	May 17-28, 1944	Lenore Shanewise
718	Those Endearing Young Charms	Edward Chodorov	May 31-June 11, 1944	Onslow Stevens
719	Murder in a Nunnery	Emmet Lavery	June 14-25, 1944	Ralph Mead
				Lenore Shanewise

TENTH MIDSUMMER FESTIVAL (Sidney Howard Cavalcade)

NO.	PLAY	AUTHOR	DATE	DIRECTOR
720	They Knew What They Wanted	Sidney Howard	June 27-July 2, 1944	Onslow Stevens
721	Lucky Sam McCarver	Sidney Howard	July 4-9, 1944	Howard Graham
722	The Late Christopher Bean	Sidney Howard	July 11-16, 1944	Lenore Shanewise
723	Dodsworth	Sidney Howard	July 18-23, 1944	George Phelps
724	Alien Corn	Sidney Howard	July 25-30, 1944	James Daly
725	Ned McCobb's Daughter	Sidney Howard	Aug. 1-6, 1944	Howard Graham
726	The Silver Cord	Sidney Howard	Aug. 8-13, 1944	Ralph Mead
727	Yellow Jack	Sidney Howard	Aug. 15-20, 1944	Morris Ankrum
728	Biography	S. N. Behrman	Oct. 2-15, 1944	Lenore Shanewise
729	Junior Miss	Chodorov / Fields	Oct. 18-Nov. 5, 1944	Howard Graham
730	The Skin of Our Teeth	Thornton Wilder	Nov. 8-19, 1944	George Phelps
731	Suds in Your Eye	Mary Lasswell	Nov. 22-Dec. 3, 1944	Lenore Shanewise
		Jack Kirkland		
732	My Dear Children	Turney / Horwin	Dec. 6-17, 1944	Howard Graham
733	Little Women	Alcott / deForest	Dec. 20-Jan. 7, 1945	George Phelps
734	Get Away Old Man	Wm. Saroyan	Jan. 10-21, 1945	Gilmor Brown
735	Mrs. January and Mr. Ex	Zoe Akins	Jan. 24-Feb. 4, 1945	James Daly
736	Uncle Harry	Thomas Job	Feb. 7-18, 1945	Howard Graham
737	The Corn is Green	Emlyn Williams	Feb. 21-Mar. 4, 1945	Lenore Shanewise
738	The Great Big Doorstep	Goodrich / Hacken	Mar. 7-18, 1945	Frederick Blanchard
739	King Lear	Wm. Shakespeare	Mar. 21-Apr. 1, 1945	George Phelps
740	Is Life Worth Living?	Lennox Robinson	Apr. 4-15, 1945	Howard Graham
741	The Barker	Kenyon Nicholson	Apr. 18-29, 1945	John R. Kerr
742	A Highland Fling	Margaret Curtis	May 2-13, 1945	Lenore Shanewise
743	Janie	Bentham / Williams	May 16-27, 1945	George Phelps
744**	Immortal	Arbuzov / Gladkov	May 30-June 10, 1945	Carl H. Roth
745	Spring Again	Leighton / Bloch	June 13-24, 1945	Howard Graham

ELEVENTH MIDSUMMER FESTIVAL (Living American Playwrights)

NO.	PLAY	AUTHOR	DATE	DIRECTOR
746	Tomorrow and Tomorrow	Philip Barry	June 26-July 1, 1945	George Phelps
747	Golden Boy	Clifford Odets	July 3-8, 1945	John R. Kerr
748	The Petrified Forest	Robert E. Sherwood	July 10-15, 1945	Onslow Stevens
749	No Time for Comedy	S. N. Behrman	July 17-22, 1945	Howard Graham
750	Mary of Scotland	Maxwell Anderson	July 24-29, 1945	George Phelps
751	The Children's Hour	Lillian Hellman	July 31-Aug. 5, 1945	Carl H. Roth
752	Counsellor At Law	Elmer Rice	Aug. 7-12, 1945	Onslow Stevens
753	Morning Becomes Electra	Eugene O'Neill	Aug. 14-19, 1945	Dan Levin
754	Kiss and Tell	F. Hugh Herbert	Oct. 1-14, 1945	Lenore Shanewise
755*	Men Coming Home	Denison Clift	Oct. 17-28, 1945	T. B. Henry
756	Snafu	Buchman / Solomon	Oct. 31-Nov. 18, 1945	George Phelps
757	Blithe Spirit	Noel Coward	Nov. 21-Dec. 9, 1945	Lenore Shanewise
758	Night Must Fall	Emlyn Williams	Dec. 12-23, 1945	George Phelps
759*	The Happy Family	Dickens / Rennie	Dec. 25-Jan.6, 1946	T. B. Henry
760	Chicken Every Sunday	J. H. / P. G. Epstein	Jan. 9-Feb. 3, 1946	John R. Kerr
761	Tomorrow the World	Gow / d'Usseau	Feb. 6-17, 1946	Dan Levin
762	Over Twenty-One	Ruth Gordon	Feb. 20-Mar. 10, 1946	George Phelps
763*	Yes Is For a Very Young Man	Gertrude Stein	Mar. 13-24, 1946	T. B.Henry
764	Harriet	Ryerson / Clements	Mar. 27-Apr. 14, 1946	Lenore Shanewise
765	When Ladies Meet	Rachel Crothers	Apr. 17-28, 1946	Dan Levin
766**	Angels Amongst Us	Frantisek Langer	May 1-12, 1946	Barbara Vajda
767*	The Avon Flows	George Jean Nathan	May 15-26, 1946	George Phelps
768	Love's Old Sweet Song	Wm. Saroyan	May 29-June 9, 1946	Brown / Glover
769**	While the Sun Shines	Terrence Rattigan	June 12-23, 1946	Lenore Shanewise

TWELFTH MIDSUMMER FESTIVAL (Clyde Fitch Plays)

NO.	PLAY	AUTHOR	DATE	DIRECTOR
770	Her Own Way	Clyde Fitch	June 26-30, 1946	John R. Kerr
771	Barbara Frietchie	Clyde Fitch	July 2-5, 1946	T. B. Henry
772	The Climbers	Clyde Fitch	July 9-14, 1946	Lenore Shanewise
773	Girls	Clyde Fitch	July 16-21, 1946	George Phelps
774	The Girl with the Green Eyes	Clyde Fitch	July 23-28, 1946	Dan Levin
775	Lover's Lane	Clyde Fitch	July 30-Aug. 4, 1946	John R. Kerr
776	The Truth	Clyde Fitch	Aug. 6-11, 1946	T. B. Henry
777	Beau Brummel	Clyde Fitch	Aug. 13-18, 1946	George Phelps
778	For Keeps	F. Hugh Herbert	Sept. 30-Oct. 13, 1946	Lenore Shanewise
779	Truckline Cafe	Maxwell Anderson	Oct. 16-27, 1946	Dan Levin
780	But Not Goodbye	George Seaton	Oct. 30-Nov. 10, 1946	Dwight Thomas
781	The Rich Full Life	Vina Delmar	Nov. 13-24, 1946	Lenore Shanewise
782	Home of the Brave	Arthur Laurents	Nov. 27-Dec. 8, 1946	Dan Levin
783	Laura	Gspary / Sklar	Dec. 11-22, 1946	Marcella Cisney
784	Mr. Pickwick	Cosmo Hamilton	Dec. 25-Jan. 5, 1947	Lenore Shanewise
		Reilly		
785	The Mermaids Singing	John Van Druten	Jan. 8-19, 1947	Lenore Shanewise

Lawrence O'Sullivan in *Our Town*

Desperate Hours

Joe E. Brown in *Father of the Bride*

June Chandler in *The Complaisant Lover*

In Appreciation
EMILIO ARECHAEDERA

NO.	PLAY	AUTHOR	DATE	DIRECTOR
786	Ten Little Indians	Agatha Christie	Jan. 22-Feb. 2, 1947	Dan Levin
787	The Late George Apley	Marquand / Kaufman	Feb. 5-23, 1947	George Phelps
788*	Stairs to the Roof	Tennessee Williams	Feb. 26-Mar. 9, 1947	Gilmor Brown / Rita Glover
789	The Hasty Heart	John Patrick	Mar. 12-23, 1947	Lenore Shanewise
790	State of the Union	Lindsay / Crouse	Mar. 26-Apr. 20, 1947	Michael Cisney
791	As You Like It	Wm. Shakespeare	Apr. 23-May 4, 1947	Dan Levin
792*	A Yankee Fable	Guy Andros	May 7-18, 1947	Jack Harris
793*	Oh, Susanna	Ryerson / Clements	May 21-June 22, 1947	George Phelps

THIRTEENTH MIDSUMMER FESTIVAL (Great Plays in Playhouse Life)

NO.	PLAY	AUTHOR	DATE	DIRECTOR
794	Mrs. Wiggs of the Cabbage Patch	Flexner / Rice	June 24-29, 1947	Samuel Herrick
795	A Midsummer Night's Dream	Wm. Shakespeare	July 1-6, 1947	Gilmor Brown / Fred Berest
796	Melloney Holtspur	John Masefield	July 8-13, 1947	Lenore Shanewise
797	The School for Scandal	R. B. Sheridan	July 15-20, 1947	Richard O'Connell
798	Arms and the Man	G. B. Shaw	July 22-27, 1947	George Phelps
799	The Great God Brown	Eugene O'Neill	July 29-Aug. 3, 1947	Dan Levin
800	Alice-Sit-By-The-Fire	James M.Barrie	Aug. 5-10, 1947	Lenore Shanewise
801	The Girl of the Golden West	David Belasco	Aug. 12-31, 1947	Victor Jory
802	The Bees and the Flowers	Frederick Kohner / Albert Mannheimer	Sept. 29-Oct. 12, 1947	Lenore Shanewise
803	Joan of Lorraine	Maxwell Anderson	Oct. 15-26, 1947	Lenore Shanewise
804	Our Hearts Were Young & Gay	Skinner / Kimbrough	Oct.29-Nov. 23, 1947	Marcella Cisney
805	Years Ago	Ruth Gordon	Nov. 26-Dec. 14, 1947	George Phelps
806	The Magic Rowan	James Shaw Grant	Dec. 17-28, 1947	Vincent Bowditch
807	Barretts of Wimpole Street	Rudolph Besier	Dec. 31-Jan. 11, 1948	Thomas Armistead
808	Apple of his Eye	Nicholson / Robinson	Jan. 14-25, 1948	Michael Cisney
809	Made in Heaven	Hagar Wilde	Jan. 28-Feb. 8, 1948	Lenore Shanewise
810	Another Part of the Forest	Lillian Hellman	Feb. 11-22, 194	Morris Ankrum
811	Woman Bites Dog	Sam / Bella Spewack	Feb. 25-Mar. 7, 1948	George Phelps
812	Love from a Stranger	Karl Vosper	Mar. 10-21, 1948	Helen Schoeni
813	Russet Mantle	Lynn Riggs	Mar. 24-Apr. 4, 1948	Samuel Herrick
814	King Richard III	Wm. Shakespeare	Apr. 7-18, 1948	Onslow Stevens
815	The Millionairess	G. B. Shaw	Apr. 21-May 2, 1948	Lenore Shanewise
816	This Young World	Judith Kandel	May 5-16, 1948	Marcella Cisney
817	The Circle	Somerset Maugham	May 19-30, 1948	T. B. Henry
818	Craig's Wife	George Kelly	June 2-20, 1948	Mabel Albertson
819	Angel Street	Patrick Hamilton	June 24-July 4, 1948	Victor Jory

FOURTEENTH MIDSUMMER FESTIVAL (Favorite Plays of Gold Coast Days)

NO.	PLAY	AUTHOR	DATE	DIRECTOR
820	The Lady of Lyons	E. Bulwer-Lytton	July 6-11, 1948	George Phelps
821	The Honeymoon	John Tobin	July 13-18, 1948	Lenore Shanewise
822	The Marble Heart	Charles Selby	July 20-25, 1948	Barbara Vajda
823	London Assurance	Dion Boucicault	July 27-Aug. 1, 1948	T. B. Armistead
824	Damon and Pythias	John Banim	Aug. 3-8, 1948	George Phelps
825	Fanchon The Cricket	A. Wauldauer	Aug. 10-15, 1948	Brown / Schoeni
826	Fashion	Anna C. Mowatt	Aug. 17-22, 1948	Vince Bowditch
827	Camille	Dumas / DeWitt Bodeen	Aug. 24-Sept. 5, 1948	Barbara Vajda
828	Dream Girl	Elmer Rice	Sept. 27-Oct. 10, 1948	George Phelps
829	The Constant Wife	Somerset Maugham	Oct. 13-24, 1948	Robert Milton
830	Road to Rome	Robert Sherwood	Oct. 27-Nov. 7, 1948	Barbara Vajda
831	An Inspector Calls	J. B. Priestley	Nov. 10-21, 1948	George Phelps
832*	Castle on the Sand	Zoe Akins	Nov. 24-Dec. 5, 1948	Robert Milton
833	The Glass Menagerie	Tennessee Williams	Dec. 8-19, 1948	Tom Armistead
834	Life With Father	Lindsay / Crouse	Dec. 22-Jan 9, 1949	George Phelps
835	Three Men on a Horse	John Cecil Holm / George Abbott	Jan. 12-23, 1949	Robert Milton
836	The Bunner Sisters	DeWitt Bodeen	Jan. 26-Feb. 6, 1949	Barbara Vajda
837	The Gentleman from Athens	Emmet Lavery	Feb. 9-20, 1949	George Phelps
838	Dark of the Moon	Howard Richardson / William Berney	Feb. 23-Mar. 6, 1949	Julia Farnsworth
839	Elizabeth the Queen	Maxwell Anderson	Mar. 9-20, 1949	Blevins Davis / Barbara Vajda
840	The Winslow Boy	Terence Rattigan	Mar. 23-Apr. 10, 1949	Robert Milton
841	The Hamlet Tetrology	Percy MacKaye	Apr. 14-May 1, 1949	
	The Ghost of Elsinore		Apr. 14 / 20, 1949	Onslow Stevens
	The Fool in Eden Garden		Apr. 15 / 24, 1949	Frederic Berest
	Odin Against Christus		Apr. 16 / 27, 1949	William Greer
	The Serpent in the Orchard		Apr. 17 / May 1, 1949	Frank Sundstrom
842	I Remember Mama	John Van Druten	May 4-15, 1949	Barbara Vajda
843	The Shop At Sly Corner	Edward Percy	May 18-19, 1949	Robert Milton
844	Command Decision	William Haines	June 1-12, 1949	George Phelps
845	Antigone	Jean Anouilh	June 15-26, 1949	Gilmor Brown

FIFTEENTH MIDSUMMER FESTIVAL (California Playwrights)

NO.	PLAY	AUTHOR	DATE	DIRECTOR
846	Bright Champagne	DeWitt Bodeen	June 28-July 3, 1949	Barbara Vajda
847	The Dove	Willard Mack	July 5-10, 1949	Victor Jory / Gordon Giffen
848	Distant Drums	Dan Totheroh	July 12-17, 1949	Onslow Stevens

NO.	PLAY	AUTHOR	DATE	DIRECTOR
849	Bird of Paradise	Richard Walton Tully	July 19-24, 1949	George Phelps / Richard Morell
850	Lightnin'	Frank Bacon / Winchell Smith	July 26-31, 1949	Morris Ankrum / James Tracy
851	Shucks!	Martin Flaven	Aug. 2-7, 1949	William Greer
852	Strange Bedfellows	Florence Ryerson / Colin Clements	Aug. 9-Sept. 11, 1949	Gordon Giffen
853	John Loves Mary	Norman Krasna	Sept. 26-Oct.9, 1949	George Phelps
854	Happy Birthday	Anita Loos	Oct. 12-23, 1949	Lenore Shanewise
855	Edward, My Son	Robert Morley / Noel Langley	Oct. 26-Nov. 6, 1949	T. B. Henry / Barbara Vajda
856	For Love or Money	F. Hugh Herbert	Nov. 9-20, 1949	George Phelps
857	This Happy Breed	Noel Coward	Nov. 23-Dec.4, 1949	Philip Van Dyke
858	The Trial	Franz Kafka / Andre Gide / Jean Louis Barrault	Dec. 7-18, 1949	Frank Sundstrom
859	The Cricket on the Hearth	Chas. Dicken	Dec. 21-Jan. 1, 1950	Barbara Vajda / Gilmor Brown
860	The Young and the Fair	N. Richard Nash	Jan. 4-15, 1950	Lenore Shanewise
861	Two Blind Mice	Sam Spewack	Jan. 18-Feb. 12, 1950	George Phelps
862	The Two Mrs. Carrolls	Martin Vale	Feb. 15-26, 1950	Onslow Stevens
863	The Tempest	Wm. Shakespeare	Mar. 1-12, 1950	Julia Farnsworth
864	O Evening Star	Zoe Akins	Mar. 15-26, 1950	Lenore Shanewise
865	Home is Tomorrow	J. B. Priestley	Mar. 31-Apr. 9, 1950	Gilmor Brown
866	As Husbands Go	Rachel Crothers	Apr. 12-Apr. 23, 1950	Barbara Vajda
867	The Heiress	Ruth / Augustus Goetz	Apr. 26-May 7, 1950	Gilmor Brown
868	O Mistress Mine	Terrence Rattigan	May 10-21, 1950	T. B. Henry
869	Many Waters	Monckton Hoffe	May 24-June 4, 1950	Barbara Vajda
870	Kitty Doone	Aben Kandel	June 7-18, 1950	George Phelps

SIXTEENTH MIDSUMMER FESTIVAL (Plays by Modern Playwrights)

NO.	PLAY	AUTHOR	DATE	DIRECTOR
871	Hobson's Choice	Harold Brighouse	June 20-25, 1950	Lenore Shanewise
872	The Traitor	Herman Wouk	June 27-July 2, 1950	Wm. Greer
873	Metropole	Wm. Walden	July 4-9, 1950	T. B. Henry
874	Peace in Our Time	Noel Coward	July 11-16, 1950	Barbara Vajda
875	One Foot in Heaven	Irving Phillips	July 18-Aug. 13, 1950	Lenore Shanewise
876	Monserrat	Emmanuel Robles / Lillian Hellman	Aug. 15-20, 1950	Gilmor Brown
877	Summer and Smoke	Tennessee Williams	Aug. 22-27, 1950	Rita Glover
878	Light Up the Sky	Moss Hart	Aug. 29-Sept. 17, 1950	George Phelps
879	See How They Run	Philip King	Oct. 2-15, 1950	Helmuth Hormann
880	The Silver Whistle	Robert McEnroe	Oct. 19-Nov. 5, 1950	Lenore Shanewise
881	Present Laugher	Noel Coward	Nov. 9-19, 1950	Barbara Vajda
882	Heaven Help the Angels	Lynn Root	Nov. 23-Dec. 4, 1950	Lynn Root
883	Little Scandal	Florence Ryerson / Alice D. G. Miller	Dec. 7-17, 1950	Lenore Shanewise
884	The Pied Piper of Hamelin	Josephine Preston Peabody	Dec. 21-31, 1950	Julia Farnsworth
885	Born Yesterday	Garson Kanin	Jan. 4-14, 1951	George Phelps
886	Anne of a Thousand Days	Maxwell Anderson	Jan. 18-28, 1951	Lenore Shanewise
887	Pagan in the Parlor	Franklin Lacy	Feb. 1-11, 1951	James Whale
888	Harvey	Mary Chase	Feb. 15-Mar. 15, 1951	George Phelps
889	The Man	Mel Dinelli	Mar. 15-25, 1951	Barbara Vajda
890	The Enchanted	Jean Giraudoux	Mar. 29-Apr. 8, 1951	Ruth Birch
891	Much Ado About Nothing	Wm. Shakespeare	Apr. 12-29, 1951	Julia Farnsworth
892	Bottom of the Pile	Ernest Vajda / Clement Scott Gilbert	May 3-13, 1951	Barbara Vajda
893	The Livewire	Garson Kanin	May 17-June 3, 1951	William Greer
894	The Swallows Nest	Zoe Akins	June 7-24, 1951	Robert Milton

SEVENTEENTH MIDSUMMER FESTIVAL (George M. Cohan Plays)

NO.	PLAY	AUTHOR	DATE	DIRECTOR
895	Seven Keys to Baldpate	George M. Cohan	June 28-July 8, 1951	Barbara Vajda
896	A Prince There Was	George M. Cohan	July 12-22, 1951	Onslow Stevens
897	The Tavern	George M. Cohan	July 26-Aug.15, 1951	George Phelps
898	Pigeons and People	George M. Cohan	Aug. 9-19, 1951	Barbara Vajda
899	Broadway Jones	George M. Cohan	Aug. 23-Sept. 2, 1951	Philip Van Dyke
900	Goodbye, My Fancy	Fay Kanin	Oct. 1-14, 1951	Lenore Shanewise
901	Detective Story	Sidney Kingsley	Oct. 19-28, 1951	Mervin Williams
902	Once Upon an Earthquake	Dan Totheroh	Nov. 1-18, 1951	Philip Van Dyke
903	The Madwoman of Chaillot	Jean Giraudoux	Nov. 22-Dec. 2, 1951	Barbara Vajda
904	Southern Exposure	Owen Crump	Dec. 6-16, 1951	George Phelps
905	David Copperfield	Chas. Dickens	Dec. 20-31, 1951	Julia Farnsworth
906	The Curious Savage	John Patrick	Jan. 3-13, 1952	Barbara Vajda
907	Come Back, Little Sheba	Wm. Inge	Jan. 17-27, 1952	Mervin Williams
908	Old Acquaintance	John Van Druten	Jan. 31-Feb. 10, 1952	Lenore Shanewise
909	Legend of Sarah	James Gow / Arnaud d'Usseau	Feb. 14-24, 1952	Mervin Williams
910	Nothing But The Truth	James Montgomery	Feb. 28-Mar. 9, 1952	Robt.Rence
911	The Golden State	Samuel Spewack	Mar. 20-Apr. 3, 1952	Barbara Vajda
912	MacBeth	Wm. Shakespeare	Apr. 23-May 4, 1952	Jack Lynn
913	Berkeley Square	John Balderstond	May 8-18, 1952	Barbara Vajda

In Appreciation
PAT & SHARON WESTMORELAND

NO.	PLAY	AUTHOR	DATE	DIRECTOR
914	Gramercy Ghost	John Cecil Holm	May 22-June 1, 1952	Bobker ben Ali
915	Life with Mother	Lindsay / Crouse	June 5-22, 1952	Lenore Shanewise
				Barbara Vajda

EIGHTEENTH MIDSUMMER FESTIVAL (Plays about Great Americans)

NO.	PLAY	AUTHOR	DATE	DIRECTOR
916	Valley Forge	Maxwell Anderson	June 26-July 6, 1952	Bobker ben Ali
917	Ben Franklin	Louis Evan Shipman	July 10-20, 1952	Barbara Vajda
918	The Patriots	Sidney Kingsley	July 24-Aug. 3, 1952	Bobker ben Ali
919	Harriet	Florence Ryerson	Aug. 7-17, 1952	Lenore Shanewise
		Colin Clements		
920	Abe Lincoln in Illinois	Robert. E. Sherwood	Aug. 21-Sept. 17, 1952	Morris Ankrum
921	Robert E Lee	John Drinkwater	Sept. 11-21, 1952	Barbara Vajda
922	Twentieth Century	Ben Hecht	Sept. 29-Oct. 12, 1952	Bobker ben Ali
		Chas. MacArthur		
923	Billy Budd	Herman Melville	Oct. 16-26, 1952	Mervin Williams
		Cox / Chapman		
924	Ring 'Round the Moon	Jean Anouilh	Oct. 30-Nov. 9, 1952	Barbara Vajda
		Christopher Fry		
925	The Yellow Jacket	Benrimo / Hazelton	Nov. 13-23, 1952	Bobker ben Ali
926	Stalag 17	Donald Bevin	Dec. 4-14, 1952	Boris Sagal
		Edmund Trzcinski		
927	A Christmas Carol	Chas. Dickens	Dec. 18-28, 1952	Jack Lynn
		Gilmor Brown		
928	The Happy Time	Robt. Fontaine	Dec. 31 -Jan. 11,	Lenore Shanewise
		Samuel Tyler	1953	
(One play a month)				
929	The Mikado	Gilbert / Sullivan	Jan. 15, 1953	Barbara Vajda
930	Bell, Book and Candle	John van Druten	Feb. 12, 1953	Bobker ben Ali
931*	Nightshade	Ken Englund	Mar. 12, 1953	Demetrios Vilan
		Sidney Field		John Bryant
932	The Country Girl	Clifford Odets	Apr. 2, 1953	Bobker ben Ali
933	Mr. Roberts	Thomas Heggen	Apr. 30, 1953	Jack Pierce
		Joshua Logan		
934	Magic	G. K. Chesterton	Not given	Douglass Montgomery
935	The Shewing Up of	G. B. Shaw	Not given	Douglass Montgmery
	Blanco Posnet			
936	The Fortune Teller	Victor Herbert	Not given	Barbara Vajda

NINETEENTH MIDSUMMER FESTIVAL (Shakespeare's Comedies)

NO.	PLAY	AUTHOR	DATE	DIRECTOR
937	The Taming of the Shrew	Wm. Shakespeare	Not given	Bobker ben Ali
938	Comedy of Errors	Wm. Shakespeare	Not given	Jack Pierce
939	As You Like It	Wm. Shakespeare	Not given	Jack Warfield
940	Remains to be Seen	Lindsay / Crouse	Sept. 17, 1953	Bobker ben Ali
941	Affairs of State	Louis Verneuil	Oct. 15, 1953	Barbara Vajda
942	Point of No Return	J. P. Marquand	Nov. 12, 1953	Thomas Armistead
		Paul Osborne		
943	Alice in Wonderland	Lewis Carroll	Dec. 17,1953	Julia Farnsworth
944	The Gondoliers	Gilbert / Sullivan	Jan. 7, 1954	Barbara Vajda
945	Lo and Behold	John Patrick	Feb. 4, 1954	T. B. Henry
946	Arsenic and Old Lace	Joseph Kesselring	Mar. 4, 1954	Victor Jory / Bela Kovacs
947	Gigi	Colette / AnitaLoos	Apr. 1, 1954	Bobker ben Ali
948	The Male Animal	James Thurber	Apr. 29, 1954	Jack Bernhard
		Elliot Nugent		
949*	Gown of Glory	Irving Phillips	May 27, 1954	Helmut Hormann
950	Mrs. McThing	Mary Chase	June 24, 1954	Barbara Vajda
951	Late Love	Rosemary Casey	July 22, 1954	James O'Connor
952	Ah! Wilderness	Eugene O'Neill	Aug. 19, 1954	Jack Bernhard
953	Street Scene	Elmer Rice	Sept. 16, 1954	Jack Bernhard
954	Bernardine	Mary Chase	Oct. 14, 1954	Barbara Vajda
955*	Mother was a Bachelor	Irving W. Phillips	Nov. 11, 1954	Bea Hassel
956	Trelawny of the Wells	Arthur Pinero	Not given	Moroni Olsen
957	The Prescott Proposals	Lindsay / Crouse	Jan. 6,1955	T. B. Henry
958	My Three Angels	Sam / Bella Spewack	Feb. 3, 1955	Jean Inness
959*	In the Spirit	Alan Mowbray	Mar. 3, 1955	Alan Mowbray
960	The Man Who Came to Dinner	Kaufman / Hart	Mar. 17, 1955	Barbara Vajda
961	A Sleep of Prisoners	Christopher Fry	May 1, 1955	Ken Rose
962	Five Plays (18 Actors, Inc.)		May 5, 1955	
963	Time out for Ginger	Ronald Alexander	June 2, 1955	T. B. Henry
964*	Please Communicate	Mary Oldfield	June 30, 1955	George Englund
965	Picnic	Wm. Inge	July 28, 1955	T. B. Henry
966	Sabrina Fair	Samuel Taylor	Not given	Mary Greene
967	Reclining Figure	Harry Kurnitz	Sept. 29, 1955	Barbara Vajda
968	The Fourposter	Jan de Hartog	Oct. 27, 1955	Lenore Shanewise
969	The Remarkable	Liam O'Brien	Dec. 1, 1955	Milton Parsons
	Mr. Pennypacker			
970	Jenny Kissed Me	Jean Kerr	Jan. 5, 1956	Jack Lynn
971	Jane	S. N. Behrman	Feb. 16, 1956	Mary Greene
972	The White Sheep of	L.duGarde Peach	Mar. 1, 1956	Lenore Shanewise
	the Family	Ian Hay		
973	The Solid Gold Cadillac	Howard Teichmann	Apr. 26, 1956	Julia Farnsworth
		Geo. Kaufman		
974	The Seven Year Itch	George Axelrod	June 28,1956	King Donovan
975	Tonight or Never	Lili Batvany	Aug. 2, 1956	Harvey Marlowe

Charlotte Stewart and Martha Scott in *Open Book*

Maudie Prickett in *The Girls in 509*

Hamlet

The House of Blue Leaves

In Appreciation
LAURA BARKER

135

NO.	PLAY	AUTHOR	DATE	DIRECTOR
976	Two Adams for Eve	Irving Phillips Heinz Roemheld	Oct. 4, 1956	Gail Shoup
977	Tonight in Samarkand	Jacque Deval Lorenzo Semple, Jr.	Nov. 20, 1956	Barbara Vajda
978	Rip van Winkle	Vincen Leccese John Colman	Dec. 20, 1956	Julia Farnsworth
979	Accidentally Yours	Pauline Williams Snapp	Dec. 27, 1956	Harvey Marlowe
980	The Curious Miss Caraway	George Batson Alex Gottlieb	Jan. 14, 1957	Stewart Smith
981	All For Mary	Harold Brooke Kay Bannerman	Mar. 28, 1957	Lenore Shanewise
982	Romeo and Juliet	Wm. Shakespeare	May 9,1957	Albert McCleery
983	A Night with the President	John Green	June 6, 1957	Mary Greene
984	Morning's at Seven	Paul Osborn	July 5, 1957	Bea Hassel
985	The Man on a Stick	Leon / Harlan Hare	Oct. 7, 1957	King Donovan
986	Janus	Grolyn Green	Nov. 14, 1957	Walter Grauman
987	Holiday for Lovers	Ronald Alexander	Dec. 26, 1957	Charles Paul
988	Inherit the Wind	Jerome Lawrence Robt. E. Lee	Jan. 30, 1958	Barney Brown
989	The Reluctant Debutante	Wm. Douglas Home	Mar. 6, 1958	Gail Shoup
990	The Teahouse of the August Moon	John Patrick	Apr. 10, 1958	Pat Miller
991	Bus Stop	Wm. Inge	May 29, 1958	Richard Morelli
992	Visit to a Small Planet	Gore Vidal	Oct. 2, 1958	M. Gardiner
993	The Happiest Millionaire	Kyle Crichton	Nov. 13, 1958	Helmut Hormann
994	Three Ponies to Peking	Richard Morelli	Dec. 18, 1958	Julia Farnsworth Richard Morelli
995	Waltz of the Toreadors	Jean Anouilh	Dec. 26, 1958	Barbara Vajda
996	The Magnificent Yankee	Emmet Lavery	Jan 29, 1959	Barney Brown
997	The Time of Your Life	Wm. Saroyan	Mar. 20, 1959	Onslow Stevens
998	No Time for Sergeants	Ira Levin	Apr. 16, 1959	James Holden
999	Plain and Fancy	Joseph Stein Will Glickman Albert Hague	May 29, 1959	Not given
1000	Who Was That Lady I Saw You With?	Norman Krasna	Oct. 1, 1959	Gail Shoup
1001	Our Town	Thornton Wilder	Nov. 6, 1959	Barney Brown
1002	The Play's the Thing	Ferenc Molnar P. G. Wodehouse	Dec. 10, 1959	T. B. Henry
1003	The Great Sebastians	Lindsay / Crouse	Jan. 21, 1960	Loy G. Norris
1004	The Fourposter	Jan de Hartog	Feb. 11, 1960	Dan Levin
1005	Desperate Hours	Joseph Hayes	Mar. 25, 1960	Ken Rose
1006	Of Thee I Sing	Geor.Kaufman George / Ira Gershwin	Apr. 29, 1960	Barney Brown
1007	The Circle	Somerset Maugham	June 16,1960	Ralph Senensky
1008	Golden Fleecing	Lorenzo Semple, Jr.	Sept. 16, 1960	Ralph Senensky
1009	Time Remembered	Jean Anouilh	Oct. 21, 1960	Bobker ben Ali
1010	The Rivalry	Norman Corwin	Nov. 25, 1960	Chas. Robt. Paul
1011	The Curious Savage	John Patrick	Dec. 30, 1960	Mary Greene
1012	The Deadly Game	Friedrich Duerrenmatt / James Yaffe	Feb. 17, 1961	Barney Brown
1013	Make a Million	Norman Barasch Carroll Moore	Mar. 24, 1961	Michael Joseph Kane
1014	The Marriage Go-Round	Leslie Stevens	Apr. 28, 1961	Oliver Cliff
1015	Father of the Bride	Caroline Francke	June 2, 1961	Alan Hanson
1016	The Pleasure of His Company	Samuel Taylor Cornelia Otis Skinner	Not given	Bea Hassel
1017	Five Finger Exercise	Peter Shaffer	Nov. 17, 1961	Bobker ben Ali
1018	The Country Wife	Wm. Wycherley	Dec. 22, 1961	Helmut Hormann
1019	The Dybbuk	S. Ansky	Not given	Morris Anluum
1020	Everybody Loves Opal	John Patrick	Not given	John McNamara
1021	Becket	Jean Anouilh	Not given	Lenore Shanewise
1022	Send Me No Flowers	Norman Barasch Carroll Moore	May 18, 1962	John Marley
1023	Under the Sycamore Tree	Samuel Spewack	Sept. 1962	Eugene Loring
1024	All the Way Home	Tad Mosel	Not given	T. B. Henry
1025	Nina	Andre Roussin Samuel Taylor	Dec. 1962	Bea Hassel
1026	The Complaisant Lover	Graham Greene	Feb. 1963	Gene de Wild
1027	Rain	S. Maugham John Colton Clemence Randolph	Mar. 1963	George Womack
1028*	Open Book	Hugh White Nat Perrin	Apr. 18, 1963	Clarke Gordon
1029	The Girls in 509	Howard Teichmann	Sept. 1963	Gail Shoup
1030	Gideon	Paddy Chayefsky	Nov. 1963	T. B. Henry
1031	Anniversary Wale	Jerome Chodorov Joseph Fields	Dec. 1963	Pitt Herbert
1032	Lord Pengo	S. N. Behrman	Jan. 1964	Don Schwarz
1033	Member of the Wedding	Carson McCullers	Feb. 1964	Coy Bronson

Mail

James Whitmore in *Handy Dandy*

Room Service

Groucho: A Life in Revue

NO.	PLAY	AUTHOR	DATE	DIRECTOR
1034	A Touch of the Poet	Eugene O'Neill	Apr. 1964	Stuart Margolin
1035	Best Foot Forward	John Cecil Holm Hugh Martin	May 1964	Not given
1036	Ballad of a City	Steve Allen	Mar. 11-27, 1965	John B .Macdonald
1037	Hamlet	Wm. Shakespeare	Apr. 9-25, 1965	Leon Askin
1038	The Shoemaker's Prodigious Wife	Federico Garcia Lorca	Oct. 1965	C. Lowell Lees
1039	The Firebugs	Max Frisch	Oct. 1965	C. Lowell Lees
1040	Peer Gynt	Henrik Ibsen	Oct. 21-Nov. 13, 1965	C. Lowell Lees
1041	The Devil's Disciple	G. B. Shaw	Nov. 18-Dec. 11, 1965	Stuart Margolin
1042	Love for Love	Wm. Congreve	Dec. 16-Jan. 15, 1966	Claude Woolman
1043	Richard III	Wm. Shakespeare	Jan. 20-Feb. 12, 1966	C. Lowell Lees
1044	Dark of the Moon	Howard Richardson Wm. Berney	Feb. 17-Mar. 12, 1966	Chas. Rome Smith
1045	Captain Brassbound's Conversion	G. B. Shaw	Sept. 28-Oct. 22, 1966	George Keathley
1046	The Decent Thing	Jay / Connie Romer	Nov. 9-26, 1966	Albert McCleery
1047	Life with Father	Clarence Day	Nov. 30-Dec. 31, 1966	Mary Greene
1048	Lady in the Dark	Moss Hart / Kurt Weill Ira Gershwin	Jan. 4-Feb. 4, 1967	Albert McCleery
1049*	Always with Love	Tom Harris	Feb. 10-25, 1967	Mary Greene
1050	Ah, Wilderness	Eugene O'Neill	Mar. 17-Apr. 15, 1967	Lenore Shanewise
1051	Affairs of State	Louis Verneuil	Apr. 26-May 27, 1967	Celeste Holm
1052	Lock Up Your Daughters	Henry Fielding	Sept. 29-Oct. 22, 1967	Malcolm Black
1053	The Caine Mutiny Court Martial	Herman Wouk	Oct. 27-Nov. 26, 1967	Not given
1054	I Remember Mama	John Van Druten	Dec. 1-31, 1967	Mary Greene
1055	Ladies in Retirement	Percy / Denham	Feb. 9-Mar. 3, 1968	Lenore Shanewise
1056	Cat on a Hot Tin Roof	Tennessee Williams	Mar. 8-Apr. 7, 1968	Victor Jory
1057	Southern Comfort	Dale / Katherine Eunson	Apr. 12-May 5, 1968	Leon Ames
1058	What Else Have You Got in The Closet	Christopher Carey	Jan. 1969	Lazlo Vadnay Hans Wilhelm
1059	The Unknown Soldier and his Wife	Peter Ustinov	Feb. 9-Mar. 3, 1969	Albert McCleery
1060	Lion in Winter	Wm. Goldman	Not given	Not given
1061	America Hurrah	Not given	Not given	John Larson
1062	Beau Strategm	Not given	Not given	Not given
1063	Arms and the Man	George Bernard Shaw	April 19, 1986	Nikos Psacharopoulos
1064	Look Homeward Angel	Ketti Frings	June 7-29, 1986	Jessica Ismana Myerson
1065	Spokesong	Stewart Parker	July 12-Aug. 3, 1986	Lewis Arquette
1066	The House of Blue Leaves	John Guare	May 3-24, 1987	Tony Abatemarco
1067	Mail	Jerry Colker	June 14-July 12, 1987	Andrew Cadiff
1068	Handy Dandy	William Gibson	July 26-Aug. 16, 1987	Tony Giordano
1069	Room Service	John Murray Allen Boretz	Sept. 6, 1987	Stephen Rothman
1070	Mail (Return Engagement)	Jerry Colker	Nov. 1, 1987-Jan. 30, 1988	Andrew Cadiff
1071	Breaking the Silence	Stephen Poliakoff	March 27-Apr. 17, 1988	Warner Shook
1072	Death of a Buick	John Bunzel	May 5-June 5, 1988	Steven Keats
1073	Born Yesterday	Garson Kanin	June 26-July 17, 1988	Don Amendolia
1074	Jacques Brel is Alive…	Eric Blau Mort Shuman	July 14-Sept. 11, 1988	Moni Yakim
1075	Harry Chapin: Lies and Legends	Harry Chapin	July 14, 1988	Kathleen Rubbicco
1076	Steel Magnolias	Robert Harling	Sep. 25-Oct. 16, 1988	Pamela Berlin
1077	Carnal Knowledge	Jules Feiffer	Nov. 13-Dec. 11, 1988	Ted Swindley
1078	Accomplice	Rupert Holmes	Feb. 5-Apr. 23, 1989	Art Wolff
1079	The Boys Next Door	Tom Griffin	May 14-June 4, 1989	Josephine R. Abady
1080	Stepping Out	Richard Harris	June 25-July 30, 1989	Don Amendolia
1081	Groucho: A Life in Revue	Arthur Marx Robert Fisher	Oct. 1-Nov. 5, 1989	Arthur Marx
1082	The Downside	Richard Dresser	Dec. 10, 1989- Jan. 14, 1990	Kenneth Frankel
1083	Flora the Red Menace	David Thompson	Feb. 11-Mar. 18, 1990	Scott Ellis
1084	The Big Day	Douglas McGrath	April 22-May 27, 1990	Don Amendolia
1085	Bus Stop	William Inge	July 15-Aug. 19, 1990	Warner Shook
1086	The Wonderful Ice Cream Suit	Ray Bradbury	Sep. 16-Oct. 21, 1990	Charles Rome Smith
1087	Holiday in Oz	B. J. Turner	Dec. 2-29, 1990	B. J. Turner
1088	Double Cross	Gary Bohlke	Jan. 20-Feb. 24, 1991	A. J. Antoon
1089	Other People's Money	Jerry Sterner	Mar. 24-Apr. 28, 1991	Kevin Conway
1090	You Never Know	Cole Porter	May 26-June 30, 1991	Paul Lazarus
1091	The Dining Room	A. R. Gurney	July 21-Aug. 25, 1991	David Saint
1092	Forever Plaid	Stuart Ross	Sept. 22-Oct. 27, 1991	Stuart Ross
1093	Solitary Confinement	Rupert Holmes	Nov. 24-Dec. 29, 1991	Kenneth Frankel
1094	Lend Me A Tenor	Ken Ludwig	Jan. 19-Feb. 23, 1992	David Saint
1095	On Borrowed Time	Paul Osborn	Mar. 22-Apr. 26, 1992	Sheldon Epps
1096	Closer Than Ever	Richard Maltby Jr. David Shire	May 15-June 28, 1992	Richard Maltby Jr.

The records for 1964–1986 were incomplete. There may be productions completely omitted here.

Helen Slater in The Big Day

Bus Stop

The Wonderful Ice Cream Suit

Double Cross

In Appreciation
BRAVO PRODUCTIONS

Staff of Theatre Corporation of America

Lenore Almanzar
Peter Ballenger
Laura Blainey
Rick Boot
Russ Campbell
Morgan B. Crofts
Deborah Dixon
Peggy Ebright
Scott Erickson
David Erskine
Drake Farrar
Lance Fritz
Loren B. Gardner
Guy Gressly
Lars Hansen
Alan Harrison
Joyce Heiman
David G. Houk
Mickey Houk
Mark Humphrey
Jeth Ilano
Matt Kennedy
Allison Kingsley
Michael Kravitz
Peter Kuhl
Amy Lackow
Mike Lancaster
Paul Lazarus
Leroy Lightfoot
Ann Loze

Donald Loze
Kevin Mahan
Melissa Malone
Denis McDowell
Judy McDowell
Betty Jean Morris
Nelson Nemec
Dawna Oak
Ken Ott
Melanie Peterson
Miguel Pous
Ivonne Pinochet
Jarmila Price
Michael Prichard
Elizabeth Pruyn
John Redmond
Rodney Rincon
Fernando Rodriguez
Laura Rodriguez
Vicente Rodriguez
Christine Rosensteel
Tim Saldain
Doug Senior
Steve Sims
Parker Tenney
Michael Thompson
Tom Ware
Jennifer Weller
Gary Wissman

The Board of Directors: Pasadena Playhouse State Theatre of California

Robin Barker
David M. Davis
David G. Houk
Jan Dior Kloke
C. James Levin

Albert Lowe
Donald Loze
Art Mann
Patrick McNally
Samuel Paul

Kathy Arntzen Roat
Ernest E. Sanchez
Margaret H. Sedenquist
Michael Sharp
Gregg Smith

William E. Thomson
William R. Treder
Katie Tuerk

The Pasadena Playhouse Advisory

Berle Adams
Lew Allen
Dann Angeloff
Robert Artz
Fitch M. Behr
Richard Capalbo
Pierre Cossette
Ralph O. Kehle
William Klove
J. Terrence Lanni

Lathrop Leishman
James Lizardi
Gary Lund
William L. MacDonald
Richard Matthews
Larry J. Mielke
Katherine Moret
Kristine A. Morris
Angelo Mozilo
Gilbert L. Neilson

George W. Ott
Greg Penske
Robert Poe
Charles Prickett
Charles Redmond
Raymond Rodeno
John Shields
Kathleen Shilkret
C. Edward Snyder
Roger Stangeland

Maurice H. Stans
Kathleen Teggares
Paul Toffel
Gerald Trimble
Miles Turpin
Patrick Westmoreland
Henry C. Yuen

The Pasadena Playhouse 90

Eleanor Albano
Betty Amato
Anthony J. Amendola
Judith Amis
Maria Anderson
Peter Brooke Bailly
Linda Baker
Joan Bonholtzer
Marco Brown
David Catlin
Lea Chazin
Sara Muller Chernoff
Candyce Columbus
David Davis

Bonnie DeWitt
Patt Dolan
Carol Ducey
Peggy Ebright
Mary B. Ferguson
Maideh Gore
Barbara Gosenson
Lars Hansen
Catherine Haskett
Paige Hendricks
Marvell Herren
Julie Hopf
Mickey Houk
Susan Hull

Charlotte Kleeman
Jan Dior Kloke
Ann Loze
Lorie MacKenzie
Jewell Matsuura
Sammi McCubbins
Judy McDowell
Kimberly Moranville
Jan Moscaret
Chris Murray
Sherry Parker
C. Anthony Phillips
Robert Pinger
Karin Rees

Kathy Arntzen Roat
Sally Rogers
Barbara Sanladerer
Nancy Shebel
Judie Shields
Gregg Smith
Phil Sotel
Nancy J. Swift
Carol Thomson
Susan M. Vincent
William Watts
Lyla White
Mel Wilson
Guido Zemgals

The Friends

Joan Aldrin
Christine Allen
Lenore Almanzar
Don Amendolia
Laura Amparan
Beverly Bahidh
Ellen Bailey
Pat Bauer
Ted Bell
Jodie Benson
Nancy Bercovitz
Corinne Bergmann
Donald Bergmann
Clark Branson
Alice Brock
Mary Jane Broderick
Evelyn Brown
Kathryn Brown
Virginia Cannon
Janice Carta
Jodie Carter
Kae Cedar
Harry Clarke
Ruth Close
Ora Clough
Donna Coffman
Mary Collins
Kevin Conway
Marilyn Costa
Bonnie Davis
Naomi Davis
Jan Dolan
Margie Duff
Peggy Ebright
Eve Edmond
Marjorie Edmonds
Amy Edwards
Gladys Eisenstat
Ginny Emett
Edith Escobar
Gail Fabbro
Frank Ferrante
Shirley Filiatrault
Monica Freeman
Helen Frey
Bridget Furiga

Robert Furiga
Gloria Gandara
Mary Gojaniuk
Greta Goran
Nat Goran
Althea Graham
Dixie Granat
Barbara Green
Jean Griffin
Pat Hardy
Joyce Hegeman
James Hendrickson
Mary Anna Henley
Sandra Herrera
Maureen Higdon
Lindy Hill
Mary Beth Hipps
Diana Hoffman
Sara Hoge
Marie Holst
Sandra Hovanesian
Vicki Huddleston
Toni Itano
Rose Lynn Jarrett
Dottie Johnson
Kim Johnson
Rosa Johnson
Mary Kearns
Bob Kody
Margot Kody
Joann Komin
Michael Kravitz
Pamela L'Heureux
Marilyn Lasky
Stan Lasky
Martin Laventhal
Doreen Lawson-Edwards
Paul Lazarus
Pauline Ledeen
Merilyn Leidig
Evelyn LeMone
Tina Lenert
Leroy Lightfoot
Ann Linck
Gail Alli Lindquist
Kristin Lowman

Ann Loze
Donald Loze
Laura Lugar-Beiler
Flo Lukens
Ingeborg Lynch
Pat MacDonald
Cecilia Magid
Morris Magid
Donna Malcomb
Lucy Marlow
Deanie Marquis
Arthur Marx
Doris Mayne
Marie McCarthy
Georgia McClay
Claudia Mendelson
Martha Meyer
Patrick Miller
Sally Montgomery
Betty Jean Morris
Megan Mullally
Gail Neiman
Phyllis Nemeth
Kathleen Noe
Carroll Oliver
Diane Olson
Esme Peake
Jill Perkins
Anne Piasecki
Irma Piasecki
Leonard Piasecki
Eleanore Pipes
Jack Rappaport
Georgia Reese
Jim Reese
Kathy Ann Roat
Vanessa Roettger
Joanne Rolle
Christine Rosensteel
Cecilia Rosenthal
Dorothy Rusch
Patricia Sahagian
Jennifer Saurenman
Kim Schaffer
Carol Schilling
Barbara Schworm

Doug Senior
Jeanne Shomaker
Ruth Skolnick
Judy Slater
Emily Smith
Jodi Smith
Laurel Smith
Mary Snyder
Maria Soldevilla
Marilyn Steinberg
Robert Steinberg
Nathan Sternfeld
Joan Stewart
Louise Stivers
Marilyn Stutenroth
John Sullivan
Tillie Sullivan
Dorothy Swanson
Betty Terlinden
Iliana Thach
James Thach
Bob Thomas
Jayne Thomas
Adelaide Thompson
Dolores Uhl
Eve Van Stralen
Lee Vessey
Chip Washabaugh
Julia Watrous
Barbara Watson
Judy Westfall
Norman Wiener
Joanne Wiggins
Jack Wills
Jean Wilson
Helen Winton
Wayne Winton
Hazel Wood
Larry Wood
Barbara Yarbrough
Caroline Yeager
Betty Young
Helen Zeller
Anneke Zeylemaker

In Appreciation
MR. & MRS. WILLIAM TREDER

The Pasadena Playhouse Alumni & Associates

Lee Abbamondi
Charlotte Abbott
Sherry Adamo
Robert Adams
Diane Alexander
Casey Allen
Lenore Almanzar
Marvin Alter
Valerie I. Amidon
Douglas Anderson
Kaye Andrews
Joan Ankrum
Blanche Ansell
Darryl Antrim
Tom Armistead
Russell Arms
James Arness
Louise Arthur
Robert Artz
Frank Atienza
Harris Ault
Bob Austin
Rick Bageley
Rowena Baggerly
Jacqueline Bagnuolo
Ellen Bailey
Dan Bailey
Robert Baisa
Margaret Baker
Richard Baldwin
Elaine Ballace
Richard Banks
Charles Barkus
Harry and Beverly Bartell
Ken Bartmess
Patricia Bauer
Arthur Bayer
Judy Baylin
Jack Beardsley
Terrence Beasor
Judy Beck
Alma Becker
Charles Becker
Robert Beecher
Emily Beery
Rudy Behlmer
Linda Shawn Bell
Charles Alvin Bell
Mal Bellaires
Phyllis Benbow
Mary Morsbach Bennett
Paul Betrand
Barbara Bierbrier
Chick Bilyeu
Eileene Blatner
Martha Blood
Patti Bloom
Joel Bloom
Marjorie Blyberg
Jerry Bono
Mary Bowditch
Mary Webster Bracken

James Bradford
Gregory Braendel
Leo Brancfield
James Bronte
Greg Brown
Anne Diamond Brownstone
Jane Brubaker
Margaret Bryant
Art Bucaro
Ralph and Ellen Burgess
Paul Burke
Jeanne Burns
Joseph Bush
David Bushner
Reb Buxton
Bob Buzzell
Ruth Buzzi
Charles Callaway
Patrick Campbell
Joan Cannon
Jill Maina Capps
Paula Carlson
Joy Carlson
Eric Don Carlson
Anthony Carras
Anthony Carras, Jr.
Anthony Caruso
Malcolm Cassell
Marjorie Cates
Roberta Cavell
Edith Cavell
Mary Cavena
Barbara Cerrato
Harry Chalfant
June Chandler
Val Chevron
Frank Chila
Craig Childress
Lloyd Gibson Chulay
Ross Clark
Kenneth Clark
Martin Clark
Patrick Clement
Hal Cleveland
Consetta Cloninger
Ronald Cody
Don Conte
Jack Cook
Hyacinth Coopersmith
Kitty Copeland
Helena Lee Corcoran
Rafe Correll
Bill Cort
Auzanne Coscarelli
Al Covaia
Candy Craig
David Crandell
Bill Crowhurst
Sydney Curtis
Paul Curtis
Donna Damon
Henry Darrow

Hershel Daughtery
Kitty Davidson
Raul Davila
Bonnie Davis
Coralee Davis
Jack Dawson
Karen Day
Jeff De Benning
Emanuel De Coita
John Dean
Charleen Decoff
Bryn DeJardin
Rickie DeKramer
Jaime Delgado
Mary Dell Sharp
Maxine Dessau
Thomas Detienne
Carroll Devine
Darey DeVinney
Gene DeWild
Tony di Milo
Will Diaz
Mary Komatar Dick
Minta Dietrich
Ronald Disalvo
Donald Donaldson
Peggy Dorsett
Harry and Barbara Double
Shirley Dougherty
Krista Dragna
Kenneth duMain
James Dudley
Angus Duncan
Claire Dunkel
Elizabeth Dunn
Darlene Duralia
Dick Durant
Ross Eastty
Sandi Eberhard
Peggy Ebright
Elsa Echezabal
Michael Edwards
Barbara Dee Ehrnstein
Grace Emery
Cliff Emmich
Bill and Fran Erwin
Jimmy Espinoza
Jennifer Essen
Ned and Milli Estey
Charlanne Evans
Rex Everhart
Susan Eyraud
Virginia Fagans
William Fairchild
Jack Fara
Jamie Farr
Marsha Fickas
Ted Field
Alex Finlayson
Ralph Fisher
Jack Fitzgerald
Danny Fitzgerald

Janet Flahaven
Ernie Flook
Jean Folsom
Donald Frabotta
Helene Frances
Camille Franklin
Rose Freeman
Harriet Freeman
Jack Freeman
Sandra Freeman
William Fucik
Dinwiddie Fuhrmeister
Robert Furiga
Frank Furniss
Rae Worthy Gaeta
Robert Gallagher
Charlene Gallagher
Bette Garren
Gwen Anderson Geerdes
Al Gemsa
Karl Genus
Robert Gerlach
Donna German
Phylis Gibbs
Sallie Gilmore
Stan Gilson
Gordon Goede
Madison Goff
Russell Gold
Elizabeth Graham
Bobbie Finn Green
James Green
Dabbs Greer
Kathleen Greer
David Grehan
Austin M. Grehan
Arlyne Grey
William Griffing
William and Louise
  Gruenberg
Bette Guithues
Leonard Gumley
Janice Gunnoe
Mehmet Gurol
Raymond Guth
Ernie Guzman
Bonnie Hall
Bruce Hamlin
Dorothy Hamner
Frances Hanna
Dwight Hanna
Lars Hansen
Peter Hanson
Patricia Hanson
Lietta Harvey
Cheryl Harwood
Tom Hatten
William Hawkes
Skip Hawkesworth
Virginia Hawkins
James Hayes
Robert Hecker

Laurie Herrick
Donna Higbee
John Higginson
Maria Hildyard
Richard Hillman
Caroline Hirshfeld
Eloise Hirt
James and Elsie Hobson
Max Hodge
John and June Hoffstadt
Earl Holliman
Susan Holloway
Henrietta Holmes
B. R. Hood
Caroline Hoover
Helmuth Hormann
Faber Hosterman
David G. Houk
Donald Howard
Tom Hubbard
Ray Hughes
Roger Hulburd
Rune Hultman
Pat Hume
Bill Hunt
Geraldine Jackson
Ben Janney
Edna Jeffrey
Eric Johns
Kim Johnson
Ila Sess Johnson
Harvey Johnson
David Johnstone
Jack Joly
Virgil Jones
Betty Jones
Claude Earl Jones
Tod Jonson
Victor Jory
Florence Ferris Jowdy
Paul and Wanda Judson
Emile Juick
Karen Kahler
Lester Kantoff
Catherine Karhoff
Christine Kasbarian
Bonnie Belle Kavelaar
Stacy Keach
Stacy Keach, Sr.
Edmund Kearney
Don Keck
Edward Kemmer
Sandra Kendig
John Milton Kennedy
James and Helene Kent
William Kepper
Frank Kesby
Paul Kielar
Richard King
Brian Kinsley
Lyle Kirk
Werner Klemperer

Frank Klier
Jan Dior Kloke
Lawrence Knechtel
Alex and Jean Koba
Charles and Helene Koon
Jamie Ann Krakowski
Beverly Kramer
George Kyron
Paul La Benz
George La Fountaine
Franklin Lacey
Stanley Lachman
Bettie Lacy
Hal Landon
John Landreth
Helen Lane
Vincent Lappas
Charles Laquidara
William Larmore
Gordon Lawhead
Sammy Leiderman
Evelyn Le Mone
Rhea Lewis
Michael Libera
Leroy Lightfoot
Harry Lindberg
Stan Lineberger
Howard London
Bud Look
Stephen Lord
Anthony Lorea
Betty Lougaris
Fannie Love
Kit Ludwig
Bonnie Lupien
Paul Lyday
Ray Lynch
Jack Lynn
Tyler MacDuff
Phyllis Bell Magee
Edward Magnus
Mason Mallory
Peter Mamakos
Shirley Jean Mann
Ruth Manning
Phil Mansour
John and Angela Mantley
Lucy Marlow
Grant Marshall
John Marshall
Mark Martin
Leo Matranga
Elizabeth Matthews
Art McCain
Stephen McCue
Ona McDonough
John McElveney
Barry McGee
Cameron McLaren
Joseph McManus
Sherman McQueen

Cliff Medaugh
Marcella Meharg
Bette Jean Meier
Norman Mennes
Esther Mercado
Charles Mertala
Roy Meyer
Albert Meyer
Barbro Meyerkamp
Leo Michelson
Victor Millan
William Miller
Patrick Miller
Tom Miller
Clarence Miller
John Mitchell
Shirli Turner Mix
Dolores Monaco
Del Monroe
Kay Hibben Montgomery
Alvy Moore
Michael Morehouse
Betty Jean Morris
Richard Morrison
Robert Muehlhausen
John Mula
Lynn Murphy
George Nelson
Richard E. Nelson
Shirley Nelson
Lloyd Nelson
James Nelson
Cathleen Neville
Josephine Nichols
Bryon Nickolson
Dave Nicolson
Leonard Nimoy
Lex North
Hedy O'Connell
Laurette Odney
Audrey O'Hara
Anne Olson
Betty Organick
Mary Orlando
Jacqueline O'Rourke
Larry O'Sullivan
Kenneth Ott
Joy Otte
Edward Oxenham
Jaclyn Palmer
Molly Paramore
Nancy Parsons
Allen Paterson
Virginia Peters
Arthur and Norma Peterson
Doyle Phillips
Dave Pierce
Charles Pierce
Cajan Lee Pimley
Patti Ritter Pitts
Joan Plemmons

Michael Pogue
Eugene Polk
Don and Peggy Porter
Lois Postel
Bryon Predika
Catherine Preston
Michael Prichard
John Radeck
Mary Radlova
William Raffeld
James Reason
Judi Record
Frances Reid
Myrna Reinoso
Mary Reynolds
Frederick Ricci
Maybelle Richardson
Jan Ridlon
Gail Ripley
Joyce Hutton Roberts
Bob and Betts Rockwell
Bea Hassel Rogatz
Ellanora Rose
Kenneth Rose
Bob Ross
Richard and Cynthia
    Rossomme
Bill and Jean Rountree
Rosejane Rudicel
Gene Rudolf
Barbara Rush
Edythe Russell
Timmy Sabor
Martha Shaw Sack
Arne Sampe
Ted Samuel
Timothy Sanchez
Rita Sanders
James Santilena
Stanley Saunders
Jacqueline Saunders
Wayne Schatter
William Schelble
Kate Schlepp
Yvonne Schneider
Bob Scholer
Michael Schropp
Jack Scott
Gordon Sears
Deborah Seed
Ralph Senensky
Doug Senior
William Severs
Judy Shaw
Helen Shaw
Sandra Shaw
Pat Sheffield
Shirley Jones Shepley
Ralph Sherman
Gail Shoup
Max Showalter

Donahue Silvas
Joseph Sinda
Richard Smart
Johni Stone Smith
Virginia Smith
George Smith
Jack Smith
Rex Smith
Carole Smither
Theodore Soares
Bonnie Alden Sommers
Paul Sorensen
William Southwood
Graydon Spalding
Naomi Spano
Kenneth Spencer
Kitty Steel
Ron Steen
Maryan F. Stephens
Edward Stephenson
Kathy Stevens
Housely Stevenson
Doni Mae Stewart
Charles Stilwill
Warren Stirling
Morgan Stock
Liz Strong
Sally Struthers
King Stuart
Paul Stuart
Marilyn Stutenroth
James Subbert
James Sullivan
Patricia Sullivan
Joyce Sullivan
Henry Sumid
Suzanne Svendsen
Bob Swan
Liz Hunter Taylor
Robert Telford
Todd Theodossin
Michael Wayne Thomas
Susan Dolph Tinsman
Paulyne Tompkins
Helen Topp
Dennis Tracy
Donna Treadwell
Brad Trumbull
Helen Turner
Winifred Turner
Joanne Underwood
Lorraine Urquhart
Virginia Van der Voort
Harry Van der Wyk
Anthony Van Stralen
Richard Vath
Fred Vaugeois
Jean Vierra
Thomas Villa
Virginia Vincent
Sterling Von Franck

Gene Vurbeff
Joe Wadlington
Karin Wakefield
Eleanor Walker
Ann Stockton Walker
Locke Wallace
Chuck Walling
Colleen Walsh
Janet K. Ward
Dale Ware
John Warford
Virginia Warren
Donna Gale Washburn
Frank Wattron
Larry Waughtel
Tara Wayne
Carmelita Wayne
C. W. Weaver
William Weber
Kenneth Weiner
Karen Welch
Vance Wells
Tedd Welsch
Beverly Welsh
Allen Welts
Jacqueline West
Maxine Wheeler
Jane White
Bernie Wiesen
Jinny Wilcott
Carla Williams
Raymond Williams
Kathryn Willis
Lois Hall Willows
Gwen Horn Willson
Ron Wilson
Phyliss Wilson
Betsy Ross Wilson
Rex Wiltse
Mary Wing
Wayne Winton
Alvin Kirk Wirick
Brenda Wittenburg
Mariann Wolfe
Charles and Anne Wood
Larry Wood
Roger Woodard
JoAnne Worley
Anna Wray
Jean Ann Wright
Maris Wrixon
Richard Wyatt
Meg Wyllie
Delores Yarbrough
Vincent Yarmel
Rosie Malek Yonan
Aysen Young
William Young
Paul Zastupnevich
JoAnn Zimmermann
John Zweers

Index

In Appreciation
SHARON & PAT WESTMORELAND

Dana Andrews

Photo Credits

The author and book designers, on behalf of The Pasadena Playhouse, would like to thank those who contributed photgraphs, newspaper clippings, and memorabilia. Professional photographers, Pasadena Playhouse Alumni and Associates—or, in some cases, surviving family members, The Pasadena Playhouse staff, local historians, and the personnel at The Huntington Library all worked to enhance this project beyond measure. Listing the following names cannot adequately compensate for the inherent trust and the many selfless gestures shown by these individuals whose willingness to cooperate can only be explained by a sincere devotion to The Pasadena Playhouse.

Endowment and the Theatre
by John Masefield

So many, many men give wealth to build

The great museums with which our towns are filled,

Our millionaires compete with so much rage

That all things get endowed, except the stage.

Men will not spend, it seems, on that one art

Which is life's inmost soul and passionate heart;

They count the theatre a place for fun,

Where men can laugh at nights when work is done.

If it were only that, 'twould be worth while

To subsidize a thing which makes men smile;

But it is more; it is that splendid thing,

A place where man's soul shakes triumphant wing;

A place of art made living, where men may see

What human life is and has seemed to be

To the world's greatest brains; it is the place

Where Shakespeare held the glass to Nature's face;

The place the wise Greeks built by public toll

To keep austere and pure the city's soul.

*A prologue read at the opening of the Liverpool Repertory Theatre and used by
The Pasadena Playhouse in 1943 as a frontispiece for a booklet soliciting gifts and bequests*